EMBRACING THE *Tide*

— A NOVEL —

JANICE WILLIAMS

Primix Publishing
11620 Wilshire Blvd
Suite 900, West Wilshire Center, Los Angeles, CA, 90025
www.primixpublishing.com
Phone: 1-800-538-5788

Published by Primix Publishing   12/29/2021

ISBN: 978-1-955177-65-8(sc)
ISBN: 978-1-955177-66-5(hc)
ISBN: 978-1-955177-67-2(e)

Library of Congress Control Number: 2021924629

To our Bobs,
Love Janice and Carole

Contents

Acknowledgment

Carole, our journey has not been easy. However, together it has been bearable. Our friendship sustained us through difficult days. Thanks for your love, support, and the opportunity to recount a light-hearted version of our story. I have to believe the Bobs are smiling. Together we have forged a beautiful friendship. The best is yet to come.

Chapter One

Till death do us part is a phrase that does not carry a lot of meaning when we are young. However, after many years of marriage, I became a widow. My husband no longer required my daily caregiving skills. I was out of a job, and consequently, my descent into widowhood was traumatic and life-changing. For the first time, I found myself at a crossroads, single and alone. Still feeling young and energetic, I needed a new direction for my life. So I escaped the well-meant intentions of family and friends. A year after losing my husband, I began the journey which would ultimately change my life.

Leaving my home in Marin, California, in August of 2017, I began a road trip to discover my new identity. Driving north on Highway One, I suddenly found myself in an unexpected downpour. California never experienced rain in August, and I could only hope that it wasn't an omen of things to come. Quickly losing visibility, I panicked as the windshield wipers lost their battle against the pelting rain. The winding coastal highway was no place to be under such horrid conditions. Reaching over to seek the comfort of my only passenger, Fritz, a miniature Yorkie, I touched my sweet fur baby. He was sleeping peacefully and unaware of my ongoing dilemma.

Making my way inland toward Mendocino, I sought the safety of a warm bed for the night. I wasn't worried about a five-star rating as I grabbed my one piece of luggage, trusty companion, and checked into a local motel. Unlocking the door, I surveyed the room. It was clean and modest. Fritz happily stretched and yawned, thrilled to escape the confines of the car. Thoughts of losing Bob and the years we shared consumed me as I changed into comfortable pajamas. I was no longer married but rather a widow, single and alone. Dimming the lights, I pulled back the floral duvet. I felt utterly lost.

How dare he go first and leave me to deal with the aftermath. Falling in love with a handsome young soldier, we eagerly married without considering the consequences. Waiting for his overseas deployment to end was the hardest thing I had ever done, or so I thought, until November 15, 2016, when he passed. Now I found myself alone and in a quandary as to the direction of my life. Unable to sleep, I reached into my bag for my laptop and turned on the television discovering an easy listening music channel for inspiration. Writing romance novels had been the sustaining force that brought me through the most challenging times. I hoped to find inspiration and time to write as I continued my trip along the scenic coastal highway. Writing until the early morning hours, I finally fell asleep. Tomorrow, I would continue my cathartic journey. With a bit of luck, I would have a completed manuscript by the time I returned.

Sunlight filtered in through the faded drapes as I sat up in bed, rubbing my eyes. Staring at my tiny companion, he was still sleeping as I picked up my cell phone. There were no missed calls or texts. It appeared my family was ready to take a break from me as I desperately tried to reinvent my life. Dealing with the harsh reality of losing their father had not been easy, and it had taken a significant toll on my entire family. However, it was time to resume our lives. Our son, Keith, had been devoted to his father during his illness, but he had a demanding job as a commercial pilot. Married with a large family, I'm sure he was relieved to know his mom was finally able to get on with her life. Our younger son, Greg, a chef, was also busy opening a new restaurant while raising a young family. As much as I loved our sons, I never wanted to become a burden.

Staring in the mirror, I cringed, noticing a few gray hairs. I needed a drastic change. Stepping inside the shower, the warm water felt invigorating. However, it was time to rethink my hair color as I reached for the shampoo. I was eager to lose the gray and take on a younger, more vibrant appearance. Caring for Bob, it had been all too easy to lose track of my youthful, carefree spirit. After numerous sleepless nights, my total lack of energy was hidden behind tired eyes and aching joints. Making a mental note to pick up hair color, I stepped out of the shower. I felt ravenous. Desperately needing a jolt of caffeine, I quickly dressed and reached for my cell phone. Searching Google for local restaurants, I discovered a nearby Denny's. Hurriedly tossing my few things back into the suitcase and walking Fritz, we were soon on our way to breakfast and, more importantly, a hot cup of coffee.

After devouring a large breakfast of Belgian waffles, scrambled eggs, and sausage, I asked for a cup to go of hot coffee. Fritz and I were once again on our way to Vancouver, stopping along the way at points of interest. Thankfully today, the sun was out in full force, a welcomed reprieve after leaving home and the Bay Area under cloudy skies the previous morning. Despite the cooler weather and fog prevalent along the Pacific Coast, the temperatures were forecast to climb into the high eighties. My breath hitched as I turned on my car radio. Elvis sang, *Can't Help Falling in Love.* I had long lost count of the times Bob had referred to it as our song. Wiping my face as tears welled within my eyes and gently cascaded down my cheeks, I missed him more than ever. Trying not to become emotional at hearing the beautiful lyrics was a battle I was clearly losing. I would never be able to listen to this song without being consumed with thoughts of our life.

I discovered becoming a widow came with many pitfalls that could easily trigger unforgettable memories. Once again, I reached over to touch Fritz. I quickly understood the term support animal. However, as much as I loved my faithful Yorkie, a part of me missed having a human connection, a spouse. For a brief second, I let myself entertain thoughts of one day finding someone. Someone to share my life with, have long conversations, enjoy movies, romantic restaurants, and warm my bed. Writing romance novels, I always believed in happy endings. Yet, I questioned if my future held the promise of once again falling in love. I truly hated being a widow, alone, and everything it denoted. I had suddenly acquired a membership in a club that I never expected to join, as I'm sure is the case with most widows.

The scenery was breathtaking as I turned my attention back to the road. Passing long stretches of sandy beaches dotted with vast jagged rocks, some of which extended into the sparkling blue waters of the Pacific, the views were spectacular. Bob and I had driven these roads numerous times, never tiring of the incredible vistas. Once, we had been fortunate to watch a whale and her calf frolic offshore in the cold waters. Not one to miss an unbelievable photo opportunity, Bob stopped the car. Exhibiting his typical rambunctious personality, which I loved, he quickly climbed to the top of a nearby boulder capturing fabulous photographs. These photos remain in our family photo album and are some of my fondest memories. It would be impossible to drive these roads and not think of him. However, I was determined to make new memories. It was my reason for taking the scenic route up the coast. I was desperately clinging to memories while trying to create new ones. Reconnecting to the man I loved and lost was extremely difficult. Every hairpin turn and every vista point brought back memories. Our shared escapades only made me miss him more as reality set in. Taking the coastal route north to Vancouver wasn't the shortest or the easiest, but I was determined to continue.

After driving for several hours, I took the next exit stopping for gas. My recent purchase, a new Toyota Camry, was economical and fuel-efficient. Still, I didn't want to risk driving on desolate roads as the evening wore on. I was only a short distance from Eureka. Perhaps, I would stop for the night and call it an early evening. Fritz and I could revisit the historic old town and spend time surrounded by the ancient Sequoias. Calling ahead, I made reservations at the landmark Eureka Inn. The renowned inn had welcomed famous guests such as Sir Winston Churchill, Walt Disney, and Humphrey Bogart. Its décor was stately old-world elegance. After a day of being surrounded by nature and fresh air, I was confident I could return to the inn revitalized. I would be ready to spend hours writing before I fell asleep. Purchasing snacks, Fritz and I continued our leisurely drive.

Arriving in Eureka a short time later, I checked in at the famous inn with Fritz and ordered room service. I was ready to relax, enjoy dinner in the solitary confines of our suite and later write until the early hours of the morning. Writing required solitude, and with Fritz once again asleep on the bed, I took out my laptop. I began pouring my emotions into my current manuscript. Metamorphically, it represented my life. A story of great love, loss, and the dream of finding the one person with whom I could again fall madly in love. I loved happy endings. However, if it were never to happen again, at least I could experience it in my book. I was a hopeless romantic. I had known the love of a wonderful man, and I felt utterly lost without him.

The following morning my cell phone rang, waking me from a deep slumber.

"Hey, mom, it's Greg. How's the trip so far?"

"Wonderful. I'm in Eureka at the inn. Is everything alright?"

"Yes. I'm just calling to let you know that someone is anxious to meet you downstairs at 10:00 a.m. for an early brunch."

"Great. Any hints to the identity of this someone?"

Greg always loved playing practical jokes, which led me to believe it could be anyone from an old high school acquaintance to Amanda, my best friend. I had deliberately not informed anyone outside of the family of my impending road trip. I didn't want to worry my friends unnecessarily. Clearly, they would think I had finally 'gone round the bend,' mentally speaking.

"Well, if you must know, it's Amanda."

"Really, Amanda?" I questioned with an air of excitement.

The past two days had been grueling with memories of Bob, and I needed the support of my best friend. Amanda and I had been neighbors for too many years to count, and she had recently lost her husband, Bob as well. No one knew me better. The fact our husbands were both named Bob and shared enough similarities to be twins was uncanny.

We had both spent difficult years caring for our husbands before they passed. Now, we both had a new title added to our name, widow.

"How does she know that I'm in Eureka?" I continued.

"After not seeing your car in the drive for two days, she called. Mom, she was worried sick. Why didn't you tell her?"

"Well, mainly because I knew she would worry, and I didn't want to stress her out with more of my problems."

"Whatever, mom. That was wrong, and just so you know, I'm following you on my Live 360 app."

"Sweetheart, you don't have to worry about me. I'm completely capable of taking care of myself. So give hugs and kisses to my sweet grandbabies, and I'll see you when I get back. Love you."

"Love you too, mom."

Wow, Amanda was in Eureka. I couldn't wait to meet her and discover what brought her all this way from the Bay Area. Racing to the bathroom, I had just enough time to shower and dress before meeting Amanda downstairs.

Taking the elevator down to the restaurant, I could hardly wait to see my best friend. Looking at us, we were an unlikely pair. Amanda was short and sturdy, and I was somewhat taller and slender. Amanda had long auburn hair, and I had short blonde curls. She had fair Irish skin to my year-round California tan. Amanda preferred casual to the max. I usually saw her in a baseball cap with a ponytail pulled through the back, jeans, and tee shirt with track shoes. I preferred dress pants and long flowing chiffon tunics with designer flats. But despite our tastes and physical differences, we were always on the same page about life. It was the reason we became best friends.

Exiting the elevator, I walked into the restaurant, where I immediately saw Amanda seated at one of the tables. Running over, I smiled.

"Oh my gosh, what are you doing here?"

"Well, I suppose I could ask you the same question?"

Amanda stood, giving me a huge hug. I knew she didn't understand my reasons for leaving without informing her.

"I desperately needed a change, and I thought a road trip would be the perfect answer," I replied, ordering coffee and waffles. "You know how devasting it is to lose a husband. I just needed to be alone and sort through the emotional rollercoaster of becoming a widow. It isn't easy to have your life turned upside down. Plus, I was hoping to finish my current manuscript. You're a writer. It's hard to write with so many distractions."

"Duly noted, but Ericka, for heaven's sake, why didn't you let your friends know about this crazy scheme of yours?" Amanda scolded, quickly turning her attention to the waiter. "Oh, I'll have the same, coffee and waffles."

"Sorry. I did tell the boys."

"And thank God for that. Without calling Greg, I would have had no idea you were on your way to Vancouver. Don't you think you're a little emotional to be wandering all over the Pacific Northwest by yourself? And why Vancouver? Why didn't you just drive up to the cabin in Tahoe for the weekend?"

"You know I've always wanted to visit Vancouver. I'm a grown woman, for heaven's sake. I've raised two sons and recently buried my husband. I need a break."

"Even more reason not to be alone and traveling desolate roads by yourself. What if you had a stroke? I'm sorry, but Fritz isn't going to be a lot of help."

"A stroke, don't be ridiculous."

"Well, it could happen. You're not young, or haven't you noticed."

"Okay, enough about me and your concerns. What's your story? Why are you in Eureka?" I questioned, taking a sip of coffee.

"You mean besides trying to save my best friend from a crazy road trip." Amanda laughed. "Eva, Bob's cousin, informed me that his Aunt Tilly's property has finally gone on the market. She's offered me the first opportunity to purchase it. Would you like to drive out to the house with me? It's not that far, and it shouldn't take long. Besides, you were a real estate agent, and I would value your opinion. I don't want to dip into my savings unless the possibility exists to make a potential profit.

"Okay. I suppose I can take a look. Unfortunately, however, I'm no longer in real estate, and you really should have a local agent pull up the comps for you."

"Well, I'm not sure that I'll even be interested. It depends on the condition of the property. It has been years since I've been back. Why don't you run up and get Fritz? I'll pay the tab and bring the car around."

Driving out to the edge of town, Amanda turned onto a single-track dirt road. We had only gone a short distance when a dilapidated barn, sprawling ranch house, and several acres of green pasture came into view.

"You didn't mention it was rural or a farm?" I hesitantly questioned.

"Oh, I thought if you knew, you might not come, and I really need your input."

"Seriously, Amanda, at your age, are you thinking of buying a farm?" I laughed.

"No. However, I could rent it out."

"Well, I have doubts about this, but we're here. So we might as well have a look."

Taking the key from under the mat, Amanda unlocked the door. Shadows of light filtered in through musty curtains, reflecting a derelict interior. A fireplace centered the small living room, which contained a sofa and two-winged back chairs covered in dust and cobwebs.

"Wow, this place is a disaster, and to be honest, it feels haunted. I think I've seen enough."

"Really, Ericka? As you said, we're here, so you might as well take the grand tour. I have a lot of fond memories of staying here," Amanda explained.

"Haunted memories," I laughed.

"I wouldn't say haunted memories, but bittersweet for sure."

"Bob was raised in this house. Tilly and Bill adopted him after his parents died in a freaky mudslide in South America. They were on a mission trip, and knowing the possible dangers, they were smart enough to leave Bob with his aunt and uncle. Thank God, Bob would have died with them. After losing his parents, Bob remained connected to this place until he passed.

"I remember you describing the horrifying details of his parent's death. I know you mentioned that he was raised on a farm by his aunt and uncle, but this is the first time I've been here. Amanda, this place is in shambles and going to require considerable work. Please don't tell me you're serious about putting in an offer?"

I was still reeling from seeing the interior of the house. Noting the amount of work needed to restore it, I couldn't, in all honesty, recommend that Amanda make such a questionable purchase. However, it was apparent that she had a strong connection to this home. Walking back to the front porch, we sat down in the high-back wooden rockers. Taking in the views, I noticed an old rusty tricycle sitting abandoned in the yard. I wanted to know more.

"Wow, check out the old trike. Do you think it might have been Bob's as a child?"

"Probably. Someone must have gotten it out of the barn. Bob had so many memories of living here. There's a trail behind the house. It leads down to a pond where he spent many hours hanging out with his cousins. At one time, many years back, the fields contained dairy cows. Bob wasn't much of a farmhand, but Bill taught him how to milk cows. He said he sat on the porch many times churning milk into butter for Tilly. Can you even imagine him sitting here with raw milk in a quart mason jar wrapped in a kitchen towel, turning it back and forth till it formed into butter?"

"No, but I'm curious. Are you seriously thinking about making an offer?"

"I've thought about it. That's why I wanted to come up and revisit when I heard it was for sale. But, at my age, it's simply too much work. Don't worry. I'm not leaving Marin."

"Oh, thank God. I love you like a sister, but I'm sorry this place requires a demolition, not a restoration, and it's probably not up to code. The work to restore it boggles my mind."

"Ericka, calm down. I know at my age, it's beyond the realm of possibilities. However, it holds so many memories of Bob. I remember how excited he was to bring me here to meet Tilly and Bill after we were engaged," Amanda smiled. "You remember how we met, right?"

Yes, but refresh my memory," I smiled with empathy, allowing her to take a sentimental walk down memory lane. Hopefully, recalling the details would give her the closure she needed while forgetting any silly ideas she might have regarding an offer. I could easily sympathize with her emotions and need to talk. It would be therapeutic and healing.

"Well," Amanda paused pensively. "I was a wreck after James left me with three small children for a girl half his age."

"Unbelievable. I remember you telling me about James. But, seriously, what kind of man does that?"

"I know," Amanda frowned. "Well, I persevered, stayed single, and worked my way through college to get my teaching credential while raising the kids. After they were grown, I got lonely. I had met several losers in nightclubs and decided that was a bad idea. One day, I picked up a newspaper running a personal ads page. I thought, well, why not advertise for a man and get what I want. *Professional woman late forties is seeking professional man late forties early fifties. No drinkers or drug users need to apply. Require financial and emotional stability.*"

"I must say that was brilliant," I interjected.

"Well, Bob read my ad and called. I agreed to meet him in a restaurant, and it was love at first sight for both of us. He was all I advertised for and more. As you know, we had our ups and downs over the past twenty-nine years, but we loved each other and worked it out. The last three years were rough, as you know. Bob's health steadily declined, and he required more and more help. It was hard to watch a happy and robust man dwindle to skin and bones. He was miserable the last few years. Ericka, I thought it would be easy for him to pass on, but it wasn't. I miss him more each day that goes by, but I know I have to go on without him. Maybe I will find another man, but not another Bob."

"Wow, the fact Bob replied to your ad gives me goosebumps. You were destined to find each other."

"Ericka," Amanda paused, wiping tears from her eyes. "It's so hard living without him. I thought purchasing this property might help bring closure to our life. But, instead, there are days that I don't think I can continue another minute without him. I feel totally lost."

"I understand your feelings and attachment to this house and property. But, Amanda, this place is too much work and money. I'm worried about you. You forget that I just recently lost my husband as well. I've walked in your shoes, and I know the horrors and devastation of losing a husband. Trust me. It's not easy. Just know that eventually, death parts all married couples. It's only the matter of who goes first unless you're both fortunate enough to pass together in an accident. Amanda, you have to *Embrace the Tide.* There's no other choice

"I suppose you're right."

"Why don't you ride with me to Vancouver?"

"I would love to, but I have appointments this week. I could meet you later. Perhaps in Seattle."

"Well, that sounds wonderful. I'll let you know what day I plan to arrive and you can meet me. We'll have a blast. I think it's time for two lonely widows to have some fun. How about a night out on the town. What do you think?"

"I like the sounds of that, but I'm not sure if I remember what fun is."

"Well, I think it's about time we put some excitement back into our lives. But, Amanda, I need to get back to the inn. Why don't you stay the night?" I inquired, noting the time on my phone. "We could pretend to make it a girl's sleepover."

"I can't. I have an appointment in the morning, and I have to drive back to Marin. So we will make up for our lost time in Seattle," Amanda mentioned, locking the farmhouse door and discreetly hiding the key.

Arriving back at the inn, I hated to see my best friend leave, but I looked forward to seeing her soon.

"Call me when you arrive in Seattle, and I'll fly up for the weekend. Until then, we can keep in touch through phone calls or texts. I've got to run," Amanda smiled. "I'll see you in Seattle."

"I love you. Drive safe. See you in Seattle," I replied.

Having breakfast with my best friend was an unexpected, enjoyable surprise. We always loved spending time together. However, the tour of the country property was surprising. Still, I was glad that I went. I couldn't have imagined Amanda going alone. The house held too many memories, and the afternoon had been emotional yet cathartic. We had both lost the loves of our lives, and the past two years had been extremely challenging. However, having each other to lean on was a blessing. No one could possibly understand the heartbreak of losing a spouse, the maze of closing out their personal affairs, and worse, learning to live alone.

The following morning, Fritz and I visited Eureka's historic downtown and later visited Sequoia Park. After spending more time than expected browsing the quaint antique shops and art galleries, I drove out to Sequoia Park. Fritz and I leisurely strolled through the living giants, inhaling the fresh air and enjoying the serenity of the stately behemoths. Having stopped for picnic supplies and dog food before reaching the park, I anxiously devoured a tasty turkey sandwich. Fritz had no problem finishing a bowl of his favorite, Blue Buffalo. Watching as families with young children enjoyed the idyllic location of being outdoors, I recalled the numerous occasions Bob and I had brought the boys to the park. Tears welled within my eyes as our past visits to the park began playing in my mind like an old movie reel. One trip, particularly when Keith and Greg had been rambunctiously chasing Max, our black lab, Greg suddenly tripped, injuring his knee. Later that night, Bob and I had debated whether we should have taken him to a local hospital. Thankfully as it turned out, he was fine. Now, I sat alone without Bob and our two sons, who were busy with lives of their own. Life was fleeting at best.

The temperature plummeted as the sun slowly faded. Feeling a slight chill, I led Fritz back to the car. I decided to stay an extra night in Eureka. I was on a roll with my book and facing a deadline with my publisher, so getting pages written was vital. Picking up fast food, burgers with fries for the evening would give me valuable time to write, not stopping my creative thoughts.

Later that evening, after hours of writing, I finally turned out the light. Resting my head on the pillow, I missed Bob. The bed felt cold and empty despite my furry companion. Without the warmth of his body, an overwhelming feeling of sadness and dread consumed me. The fact I would never feel his strong arms embrace me in the middle of the night or the tenderness of his gentle kisses brought on a deluge of tears. My breath hitched as I wiped my eyes, envisioning his quirky smiles. It was moments like this in which I wasn't sure if life without him was possible. Losing a spouse after fifty years of marriage was by far the hardest thing I had ever faced. But, unfortunately, no amount of tears would ever bring him back. Pulling the covers over my head, I finally fell asleep.

Waking to the brilliance of the morning sun as it washed over the room in a soft glow, it was time to embrace a new day. I tossed back the covers and walked into the bathroom. The warm water from the shower felt refreshing and cathartic. Deciding to order room service, I leisurely enjoyed breakfast in my room. There was nothing like a hot cup of coffee in the morning with pancakes and sausage to get the day started. Today, I promised myself that I would put aside my emotions and simply enjoy the journey. Crescent City was my next stop. Even though it was less than two hours north on Highway 101, I had beautiful memories of Bob and me touring Battery Point Lighthouse. I was excited to retrace our steps and create new memories.

Chapter Two

Arriving in Crescent City, Fritz and I checked in to a local motel with ocean views. Even though it was still early in the day, August was the peak of tourist season, and I wanted to secure a room. In retrospect, the road trip held no time restraints. I wasn't in a hurry to arrive in Seattle to meet Amanda or my final destination, Vancouver. It was simply a healing journey to discover my new identity.

I unpacked, changed into comfortable tennis shoes, grabbed my light jacket, Fritz's leash, and walked downstairs to the car. Our lodging wasn't a five-star luxury resort, but it was on the ocean and close to where I wished to visit. Our first stop today was the Battery Point Lighthouse. Tides permitting, it was only open till 4:00 p.m. The lighthouse was registered as a California Historical Landmark and on the National Register of Historic Places. Grabbing Fritz, we anxiously made the trek across the sandy, rocky beach. Unfortunately, tours were only possible during the low tide. I shivered, remembering my previous visit with Bob and the boys. Young and energetic, Keith and Greg stopped to pick up small rocks, and I was frantically worried we would be swept out to sea by a sneaker wave. Oh, the worries I had raising two small boys only eighteen months apart.

Touring the historic lighthouse, the views of the rugged coastline were breathtaking. The continued onslaught of the incoming surf as it crashed against jagged rocks, hurling a spray of mist skyward, was mesmerizing, just as I remembered. However, the rumbles in my stomach reminded me that I had skipped lunch. As a result, I was starving when I reached the parking lot. Craving seafood, I quickly searched for the best seafood restaurants. Finally, I stopped by the motel, changed into a modest sundress and heels, ensuring Fritz was comfortable and well-fed before leaving.

Deciding to eat at Fishermen's Restaurant, many described it as one of the best places on the Pacific Coast to enjoy seafood. Walking in, the waiter questioned if I was eating alone or if someone would be joining me. Without Bob, I felt abandoned as the waiter seated me at a table near the back. Reaching into my purse for my reading glasses, I looked over the menu. Deciding to order a drink to relax, white zinfandel, and the seafood combo, I hoped not to be disappointed with my selection. As the waiter sat a piping hot plate of battered beer prawns, deep-fried clam strips along with fresh cod in front of me, it looked scrumptious. Tasting the prawns, they were delicious. The seafood far exceeded my expectations. Lifting my glass of wine, I suddenly felt the intense stares from a gentleman seated two tables away. He was extraordinarily handsome and charming by any stretch of the imagination. Appearing to be in his early seventies, his distinguished profile, gray hair, and physique made it apparent that even at his age, he kept in shape. Looking around, I questioned if I was possibly the focus of his attention. Taking a quick glance, I blushed to discover we were the only ones seated in this part of the restaurant. Feeling insecure, I reached into my purse for a small mirror. I was horrified by the thought that perhaps I had the remains of food on my face. After a close inspection, I didn't. Thank God. However, before I could close my compact, he walked over. Tall and exuding an air of confidence, I was captivated by his sudden appearance.

"I don't mean to interrupt your meal. I noticed you as you entered the restaurant and that you were eating alone. May I join you?"

Unsure of what to say, I briefly hesitated. Then, charmed by his warm smile, it led me to believe there was no harm in allowing him to join me. After all, we were in a public space.

"Yes," I smiled as the words slowly slipped from my lips.

"Thank you. By the way, I'm Liam. I've always hated eating alone."

"I know the feeling. I'm Ericka."

"May I get you another glass of wine? Zinfandel, right?"

"Yes. Thank you," I smiled, questioning his intuition. "Lucky guess?"

"Not really. Most women love white zinfandel," he replied with a smile, motioning for the waiter.

"So, Liam, what brought you here this evening?"

"I'm visiting my brother, and I come here often when I'm in Crescent City."

"And," I hesitated demurely, unsure of his intentions. "Why isn't he with you?"

"Well, for starters, he's at work, and more importantly, he's always been allergic to shellfish and most seafood," Liam grinned, somewhat amused at my curiosity.

As the waiter approached our table, Liam ordered a glass of white zinfandel for me and a beer.

"Okay, Ericka, if I can be so bold, what brought you here?" he questioned with a curious stare revealing the intensity of his blue eyes.

"I lost my husband last year. He was the love of my life. We were married for fifty years, and I decided a road trip might give me the clarity I needed to start over in life."

Geez, I'd just blurted out the synopsis of my life and the fact that I was traveling alone. Clearly, the wine had gone straight to my head. What if he were a murderer looking for his next victim? I could only pray his intentions were not nefarious. However, his warm smile and my gut instinct told me otherwise.

"I'm sorry for your loss. I know that has to be challenging."

As the waiter returned with our drinks, I lifted my glass, taking a long sip. There was an air of familiarity about Liam, which allowed me the comfort of explaining my entire life to someone I barely knew.

"So, are you married?"

"Divorced."

"Sorry."

"Unfortunately, my job wasn't conducive to a great marriage, and after years of being away from home, she finally left," Liam answered, taking a sip of his beer.

"Do you have any children?" I questioned.

"No. Considering the circumstances, it was a blessing. Do you have kids?"

"Yes. I have two boys. Of course, they're both grown now. My oldest is a pilot, and my youngest is a chef. He's opening a restaurant," I smiled, finishing my glass of wine.

"May I get you another glass?" Liam inquired, finishing his beer.

"Thank you, but I've reached my limit. I should be going," I smiled, gaining the attention of the waiter.

"Please, let me get this. I can't let a beautiful young lady pay for her meal. After all, I intruded on your meal," Liam winked flirtatiously.

"Thanks, but that's not necessary."

"I insist," Liam smiled, placing a Black Amex Card on the table. "Ericka, I would love to see you again. I know you mentioned the fact you're on a road trip. Here's my cell number. I live in Canada. Call me anytime. I can arrange for us to meet," Liam smiled, quickly writing his number on a paper napkin before standing to pull back my chair.

"Thank you. I'll give it some thought," I blushed, taking the folded napkin with his number.

As I left the restaurant, I felt an unexplainable connection to Liam. Truth be known, I wanted to see him again. Getting into my car, I unfolded the napkin. Staring at his number, I questioned what had just happened. I couldn't remember another time in my life when anyone other than friends or family had approached me in a restaurant. Yet, I couldn't wait to reach the motel and call Amanda.

Unlocking the door to my room, I scooped Fritz into my arms and fell back on the bed. For a brief moment, I felt like a giddy high school teenager who the star quarterback had approached. Then, reaching for my cell phone, I called Amanda. She answered on the first ring.

"Hey. What's up?" Amanda answered.

"You're not going to believe what happened earlier tonight," I stated rather excitedly.

"Well, from the sound of your voice, I'm guessing it wasn't a stroke."

"Geez, Amanda, you and your ridiculous ideas. I'm as healthy as a horse."

"Okay. I give up. What's going on? Whatever it is, it better be good because I'm in the middle of a Hallmark movie."

"Right? Don't be funny. I met someone tonight."

"What do you mean met someone? Like where, at a gas station, liquor store?"

"Amanda, stop with the crazy scenarios and let me explain. Have you been drinking?"

"Well, I might have had a glass of wine."

"I met a guy in a restaurant this evening. It was unbelievable, like a scene out of a romance novel."

"Of course it was. You write romance novels, probably just a figment of your wild imagination."

"Amanda, don't be silly. I was in a restaurant this evening in Crescent City, the Fishermen's, and this guy approached my table and asked if he could join me. He said he had noticed me as I walked in and that he hated eating alone. He was drop-dead gorgeous. I have butterflies just thinking about him. He bought me a glass of wine and even offered to pay for my meal."

"Well, I hope you let him pay."

"I offered, but he insisted on paying."

"Please don't tell me you brought him back to your room," Amanda giggled.

"Be serious. You know me better than that, and it definitely wasn't that type of encounter. His name is Liam. He said his brother lives in Crescent City and often frequents the restaurant when he's in town. He's divorced. Amanda, I can't explain it, but there was something familiar about him. He gave me his cell number, and I want to see him again."

"Wow, that's unbelievable. Are you going to call him?"

"Probably, I'm not sure. It all happened so fast. I haven't dined with a guy since Bob passed. It's new territory for me."

"Well, you're on a journey to discover your new identity, and perhaps, Liam is supposed to be a part of it. So I would definitely give it some serious thought."

"Thanks, Amanda. I'll let you get back to your Hallmark movie," I laughed. "We'll talk later. Love you."

"Love you too. Stay safe. I'll see you in Seattle."

Laying my cell phone on the bedside table, I put Fritz on the bed. Then, dimming the lights, I pulled back the covers. Tomorrow was a new day. I planned to drive the four and half hours to Eugene, Oregon. I promised Bob's younger brother, Randal, that I would stay with them this weekend. Since Bob's services, I hadn't seen Randal, his wife, Pam, or their brood of five adorable grandchildren.

Waking early the following morning, I desperately needed coffee. I had a long day of driving ahead, and I wanted to stop at Sea Lion Caves. It had always been a favorite of Bob's and the boys, and I didn't want to miss it. However, if I were going to stay on schedule and reach Eugene, I needed to leave before late evening. Hurriedly getting dressed, I repacked my suitcase and fed Fritz. Reaching for my phone, I searched for the nearest café. Discovering a waffle house nearby, I once again gathered my few belongings and Fritz. A balmy invigorating breeze wafted in from the ocean as I quickly walked Fritz. Afterward, putting him in the car, the morning sun's penetrating warmth assured me the weather forecast from the night before seemed accurate. It would be a good day for driving, and time permitting, I hoped to make a few stops along the way.

After consuming too many waffles covered in butter with warm maple syrup and downing several cups of coffee, I set off on my journey once again. Entering Highway 101, Fritz, as usual, fell asleep. It had become his normal routine. Turning up the SiriusXM volume, the romantic songs of Frank Sinatra were comforting. The calming music made the long trip less stressful, and there was nothing better than driving while listening to your favorite artists. For me, it was Nat King Cole and Sinatra. Hearing the beautiful lyrics of *Strangers in the Night*, my thoughts rushed back to meeting Liam the previous night.

For once, I allowed myself to entertain thoughts of finding love for the second time. Was it too early after losing Bob? Were their unspoken rules to becoming a widow? How long was it appropriate for a widow to mourn? It had been over a year. Would the boys think it an irreverence to their dad's memory? Consumed with thoughts, my membership in the widowhood club came with no handbook. There were no monthly meetings or rules of etiquette. Women who had lost their spouses were simply left to seek the comfort of family and friends and perhaps support groups. As usual, we were expected to keep our emotions checked when met with well-meant condolences while privately crying ourselves to sleep at night. Despite all the reasons for not pursuing another relationship, I had to believe that Bob would approve. I knew he would want me to be happy. Moving on didn't mean that I would no longer mourn the loss of him or the loss of our lives together. I was simply allowing myself to embrace a new identity. My decision was made. I was going to call Liam.

Finally, after numerous pit stops for gas, snacks, and restroom breaks, I reached Florence, Oregon, and Sea Lions Cave. Finding a place to park, I opened the trunk of the car and grabbed Fritz's doggie carrier. Memories of a previous visit with Bob and the boys flooded my mind. I remembered how anxious they were to see the sea lions and repetitively asked how much farther until we arrived. Grabbing a light jacket before leaving the car, I recalled the cave's cool, damp temperatures.

Joining the next tourist group, I waited to enter the elevator, which descended through two hundred and eight feet of rock. Entering an impressive cavern formed twenty-five million years ago, it soared to the height of a twelve-story building and stretched to the length of a football field. Water swells flowed over the rock ledges as I stood near the ocean floor. The outcroppings contained numerous sea lions and their pups. Instantly, I knew why this was a favorite attraction of the boys and Bob, who was often a kid at heart. He was a great father and took every opportunity to enlighten them with his vast array of knowledge. He took pride in pointing out the lichens, algae, and mineral stains that painted the cavern walls in various colors. The colors depicted distinguishable figures as Lincoln's head, the Indian Maiden, and the Goddess of Liberty combined with the rough surfaces. My eyes moistened with memories as I snapped photos of the stellar sea lions. However, it didn't take long for the nose-pinching stench to force me back to the elevator.

After visiting Sea Lions Cave, Fritz and I entered the car for the short sixty-mile drive to Eugene, Oregon. I was anxious to see Pam, Randall, their kids, and their grandkids. However, I underestimated the emotions I would experience. Randall resembled Bob in every way, including his mannerisms. Sharing the same DNA, they were fortunate to have handsome features. Their father, Robert Reed, Sr., a corporate attorney, was a prominent figure in the bay area before he passed. However, neither of his sons followed him into the realm of the legal world. Randall chose to teach at UC Berkeley before retiring to Eugene. Bob had followed his heart, choosing a career in aviation. His love of flying and everything connected to it was evident as he retired from the airlines after thirty years as a commercial pilot.

Taking a glance at the time, I knew it would be late evening when I arrived. However, I knew Pam and Randall would welcome Fritz and me with open arms despite the late hour. Deciding to stop for fast food, I didn't want to arrive with a ravenous appetite. However, knowing Pam, I was sure she had spent the entire day in the kitchen preparing a small feast.

As the impressive stately home came into view, I had arrived. Located in one of Eugene's older, affluent downtown neighborhoods, it was apparent that they had retired in luxury by its outward grandeur. Parking in the circular drive that fronted the property, I grabbed Fritz. Approaching the front door, it opened before I had a chance to knock. A young girl with locks of red curly hair and brilliant blue eyes stared up at me.

"Hey, Auntie Ericka, I'm Robin. We've been waiting for you. Nana said you were coming," she smiled, pulling me inside. "Can I hold Fritz?"

"Of course," I smiled, placing him in the hands of an adorable ten-year-old. "Wow, look at you. You've gotten so big."

"Hey Sis, it's so good to see you. How was the drive?" Pam inquired.

"Not bad."

"Come in. Let's go into the living room. Can I get you anything? Perhaps something to drink?"

"No. I'm fine."

"Sorry, Randall isn't here. Unfortunately, an unexpected meeting came up at the university. You know Randall, he never actually retired. He said he will see you in the morning."

"Oh, not a problem. I understand."

"Have a seat while I ask one of the grandkids to take your luggage upstairs to the guest room. We promised Charlie and Jill the kids could stay with us this weekend. They're away on business."

Watching as Pam walked back to the family room, she had not changed in appearance since I last saw her at Bob's services. Sculpted like a model, tall, slim with gorgeous auburn hair pulled back into a ponytail, she never seemed to age. It was easy to see how Randall had fallen in love with her while attending the University of California, Los Angeles. They appeared to have the perfect marriage. But, looking around their immaculate home, I was jealous. How was it that some people had all the luck?

"Are you sure that I can't get you anything?" Pam asked cordially, walking back into the living room.

"I'm okay. Thanks."

"We haven't seen you since the funeral. How are you? I know this past year hasn't been easy."

"I'm fine, but it has been a challenging year since Bob died. I really miss him."

"Ericka, I'm so sorry. I can't even imagine what you've gone through. It hasn't been easy on Randall either. He misses Bob."

"You look tired. Why don't I let you turn in for the evening. I'm sure the drive was exhausting. The guest room is ready upstairs, and we can talk more in the morning."

"Honestly, that sounds great. It has been a long day. Thanks for having me for the weekend."

"Ericka, don't be silly. You're family. It's been too long since we last saw you. I know you've had a lot to take care of since Bob died.

We're happy to have you. Is there anything I can get Fritz before you retire upstairs?"

"No. Fritz is good. I'll see you in the morning."

"Okay. Get some rest."

"Thanks."

Scooping Fritz into my arms, I walked over to the intricate wrought iron staircase which led upstairs to the guest room. Beautifully executed, the room's décor emphasized patterns of blue French toile. Deciding to shower before bed, I unpacked my clothes, leaving out my nightgown. Invigorated from the warm shower, I turned back the duvet and reached for my laptop. However, before I could organize my thoughts, my cell phone buzzed. It was Amanda.

"Hello."

"Hey, I didn't hear from you today? Are you okay?" Amanda quizzed.

"Yes. I'm in Eugene, Oregon, at Randall and Pam's home."

"How's that going?"

"Oh, great. The grandkids have really grown."

"What about Liam? Did you call him?" Amanda asked curiously.

"No. Geez, Amanda, I just met him last night. I don't want to seem too eager."

"Well, I wouldn't wait too long."

"How are things with you?"

"Good, except I'm missing Bob. There are days that I feel like a tsunami of emotions has overtaken me. Today was one of those days. Bob was my anchor, and now, I feel adrift."

"I totally understand. It's tough. Today I visited Sea Lion's Caverns, and memories of Bob and the boys flooded my mind."

"Ericka, don't be too hard on yourself. I know this trip is important to you, but it's about starting over, not dwelling on the past. Hang in. I'll talk to you tomorrow."

"Thanks, Amanda. We'll talk tomorrow."

Closing my laptop, I pulled the covers up to my chin. I felt lonely. I knew precisely the feelings and emotions that Amanda was experiencing. I, too, missed my husband. Widowhood came with many pitfalls, and tonight I was falling once again into the depths of despair and loneliness. Wiping tears that moistened my eyes, I finally fell asleep.

Waking early to the noise of boisterous children, I had forgotten what Saturday mornings felt like with young kids. Becoming empty nesters, Keith and Greg had long moved out of our house. It meant no early morning cartoons blaring from the family room or messy bowls of fruit-colored cereal left on the kitchen island. My Saturday mornings were now eerily quiet. Hurriedly, I pulled on sweat pants with a matching top before walking downstairs with Fritz. The smell of fried bacon drew me to the kitchen.

"Good morning," Randall smiled, giving me a huge hug. "Sorry I missed seeing you last night. I'm on a few committees at the university, and I had an unexpected meeting last night. It's so good to see you. I hope you're hungry. Coffee?"

"Yes, please, only cream, no sugar. No problem about last night. I totally understand. Can I help with breakfast?"

"Thanks, but I've got it under control. I hope the grandkids didn't wake you," Randall questioned, flashing the familiar Reed brothers' smile. "We have them for the weekend. Charlie and Jill are away on business, and unfortunately for us, John and Cindy have recently relocated to Florida. However, they said to give you their best. They're hoping to see you during the holidays."

"Sorry, I missed them."

My heart melted at the mere sight of Randall's upturned lip and quirky smile. I had to steady myself as I reeled with sudden flashbacks of my Bob. Randall and Bob had always mirrored each other in their youthful, handsome appearance and personality. Regardless of their ten-year age gap, I'm sure most people at a glance thought them to be twins.

"Ericka, sit and enjoy your coffee. I always cook breakfast on the weekends allowing Pam to sleep in," Randall mentioned, handing me a hot cup of coffee. "I hope you like waffles and bacon."

"My favorites. Trust me. I could eat waffles every morning."

"Ericka, I know the past year has been brutal. I miss Bobby more than you know. How are you holding up?"

"Well," I paused, taking a sip of the hot beverage. "I suppose you could say that I'm doing the best I can under the circumstances. It's not easy. After being married for fifty years, it's left a huge hole in my heart. I miss Bob more than you could possibly imagine."

"I'm so sorry. I know losing Bob hasn't been easy. I miss him—a lot. Have you thought of selling the house and downsizing?"

"I have, but I don't know if I could. Our home holds so many memories, and I'm not sure the boys would want me to sell."

"Ericka, there are times in life when you have to focus on yourself. The boys are grown and have lives of their own. You need to think of what's best for you. I'd be happy to talk to them."

"Thanks. I'll let you know."

"Good morning," Pam smiled, slowly strolling into the kitchen. "I hope the grandkids didn't wake you. Randall gets up early and makes breakfast on Saturdays. It can be hectic when the kids are here, so he lets me sleep in," Pam added, pouring herself a cup of coffee.

"No. I didn't hear a thing," I mentioned, deciding to err on the side of kindness. "I always get up early to walk Fritz."

"Randall and I have made arrangements to take you on a wine tasting tour. You can't come to Eugene without tasting the local wines. I called my friend, Gail, and she's agreed to watch the kids," Pam stated. Pulling out one of the wrought iron stools that lined their extensive granite island, she sat next to me.

"Sounds wonderful. I hope your friend didn't have plans. I would hate to have her change her schedule because I stopped by for the weekend," I inquired.

"Are you kidding? She doesn't have any children, and she loves watching the grandkids. Besides, Randall and I have been discussing the fact we need to restock the wine fridge."

"First breakfast. I didn't slave over a hot stove for no reason this morning," Randall laughed, sitting plates of yummy waffles and bacon on the island.

After finishing breakfast, and another cup of coffee, I ran upstairs to change. Today called for comfy shoes and dressing casually in jeans instead of the baggy sweat pants I wore. I hated not spending the day with Robin and her brothers, but it appeared Pam had the day planned.

Later, arriving at our first stop, one of Pam and Randall's favorite, King Estate Winery, was gorgeous. It was family-owned and located in Oregon's Southern Willamette Valley. It overlooked stunning vineyards and the surrounding valley. Pam and Randall bought a mixed case of pinot gris and pinot noir, along with several bottles of white zinfandel. I also purchased two bottles of pinot noir for later consumption.

Moving on to our next winery, we visited Sweet Cheeks Winery. It was known for its beautiful outdoor setting and ever-growing list of wines, including pinot gris and pinot noir. Bob and I shared a love for chardonnay, so I purchased a bottle and one bottle of riesling, my personal favorite. Sharing his brother's love for chardonnay, Randall added another six bottles to their ever-growing list of purchases.

The next stop on our wine tasting tour was Silvan Ridge. Located just twelve miles from downtown Eugene, it offered a great selection of Willamette Valley wines. Pinot noir and pinot gris and their delightful effervescent muscat, along with their micro-production varietal wines from the Rogue Valley region, were among their best. Known for incredible long sunset views and the surrounding hills, it was beautiful. Finally, it was time to end the day with dinner after making our last purchases.

Dinning in downtown Eugene at Marche, it was known for its French-inspired menu. Tucked away between upscale boutiques at the chic Fifth Street Public Market, it was romantic and the highlight of our outing. Surveying the menu, we ordered the lamb, a grilled chop with pistachio-cilantro pesto, grilled asparagus, and scallions. It was finally time to call it a day after several drinks and dessert.

Arriving back at Pam and Randall's beautiful two-story Tudor home, we sat in the living room with glasses of wine and reminisced about our lives with Bob. Again, Randall's love for his brother was evident. More than once, I watched him discreetly wipe his moist eyes. Finally, after thanking them for the lovely day, I once again retired upstairs to the guest room.

Laying my head on the pillow, memories of Bob hit me like a

Tsunami. I knew that grieving came in waves, and I felt like I was drowning in a sea of emotions. But, I also knew there were five steps to grieving, denial, anger, bargaining, depression, and acceptance. It had been over a year, yet I still felt trapped between denial and anger.

The following afternoon, I said my goodbyes. It was hard leaving Pam, Randall, and their grandkids as they were the only family I had other than Keith, Greg, and their families. Being an only child, I never had siblings. Then, not long after Bob and I married, my father had a fatal heart attack. Unfortunately, my mother was diagnosed with advanced breast cancer only two years later and passed the following year. I wasn't immune to tragedy or heartbreak but losing Bob seemed to throw me into another dimension of time and space. Often, I felt disoriented, out of reality, not to the point of harming myself or others, but perplexed about my life's direction. Why had Bob gone first?

Entering Highway 101, I selected my favorite Sirius XM channel and reached over to find comfort in Fritz. My plans for today included a stop at Tillamook. Purchasing enough groceries to last for several days plus cheese to go with my selection of wines would be the perfect complement to endless hours of writing. Before leaving Marin, I rented a small cabin on the coast through a local realtor for the week. I couldn't wait to experience the solace of being alone, gathering my thoughts, and escaping into my fictional fantasies. Then, perhaps, I would finally call Liam.

Chapter Three

After leaving Tillamook, I exited onto a remote side road, carefully driving down a steep, narrow dirt road toward the ocean. Slowly rounding the last curve, the views were breathtaking. A desolate sandy beach stretched for miles, exposing a beautiful rustic cabin tucked away at the edge of the forest. I was excited at the possibilities of being alone with only my thoughts and Fritz. Working under a deadline with my publisher was often stressful. The cabin would provide a picturesque, tranquil setting to accomplish my goals.

It appeared a storm front was quickly moving in as I inhaled the crisp salty breeze blowing in from the ocean. Gray clouds swirled menacingly over the horizon, demanding that I hurry as I unloaded the car. Getting Fritz, the luggage, and groceries inside to the safety of the cabin was paramount. As I opened the door, the interior was stunning. Vaulted timbered ceilings highlighted the large floor-to-ceiling windows, which exposed dramatic ocean views and endless miles of beach. I looked forward to getting a warm fire started taking note of a massive fireplace with an ample supply of logs that centered the spacious room. Hurriedly attempting to walk Fritz before the dark clouds unleashed a fury of rain, my luck ran out. Drenched as the heavens opened, releasing a heavy downpour, I grabbed Fritz as we raced towards the safety of the front porch.

Quickly starting a roaring fire in the fireplace, I ran upstairs. The master bedroom offered all the comforts of home. A king-size four-poster bed faced French doors, which led outside to a balcony. Once again, as I drew back the curtains, the views were phenomenal. Deciding a warm shower would stave the chill off my bones, I walked into the bathroom. The warm water felt like heaven as it cascaded over me. Finally, stepping out of the shower, I quickly grabbed a towel, drying myself as I wrapped my hair in a turban. Dressing in a pair of sweats, I walked over to the mirror to dry my hair. Suddenly, gazing at the vanity, I felt faint. Sitting with the toiletries was a bottle of Aramis Cologne. I had always connected the leathery spicey scent with my husband, Bob. He had worn this fragrance since I met him in the late sixties. My eyes moistened as I picked up the bottle and slowly inhaled the scent.

How was it even possible that a fragrance made popular by Estee Lauder in nineteen-sixty-five would appear on the vanity at the cabin. Was it likely his spirit was watching over me? Instantly, I knew in my heart without a doubt it was a sign. He was indeed aware of my life. Letting my emotions consume me, I wiped tears from my eyes as I walked over to the bed. I missed him more than ever. Reaching for a pillow, I hugged it close to my chest for comfort. I wondered if he could possibly understand the degree of my grief or how devastating it was for me to live without him. Returning the bottle of Aramis to the vanity, I slowly walked out of the bathroom. I needed to face reality and the fact he was never coming back. Feeling lost, I went downstairs to the kitchen. There was only one thing that could help. It was still in the bags I had brought in from the winery.

Searching through the numerous bags, I found just what I needed, a bottle of riesling. Uncorking the bottle, I poured a glass and reached for the cheese and crackers. Taking my bounty into the living room, I curled up on the couch beside Fritz. The warmth of the fire made the spacious room feel cozy and comfortable. Suddenly startled by the buzz of my cell phone, I jumped off the couch and ran over to collect it from my purse. It was Amanda.

"Hey, just checking in. How are you?" Amanda quizzed.

"I'm okay," I answered softly.

"Well, you don't sound okay. What's wrong?"

"It's nothing. Really."

"Ericka, I'm sorry. I know you too well. Something is bothering you," Amanda insisted.

"I'm just missing Bob. I found a bottle of his favorite cologne earlier this evening. I rented a cabin by the ocean near Tillamook, and it was sitting on the bathroom vanity. Someone had obviously left it. Aramis was always his fragrance, and it just brought back so many memories."

"Ericka, you never mentioned renting a cabin, and finding the cologne sounds freaky. So what are you doing in a cabin?"

"I wanted to find a quiet place to write. You know I'm up against a deadline with this book."

"I understand, but for heaven's sake, next time, let me know. Why don't I fly up? I can reschedule my appointments. I don't think it's good for you to be alone. You do know what happens to people who are alone in isolated cabins, right?" Amanda laughed.

"Amanda, I'm fine. You write horror. None of that is true, and there's no need for you to fly up. I'll see you in Seattle."

"Well, I wouldn't exactly say that. It happens. If you need me, remember I'm only a phone call away. Stay safe, and I hope you get your book finished. See you in Seattle."

"Thanks, Amanda. We'll talk later."

Leave it to my best friend to plant seeds of doubt regarding the safety of my being alone, I mused, hanging up the phone. She did make a good point. No one knew that I was here, not even the boys. Perhaps, she was right. I should have given them the full details of my trip. Oh well, I had a manuscript to finish, and I needed the quiet that only seclusion offered. Locking the door, I rummaged through my luggage, finding my laptop. It was time to gather my thoughts and continue the arduous task of completing my book. I knew that my publisher would be thrilled to receive a finished novel by the end of my journey, providing I could stay focused. The words seemed to flow as I sat back on the sofa, sipping a glass of wine. Inputting my thoughts into my laptop, I managed to complete the following ten chapters in the wee hours of the morning. Closing my computer as the sun slowly made its appearance, I felt exhausted. Finally, making my way upstairs, I slipped into bed and pulled the covers over my head. Setting the alarm on my phone for 4:00 p.m., I didn't want to sleep the entire day away. I still had chapters to finish.

Waking at the sound of my alarm, I felt ravenous and desperately needed coffee. I quickly styled my hair, dressed in my sweats from the previous day, and ran downstairs to make coffee. Quickly finding a Keurig Coffee maker, I selected the most robust K-Cup and started breakfast. The aroma of fried bacon soon infused the air. I wasn't a culinary chef like my son, Greg. Still, my attempt at breakfast this morning could easily rival Denny's. Filling my plate with an overabundance of bacon, eggs, and hash browns, I savored every morsel. After putting the dishes away, I rummaged through the luggage for my San Francisco Giants baseball cap. Finding my sunglasses, I grabbed my sweater and Fritz. Hopefully, a long walk on the beach would give me the revitalization I needed to continue writing.

Any thoughts of a long walk quickly turned into a fast-paced run as I frantically chased after Fritz. Spotting a flock of seagulls in the distance, Fritz had decided a closer inspection was in order as he pursued the gangly squawking birds down the vast sandy beach. Finally catching up to my furry companion and feeling the heat from the intensity of my run, I stopped to discard my sweater tying it around my waist. Catching my breath, I took a moment to take in the spectacular surroundings. The views of the ocean and sky above appeared like a postcard. The Pacific's cobalt waters sparkled and danced as it brilliantly reflected the rays of the evening sun.

Slowly making my way back toward the cabin, I was in for a surprise. Noticing an unfamiliar car as it parked, for a brief second, I let my mind entertain thoughts of Amanda's warning. Perhaps being alone in an isolated cabin wasn't such a great idea. However, as I got closer, a familiar voice rang out.

"There you are," Amanda yelled. "I came as fast as I could."

"Amanda, what are you doing here? How in the world did you

find me. No one knew I was here," I exclaimed, totally shocked by her sudden appearance.

"Well, I couldn't let my best friend be murdered or become the victim of someone's evil, demented plans. The thoughts of your body not being discovered for days were horrifying," Amanda laughed.

"Amanda, that's ridiculous. You didn't answer my question. How in the world did you find me? No one knows I'm here?"

"Greg. You can run, but you can't hide," Amanda added with a giggle."Isn't technology incredible? He's been tracking you with an app. Can you even believe it? The GPS coordinates lead me straight here. Oh, I brought wine, lots of wine. I hope this place has a decent kitchen. I picked up some steaks and all the fixings in Tillamook."

What could I say? I loved Amanda. No one could have a better friend. However, her crazy scenarios were often hilarious. Despite her wild imagination and reason for being here, I was thrilled to see her.

"I brought someone," Amanda smiled, reaching inside the car for Hazel, her adorable white chihuahua.

Taking Hazel as Amanda unloaded her rental car, Fritz barked excitedly, recognizing his furry friend.

"Come inside. Let's get you settled. There's a second bedroom upstairs," I explained, hugging my best friend. "I'm glad you're here."

"Thanks. I know you want to work on your book, but no worries, I can be quiet as a church mouse. And, besides, I'm a great cook."

"Amanda, I hope you know that you never have to have a reason to show up. I love you. However, keep your violent thoughts in your books. You freaked me out."

"Sorry. Now show me this fabulous place you rented."

After giving Amanda a quick tour, we went into the kitchen. Unpacking the groceries, I laughed. She had brought items to make s'mores and enough wine to last for months.

"S'mores. Now I know why we continue to be best friends."

"Well, I hope there's an outdoor fire pit. Otherwise, we have to rely on our skills as former girl scouts and pick up pieces of driftwood to make one."

"You're in luck. There's a fire pit on the beach."

"Awesome, I see nights under the stars, s'mores, and wine," Amanda giggled. "Ericka, don't let me keep you from writing. I'm going to start dinner, steaks smothered in mushrooms, baked potatoes, green beans, and salad. I see pans in the sink? Did you cook?"

"Earlier. I had a late breakfast. I spent the entire night writing and slept in this morning."

"Wow. You were up all night writing?"

"Of course. Writing in the quiet of the night is truly productive."

"Well, I'll pour us a glass of wine. Find your laptop and just pretend that I'm not here."

"Right. You're crazy, but I love you."

"Girl, we both define crazy. We have conversations with people who don't exist and create fictional worlds. What can I say? We're both writers," Amanda laughed.

"Good point," I giggled, picking up my laptop. "I'm going upstairs to the balcony. Let me know when dinner is ready."

Taking a seat in one of the wicker lounge chairs, I leaned back, making myself comfortable. The tranquil sound of waves softly washing ashore, along with an impressive sunset that painted the evening sky in hues of deep violet, pinks, and orange provided the perfect ambiance to write romance. I was on a roll as the words flowed freely. At this rate, I might actually finish the manuscript. Completing the following three chapters, I heard Amanda's voice.

"Dinner is ready. Are you at a place in the book where you can take a break?" Amanda announced, suddenly walking out to the balcony. "I must say these views are stunning."

"Yes, they are, and the aroma coming from downstairs is mouthwatering. I'm famished."

"Well, just wait till you taste the steaks, two ribeyes cooked to perfection with all the trimmings."

"Sounds scrumptious," I smiled, following Amanda downstairs.

Glowing candles centered the dining room table giving the room a warm ambiance. The table was impeccably set for two people and held an opened bottle of merlot next to crystal wine glasses.

"Wow, Amanda, you've outdone yourself," I laughed.

"It's the least I can do for interrupting your writing retreat."

"Seriously, I'm happy you're here. Let's eat," I smiled, cutting into my steak.

"I have all the items needed for s'mores. Later, after dinner, we can enjoy dessert on the beach," Amanda mentioned, taking a sip of wine.

Later that evening, the night sky appeared like an expansive canopy of twinkling stars as we carried the makings for s'mores down to the beach. Fritz and Hazel followed close behind as I precariously balanced a tall pitcher of strawberry margaritas and glasses down to the shore. Amanda carried a platter and skewers. After getting the fire started, we pulled two rustic wooden Adirondack chairs near the fire pit. Threading our marshmallows onto skewers, we put the melted gooey sweetness between graham crackers and chocolate. It was simply divine.

"Wow, I wonder what our Bobs would think if they could see us sitting here under the stars eating s'mores?" Amanda questioned, downing her second drink.

"Well, I'm sure they would smile. We're doing the best we can under the circumstances."

"Ericka, I really miss Bob. But, I have to be honest. There are days when I think I can't go on. Sorry. I don't mean to put a damper on the evening," Amanda grieved, wiping tears from her eyes. "My memories of Bob will forever be engrained in my mind. Bob was rock solid. Even as he became older, his shoulders remained hard to the touch. I loved his ruddy cheeks and blue eyes and the fact that he had a head full of stark white hair in his elder years. He was always calm when I was going off the rail over something or another. He wasn't tall like your Bob, but he was imposing. Oh, Ericka, I don't know how I'm going to live without him." Amanda wept.

"You're going to be fine. You're the strongest person I know," I replied, completely understanding her emotions as I refilled our glasses.

"If I only had your optimism. I don't feel strong. I wished I had gone with Bob," Amanda cried softly, pulling Hazel to her chest.

"Amanda, life doesn't work that way. You have to carry on. You can't give up."

"Well, I'm not so sure. It's tough to lose a spouse after twenty-nine years."

"Amanda, I miss Bob every day. Trust me. I know how hard it is to lose a husband. Do you even remember the days, months, years we spent caring for them? You do remember how difficult it was, right?"

"Yes, but I'm out of a job. I feel lost. Do you know how hard it is to go to bed and in the middle of the night you reach for him, but he's not there or roll over to his side of the bed where he slept, and his side of the bed is cold and empty," Amanda sobbed. "Ericka, the better half of me is missing. I have no one to talk with, go to the movies, or enjoy a great meal together. I hate being alone. How do you do it?"

"Amanda, I don't. You have no idea. Last night when I discovered the bottle of Aramis on the vanity, I almost fainted. I walked into the bedroom, pulled a pillow to my chest, and cried a river of tears. I guess if there's anything we can take comfort in, it is the fact that we're not alone in our grief and despair. There are millions of women like us who have lost their spouses. I feel for the young women who unfortunately didn't have their husbands with them for most of their lives. There's no doubt our Bobs were unique, two of a kind, and unbelievably, they suffered from the same enormous list of ailments. They both broke their shoulders over the holidays and were in and out of the hospital and convalescent homes more times than I like to remember," I reminisced.

"I cherish my memories of the guy that I fell in love with. Bob, you know, was a big guy, a head and shoulders above most men, and that always made me feel safe and protected. He was an alpha male for sure, but he had a boyish side. I loved his quirky smile and the way he threw his head back to laugh, blue eyes brimming with child-like delight. Amanda, they loved us. But you know the most important thing they had in common, they had us. I love you, and you'll never be alone. Tonight has been cathartic. Let's take the doggies inside. Tomorrow is another day."

The following day we woke to blue skies and sunshine. It was the perfect day for long walks on the beach with the dogs, meandering through local antique stores, and curling up with a great book on the balcony. However, for me, it meant another day of writing and revisions.

Rummaging through my luggage, I was determined not to spend another day in baggy sweat pants. Discovering a cute polka dot dress hidden among the clothes, I laid it on the bed and jumped into the shower. A delectable aroma of coffee and fried bacon infused the air as I walked out of the bathroom. Hurriedly getting dressed, I ran downstairs.

"Good morning," Amanda smiled, handing me a cup of coffee. "I hope you finally got a good night's rest and didn't write till the wee hours of the morning."

"No. I actually slept for once. Thanks for the coffee," I smiled, walking over to the stove. "Wow, bacon, omelets, and waffles. You've cooked enough for an army, but I must say it smells scrumptious."

"Well, you know what they say about breakfast being the most important meal of the day. So make your plate, and let's eat."

"Wow. The eggs are incredible," I smiled, cutting into my omelet. "What are your plans for the day?"

"I haven't given it much thought. It's a beautiful day. I might take a book and hang out on the beach—a glass of wine, relaxing in one of the wooden chairs with Hazel. Sunshine, fresh ocean breezes, and the tranquil sounds of the waves do it for me. My happy place has always been anywhere that has beautiful beaches."

"Well, I agree. Sounds totally relaxing."

"Ericka, changing the subject, did you ever contact Liam?"

"No. I guess I've just been waiting for the perfect time."

"You and I both know that's a cop-out. It's a flimsy excuse, so why are you avoiding him? You said you felt a connection, and trust me, no man walks over to a woman's table, introduces himself, and pays for her meal unless he's interested. So you should call him."

"I know. I've thought about it, but sometimes I feel like I'd be cheating on Bob."

"Ericka, you're a widow. Bob's been gone for over a year. I don't think he wants you to remain single for the rest of your life. Seriously, you're still young, and life is for the living. Fall in love. What are you afraid of?"

"It's not that I'm scared to call him, but what if he doesn't share the same feelings. What if he was just lonely, like me, and simply needed a dinner partner. I'm not sure I want to take the risk of being rejected. I loved Bob more than you know, we were married for fifty wonderful years. But, I'm not sure another man like him exists for me."

"Ericka, I know you loved Bob. But, I'm sorry, he's not coming back, and all I heard were excuses. You're not trying to replace him. He'll always be with you. The bottle of Aramis should have confirmed that. I have a strong feeling that if you let Liam slip through your fingers, you're going to regret it. So, for once, become the strong, confident woman that you so often write about in your books. Besides, I want to know how this story ends," Amanda giggled, downing the last of her coffee.

"Okay. I'll call Liam later tonight, but no more pressure. I'm not sure that I'm ready at my age to jump back into the dating scene," I mused. "I haven't dated anyone since high school. Do you even know how long that's been?"

"Unfortunately, I do. You forget we're the same age. Now finish your book. I'm going down to the beach with Hazel to soak up the sun."

That evening, after devouring a huge portion of Amanda's phenomenal homemade lasagna, and too many glasses of wine, I retired to the bedroom to call Liam. Reaching into my purse, I found the napkin. Carefully unfolding it, I lounged back on the bed, staring at his cell number. Did the number hold the promise of something more, or was I reading too much into his simple invitation to join me. Questions swirled through my mind as I stared at the napkin. However, there was only one way to get the answers I needed. Anxiously picking up my cell phone, I entered his number and hit call.

"You've reached the voicemail for Liam Lachowski. Unfortunately, I'm unable to take your call at this time. Please leave your name, number, and a brief message. I will return your call as soon as possible."

Well, that was it. I didn't bother to leave my name or the reason for the call. The universe was sending me a message. It simply wasn't meant to be. I had merely misconstrued his intentions, and unfortunately, let myself entertain feelings that were not shared. Picking up the remote to the television, I began channel surfing. Stopping briefly on the Hallmark Channel, I smirked. A company sends a beautiful young woman to revitalize a landmark inn. In comes the cookie-cutter local guy in a plaid shirt with a dog to help with the restoration. Falling in love, the movie ends. Seriously, how corny could these movies get? They were beyond predictable. Resting my head on the pillow, I found myself drifting off. Suddenly, the sound of my cell phone woke me. Sitting up, I instantly recognized the number. It was Liam. Unsure of what to do, I decided to take the call.

"This is Liam Lachowski. I'm returning your call."

"Liam, this is Ericka Reed," I mumbled, trying to sound alert.

"Ericka," Liam paused. "I thought I would never hear from you. So why didn't you leave a message?"

"To be honest, I'm not sure."

"Well, I'm glad you called. Sorry I didn't answer. I was on another call. How are you?"

"Good. How about yourself?"

"Great. It's so good to hear your voice. I've not been able to get you out of my mind. I was hoping you would call."

"I suppose I should thank you again for dinner."

"No need. The pleasure was all mine. Are you free tomorrow?"

"I could be. Are you asking to see me?"

"Yes, as a matter of fact, I am. Just give me an address. I'd love to take you to dinner."

"Liam, it's rather remote."

"No worries. Remember I told you to give me a call, and I could arrange for us to meet."

"Well, I've rented a cabin on the beach near Tillamook. It's sort of a writing retreat."

"Wonderful, text me the address, and I'll pick you up tomorrow at 7:00 p.m."

"Okay. I'll text you. See you tomorrow evening."

"Tomorrow it is. Have a good evening."

Tossing the phone on the bed, I couldn't believe that I would be seeing him the following evening. How was that even conceivable? My mind was racing, and sleep was going to be elusive. Picking up my laptop, I decided to write. Pouring my thoughts into my book was a better option than staying awake all night.

The following morning, I walked into the kitchen with a huge smile.

"Okay. What gives? You look like the Cheshire cat who swallowed the canary," Amanda teased.

"Well, let's just say I've been invited to dinner this evening."

"Oh my gosh, you called Liam."

"Yes. He will be here at 7:00 p.m."

"Wow, that's unbelievable," Amanda exclaimed. "I'm so excited for you. But, wait just a minute, how does anyone drop whatever they do for a living and show up in a remote location? Is he in Oregon?"

"I'm not sure, but it's possible. Liam's brother lives in Crescent City. He's probably retired. It doesn't matter. What does matter is that I have no idea what I'm going to wear this evening?" I worried, helping myself to scrambled eggs, sausage and toast.

"Well, we can drive into town. I noticed several fashionable boutiques along Main Street when I drove through town."

"Oh, my hair," I panicked. "I've been planning to color it for days. Amanda, I have to color it before tonight. Can you help?"

"Calm down. No worries. We can go by a drug store while we're in town and buy a box of hair color."

"Amanda, what would I ever do without you. Without your help, this evening wouldn't be possible."

"You've got this. Now let's run into town."

Making a quick trip into town for a new dress and hair dye, I was excited to see what possibilities the boutiques along Main Street might offer. Luck was on my side, as the second shop, Elegant Threads, had the dress of my dreams. Purchasing a black halter gown covered in shiny black sequins was perfect. My purchases were complete after adding a pair of matching black heels. Finally, I had my ensemble for the evening. Amanda and I decided to stop for burgers. A drizzle of rain fell as we left the café. I hoped the weather would clear before Liam arrived. Unfortunately, the road leading down to the cabin was treacherous at best. Glancing down at my watch, we had just enough time to make a stop at the pet store to stock up on treats for the dogs. Finally, leaving Tillamook, I had my attire and hair coloring. Now, I was anxious to return and color my hair.

Wagging tails met us at the door as we arrived at the cabin. Hazel and Fritz were happy to see us. Amanda gave them each a snack before we ran upstairs to begin the process of covering my gray hair. Choosing a medium shade of blonde, I hoped to accomplish a more vibrant, youthful appearance. I could only pray that the shade I decided to purchase didn't result in a garish brass color. There was no time for a second trip into town or a do-over. Following the instructions on the box, I polished my nails while I waited for the color to process. I felt like a giddy teenager. I hadn't been on a date in over fifty years other than with my husband, and I was extremely nervous. Was it possible to start over in life? By the end of the evening, I hoped to have the answer.

"I brought you a glass of wine. I figured you might need it."

"Thanks. Amanda, I'm having second thoughts. Why did I call him? Honestly, I think I'm too old for this. Dating is for young people."

"Ericka, you're just getting cold feet. It's understandable to be nervous. How long has it been, fifty years since you've been on a date with someone other than Bob? Listen, you've been to the rodeo, and it's about time you get back on the horse."

"Thanks. That's comforting," I laughed.

"Hey, I'm your best friend. Relax. You're going to have fun. Let me know if he happens to have a best friend who's available."

"Oh, trust me, if he doesn't, I'm sure Seattle will have lots of eligible men our age. I can't wait to set you up with someone. Any criteria other than breathing," I laughed.

"Yes, no smokers or drug users, need I continue. Oh, and I don't ride bikes, especially motorbikes, hike, skydive, or ski either on snow or water. Do you get the picture?"

"Amanda, you're hysterical. I love you."

Holding my breath, I shampooed my hair and reached for the hairdryer. One look in the mirror, and I smiled. The color was perfect. Sporting a new shade of blonde easily took years off my appearance.

Walking into the bathroom, I stepped into the shower. Unexpectedly as the warm water washed over me, I suddenly became emotional. Once again, my eyes moistened as I thought of Bob. Would he be okay with me seeing Liam this evening? Why did it still feel like cheating on him and the incredible life we shared. Wiping my eyes, I stepped out of the shower and reached for my bathrobe. My eyes were once again drawn to the bottle of Aramis as I sat down at the vanity to style my hair and apply makeup. Picking up the bottle, I held it as I inhaled its fragrance. For a brief second, it felt like someone lightly touched my cheek. Quickly glancing in the mirror, there was no one in the room, yet undeniably I sensed Bob's presence. A myriad of tears ran down my face. Then, in a low, faint whisper, I distinctly heard Bob's voice. "It's okay. Be happy. I love you." I couldn't be sure if I had honestly heard it audibly or in my mind, but I knew he was there to give me closure on our life. "I love you. I'll always love you forever," I cried softly. Shocked and motionless from the unexplainable encounter, a feeling of warmth consumed me. It was a private moment shared between lovers. And whether it actually happened or was a figment of my imagination, I would never know. However, I would always believe in my heart Bob came to me when I needed him most.

After finishing my hair and makeup, I took the beautiful garment from its hanger. Carefully stepping into the gown, I didn't want to accidentally get makeup on the gorgeous sequined material. Then, slipping into matching heels and reaching for a shawl to keep me warm during the cooler evening temperatures, I walked downstairs. Still reeling from the experience, I tried to hide my emotions. However, knowing Amanda, I felt sure she would sense something was amiss.

"Wow. That gown was made for you. You're stunning. Liam is a lucky guy."

"Thank you."

"Ericka, what's wrong? You look like you've seen a ghost. You should be excited."

If she only knew. "I'm just tired. It's been a long day."

"Well, sit down. I have just what you need," Amanda explained, walking into the kitchen. "Toss back this shot of Jameson. It's Irish whiskey."

"Geez, Amanda, that's strong," I gasped.

"Do you want another?"

"No. Thanks. I need to be able to walk when Liam arrives."

Waiting nervously for his arrival, I sat on the sofa, reliving the encounter. I smiled, knowing that I would be fine regardless of how the evening went.

Awestruck, I watched from the tall windows as a luxurious Maserati slowly made its way up to the cabin and parked. Maybe there was more to this man than I knew. I didn't realize that my life was about to change in ways that I could never imagine.

Chapter Four

I was about to enter the world of Liam Lachowski, and my life would never be the same. Hearing a light knock at the door, I walked over. A debonair handsome man entered my field of vision. My breath hitched, taking in his distinguished familiar traits, which I remembered from the restaurant. Dressed in an impeccable three-piece tailored suit and holding an exquisite floral bouquet of pink peonies, I was completely mesmerized at the mere sight of him.

"We meet again," Liam smiled.

"Yes," I mumbled, totally speechless.

"May I come in?"

"Of course."

"I believe these are for you," he winked, handing me the bouquet.

"Thank you," I blushed, slowly regaining my voice. "The flowers are gorgeous. Come inside and have a seat while I find a vase." Watching him from the kitchen, I was breathless.

Suddenly, met with wagging tails and the excitement of Fritz and Hazel, Amanda was exasperated, chasing behind them.

"Sorry. I was trying to keep the dogs contained in the family room," she smiled, unable to pull her eyes away from him.

"Liam, this is Amanda. We're neighbors and best friends, I might add."

"Amanda, it's nice to meet you," Liam acknowledged, flashing one of his quirky smiles.

"It's nice to meet you as well," Amanda replied, turning her focus on the dogs as she attempted to herd them back into the family room.

"They're fine," Liam grinned, stooping down to give Hazel and Fritz a quick rub behind their ears. "I have a black lab. She's the love of my life."

"Well, as you can tell, we love our furry companions," I added, watching as Liam continued with his playful affections. Finally, he looked up with a smile.

"Shall we go? I made reservations for 7:00 p.m."

"Yes. Let me get my shawl. It can be unusually cool near the ocean after dark."

Taking the chenille wrap, Liam wrapped it loosely around my shoulders as we walked towards the door.

"Have a wonderful evening," Amanda smiled.

"Thanks. I'm sure we'll meet again," Liam replied, turning to leave.

Walking to his car, I wasn't sure if I was more impressed with the fact he was driving a new Maserati or the fact he was able to maneuver it down the steep, narrow descent.

"Ericka, you're stunning," Liam complimented, opening the car door. "Your hair is different. I like it. So blonde, is it?" he teased with a wink.

"Yes. Thanks." I was impressed that he would have noticed.

The car's interior was pure luxury and smelled of Italian leather as I stepped inside.

"I've made reservations at Bella E Buona. It means, 'Beautiful and Good.' It came highly recommended, and it's only a short drive. I hope you like Italian."

"Yes."

"Great. Ericka, I have to say once again how thrilled I was that you called, even though you didn't leave a message," he smiled.

"Sorry. Honestly, as I said, I don't know what came over me."

"No worries. It's fine," Liam laughed. "I'm only teasing. Geez, I must say these roads are dangerous."

Arriving at Bella E Buona, the restaurant was exquisite. A fountain greeted us as we entered, and the ambiance of the Tuscan décor was breathtaking. Following the maître d' to our table, Liam gently placed his hand at the small of my back, guiding me to a table. He exuded the word 'gentleman' as he pulled out my chair. After we were seated, Liam smiled, looking up from his menu.

"May I take the liberty of ordering for us?"

"Yes, of course." I knew I was in excellent hands.

"To start, we would like a bottle of pinot grigio. Then, for our entrée selection, we will have the salmon with artichoke spinach ravioli with olive tapenade and butternut squash," Liam graciously instructed the waiter.

"Yes, sir, I'll be right back with your wine."

"Thanks."

"Ericka, tell me once again everything there is to know about you," Liam asked, thoughtfully focusing his undivided attention on me.

"Well, I'm afraid you will find my life rather mundane and boring. You know that I lost my husband, Bob, last year after fifty years of marriage."

"Yes. Again my condolences. I know that had to be difficult."

"Thank you. It has been overwhelming at times. Of course, you know that my oldest son, Keith, is a commercial pilot, and my youngest son, Greg, is a chef.

"Commendable professions," I must add.

"Thanks. I have four grandchildren. Keith and his wife, Briella, have two small boys. Jeffry is ten, and Bobby is six and named after my husband. Greg and his wife, Samantha, have twin girls, Abby and Bella. They just celebrated their second birthday. They're the loves of my life."

"No doubt. I think if there's one thing I regret in life is not having children."

"I'm sorry."

"No need. It was a decision my wife and I made. But, unfortunately, our marriage was rocky at best and, as you know, ended in divorce."

"Your entrees will be out momentarily," the waiter stated, leaving the bottle of pinot grigio.

"Taste this. I think you'll love it," Liam said, filling my glass.

"You're right. It's wonderful," I replied, taking a sip. "Thank you."

Returning with our meals, the waiter sat two piping hot plates on the table. Our entrees were entirely delectable. The salmon was flaky and tender, and the artichoke ravioli with olive tapenade and butternut squash was phenomenal. This meal definitely came with bragging rights, as I finished every morsel.

"Would you like dessert? I hear they make a delicious tiramisu," Liam inquired.

"Oh, I'm not sure, it sounds delicious, but I think I overindulged?"

"Nonsense. Why don't we split one?"

"Okay," I hesitated. "I suppose I should at least try it."

"Good girl," Liam smiled, motioning for the waiter. "We would like to share a tiramisu, and could you please bring two coffees," he added.

"Yes, of course, sir, I'll have it brought out immediately."

Sampling the tiramisu was incredible and just as scrumptious as Liam had described.

"So, Ericka, tell me about you. You've told me about your family, but I want to know more about you? What are your hobbies? Did you have a career?" Liam questioned, taking a sip of coffee.

"Well, please don't laugh, but I write romance novels. It's my passion, and I'm currently working on my nineteenth manuscript. In fact, I'm working against a deadline with my publisher as we speak. It was my reason for renting the cabin, and I was hoping to complete it this week."

"Wow, impressive. Are your books widely available?"

"Yes. The books are available at all major book stores and online," I smiled. "I have an upcoming book marketing campaign. It kicks off next week in Portland. My agent scheduled a couple of promotional book signings when she found out that I was taking a short road trip up the West Coast."

"That's a huge accomplishment. I'm sure becoming a published author is a lot harder than it appears. It's definitely a talent most people don't possess. Do you write under a pseudonym or use your given name?"

"Oh, I've always written as Ericka Reed."

"Well, Ericka Reed, the novelist, I feel honored you accepted my dinner invitation," Liam winked teasingly.

"It's not such a big deal," I blushed. "So, Liam Lachowski, what career path brought you to your retirement years?" I taunted, in turn referencing his full name.

"Well, I still manage a small company in Canada," he answered, flashing his sexy smile.

Liam exuded an air of confidence that I found alluring and sensual. The man sent shivers of excitement racing throughout my body. There was undeniable chemistry between us, and I knew I wanted to see him again.

"Ericka, I want to see you again," he paused as if he were reading my mind. Reaching across the table, he held my hand. "Sweetheart, we're in the home stretch of our lives. Why don't you come to Canada with me?"

"Liam," I slowly hesitated, surprised by his sudden invitation. "There's no doubt that I would love to see you again, but asking me to go with you to Canada is out of the question. We hardly know each other, and I have a book to complete. I'm going to be in Seattle later this month. Why don't you join me?"

"I suppose that's a hard no for leaving with me tonight," he laughed. "Yes. I would love to meet you in Seattle," he grinned without hesitancy.

"Liam, I'm afraid it's definitely a hard no for tonight. However, Seattle sounds exciting."

Truth be known, I was utterly flattered by his invitation. The mere thought of doing something as daring as running away with prince charming was exhilarating. However, I wasn't a character in one of my books. I was Ericka Reed, a recent widow who didn't contemplate flights of fantasy. I only wrote about them.

"Well, I should get you back. It's late, and I'm sure you have some writing to finish."

"Yes. Thank you for dinner. It was exquisite."

Driving back, we listened to classical music. The wine had me feeling a tad dizzy, so I leaned my head against the seat. Glancing over at this incredible man, for once, I entertained thoughts of falling in love again. Parking in front of the cabin, Liam opened my door and walked me to the front porch.

"Ericka, thank you for a beautiful evening. Is it alright if I call or text?"

"Yes. Definitely."

"Sweetheart, if you change your mind regarding my offer, my door is always open," he whispered softly against my ear, lightly kissing my cheek. "See you in Seattle," he smiled.

Watching as he drove away, my emotions were all over the place. How was it this incredible man had shown up in my life? I couldn't wait to see him again. Walking inside, I knew Amanda would be awake and wanted a detailed account of our evening. Lounging back on the couch, I waited for the questions to begin.

"I thought I heard you come in. How was your evening?" Amanda asked.

"Dreamy."

"Wow. Coming from you, that's quite a statement."

"Amanda, I don't know how to explain it, and at my age, it probably sounds absurd, but I'm totally attracted to him. He even asked me to leave with him tonight, and for a brief second, I almost considered it."

"Oh dear Lord, you've finally lost your mind. No more dating for you. He could have kidnapped you or, worse yet, sold you into human trafficking," Amanda exclaimed.

"Amanda, that's ludicrous," I laughed. "I might be tipsy, but that's the funniest thing I've ever heard. I don't think I would be worth much at an auction. Besides, you met him. He's a really nice guy."

"Ericka, they all seem friendly at first. You don't even know this guy."

"Well, I'm a good judge of character. He's charming, sexy, and I'm going to see him again. We've agreed to meet in Seattle, and I can't wait to see him."

"I suppose he's retired."

"Yes. However, Liam still manages a small company in Canada."

"Well, that's vague. He didn't elaborate?"

"No, and I didn't ask. I don't really care. But, Ericka, I think I might be falling in love with McDreamy."

"Seriously, and this is coming from the woman who referred to dating as cheating on her deceased husband. Oh, Ericka, you've got it bad for this guy. I can tell. God help you. I can't wait to see how this plays out. Just remember, he's not a character in one of your romance novels, and this is real life, not a fictional script you are writing. I don't want to see you get hurt. Geez, I feel like I'm talking to a ditzy teenager who's got a humongous boy crush. And, on that note. I'm off to bed."

Alone on the sofa with only my thoughts and Fritz, my mind kept replaying the events of the evening. Amanda was right. I did have a humongous boy crush, and his name was Liam Lachowski. Heaven help me. She was right on so many levels. But one thing Liam said stood out in my mind, we were in the home stretch of our lives, and to sit on the sidelines and watch the game wasn't for me. I was going to be in the game, whatever that meant. Batter up. I loved baseball, especially the San Francisco Giants. Pulling Fritz close to my chest, I was ready to risk everything for a relationship with Liam.

Turning in for the night, I grabbed Fritz and went upstairs. Getting out my laptop, I poured my emotions into my writing. Three more chapters down, but I was still far from completing my story. Truth be known, the story just took an unexpected twist. Writing till the sun peeped in under the brocade curtains, I was exhausted. Unfortunately, I wouldn't be up to enjoy one of Amanda's incredible breakfasts, and she would have to spend most of the day alone. Setting my alarm for 3:00 p.m., I pulled the covers over my head. I finally fell asleep.

Waking to the sound of my cell phone, I instantly jumped up from the bed, thinking perhaps it was Liam. However, looking down at the screen, it was Amanda.

"Hey, sleepyhead, sorry to wake you. I came into town with Hazel to check out the antique stores. I have a maid service coming by within the hour. I wanted to make sure you were awake and knew other people would be in the house. I didn't want there to be any surprises. Do you know it's almost 2:30 p.m.? Anyway, I also called to see what you wanted for dinner. I discovered they have a fabulous farmers market. I was thinking perhaps a veggie soup with organic homegrown vegetables. Are you on board?"

"Sounds delicious. While you're in town, why don't you see if there's a local bakery and pick up dessert."

"I've got a better idea. I'll bake us one of my famous chocolate cakes and pick up some ice cream."

"Oh my God, I love you. You're one in a million. I can't wait. See you soon."

Turning off my alarm, I jumped in the shower, anxious to be out and dressed before the maids arrived. Unfortunately, I forgot that we had signed a cleaning service on the rental agreement. Tomorrow was our last day at the cabin. I would be driving over to Portland, and Amanda was flying back to the Bay Area. Stepping out of the shower, I hurriedly wrapped my hair in a turban and walked over to the vanity to apply a light touch of makeup. A quick glance told me something was askew. My heart stopped taking a closer look. The bottle of Aramis was missing.

Rubbing my eyes, they surely deceived me, but I found that wasn't the case as I slowly opened them. The Aramis was gone. Tears filled my eyes, and goosebumps covered my entire body as I immediately searched the drawer, thinking somehow it was there. To my astonishment, the drawer was empty. Staring into the mirror, it reflected my utter shock. Tears flowed down my face. No one would ever believe the bottle of Aramis had vanished. I wasn't sure that I understood it myself. Wiping my eyes, I knew it represented Bob, his love for me, and our life. It signified him taking a step back to allow me to live my life. It didn't matter if anyone ever believed me. My heart knew the truth. Looking upward, I wept. "Sweetheart, I love you. Rest in peace." Bob had lovingly given me the closure I needed to move forward with my life. Wiping my eyes, I finished applying my makeup, covering any outward signs I had cried rivers of tears. If it were only that easy to hide my emotions, I thought.

Hearing someone come in, I hurried down the stairs. Amanda

walked inside, encumbered with numerous shopping bags. She looked like a pack mule.

"Wow. I guess if those bags are any indication, you discovered a lot of nice things at the antique stores," I laughed.

"Are you kidding? I think I did major damage to my budget."

"Seriously, Amanda, that's funny. I don't think I've ever heard you use the word budget."

Helping unload the bags, she had all the necessary ingredients to make the veggie soup. But, most importantly, she had everything needed to make the chocolate cake. Tonight, of all nights, I needed the comfort of chocolate and wine.

Amanda took over the kitchen. Finally, the maids arrived late, taking over the house cleaning, and I took my laptop out to the balcony to write. The evening was getting off to a great start. However, tears once again swept over me like a tsunami as I poured my emotions into my writing. Thoughts regarding the missing bottle of Aramis consumed me. There was no doubt that Bob wanted me to move on with my life. However, I knew that he would always be with me in spirit. Knowing that gave me comfort and the courage to pursue happiness, hopefully exploring a relationship with Liam.

After completing two additional chapters, my tummy's rumbling and the delectable aroma coming from the kitchen sent me running downstairs.

"Something smells divine."

"Oh, trust me, it is. Taste this," Amanda smiled, dipping a large spoon into the vast pot simmering on the stove.

"Oh my gosh. The soup is amazing."

"It's the ingredients. The farmers market only offers the best local homegrown organic vegetables. It's probably the healthiest meal we've had since being here, and the cake is almost ready to take out of the oven. I think there are about ten minutes left on the timer."

"I can't wait."

"I opened a bottle of chardonnay earlier. Pour yourself a glass, and I'll set the table."

After consuming one too many bowls of soup, Amanda finally

served up her famous chocolate cake with vanilla ice cream. Over the years of knowing Amanda, it had quickly become a much-requested dessert at every holiday.

"Wow. As always, it's delicious," I remarked.

"It's the cocoa powder. You need high-quality cocoa," Amanda suggested.

"Well, whatever your magic ingredient is, it never disappoints."

After cleaning the kitchen, we decided to take our wine and the dogs down to the beach. Hazel and Fritz needed to escape the confines of the cabin. It was our last evening, and the stars were out in abundance. The night sky was inundated in the brilliance of sparkling diamonds. Relaxing in the Adirondack chairs with a glass of chardonnay, it was the perfect ending for our stay at the cabin.

"Ericka, thanks for letting me intrude on your writer's retreat."

"Amanda, having you and Hazel wasn't an intrusion. Trust me, I love you, and the meals you prepared were worthy of a Michelin three-star rating. Our next retreat might have to be centered around weight loss," I laughed.

"Well, as you know, I enjoy cooking, but I'm looking forward to Seattle. I can't wait."

"Me too. I'll make reservations for pet-friendly accommodations, so no worries about Hazel. By the way, did you happen to move the bottle of Aramis from the counter in my bathroom? It's missing."

"What are you talking about? First, I don't use cologne, and second I use the bathroom in my bedroom. So why would I go into yours?"

"Well, it's gone, and I was just curious."

"The maids could have moved it. Remember, they were in the bathrooms cleaning earlier today."

"Guess that's possible," I answered. However, I knew that wasn't the case. The maids had arrived late, and it was missing before they entered the cabin.

"Changing the subject, have you heard from Liam?"

"No. It's probably a little soon. We just had dinner last night."

"Ericka, I don't want to see you get hurt. That's all."

Later that evening, after consuming several glasses of wine, we gathered the dogs and walked back towards the cabin. Scooping Fritz into my arms, I observed a shooting star as it brilliantly raced across the night sky. Instantly, I made a wish.

"Wow. Did you see that?" Amanda exclaimed.

"Yes. Did you make a wish?"

"Of course. I need all the help I can get these days. My life hasn't exactly been great since Bob passed."

"Well, you just never know. Maybe it's about to change," I remarked.

"From your mouth to God's ears."

Reaching the cabin, we both decided to turn in for the evening. I opened another bottle of wine to make a quick toast before we retired to our rooms. After pouring two tall glasses of white zin, I handed a glass to Amanda.

"Here's to Seattle and an unbelievable weekend," I toasted.

"Yes. I'll toast to that. I can't wait. It's my birthday weekend. We should make it spectacular."

"Definitely. Get some rest. I'll see you in the morning. Don't forget. We have to vacate the cabin before noon."

"Okay. I'm mostly packed, and the maids did a superb job, so there's not much to do. See you in the morning. Good night."

Walking into my room, I felt melancholy. The cabin would always hold the memories of meeting Liam and our unforgettable dinner. Trying to put the worries of him not having called out of my mind, I finished my glass of zinfandel, put on some soft music, and stepped into the shower. The warm water, even though refreshing, and the wine did not calm my sense of worry. Emerging from the bathroom, I wrapped my damp hair in a turban. Oddly as it seemed, I felt no compulsion to write. I decided reading offered a better option to refocus my mind away from Liam. Grabbing my latest reading material, a mafia romance, I simply got into bed. After reading for several hours, I turned off the light. Lying in bed, unable to sleep, I reached over to check my cell phone one last time for missed calls or texts. I had none. Being logical, I knew there were many explainable reasons he might not have called. Finally, as my mind gave way to sleep, I was suddenly awakened by the sound of my phone. My heart raced as I bolted upright, discovering Liam's name brightly displayed on the screen.

"Hey, sweetheart, how are you this evening? Sorry to call so late. I've been tied up in meetings all day."

"I'm good. It's so great to hear your voice. How are you?" I asked groggily.

"Missing you. I hope I didn't wake you or interrupt your writing. I know we planned to meet in Seattle. But, unfortunately, that's a few weeks away, and honestly, I don't want to wait. So, what are your plans for this week?"

"Well, as I said, I'm signing books. It's part of the marketing campaign in the Portland area. I'm staying at the Marriot. Maybe we could meet for dinner after one of the book signings."

"That sounds perfect. I hate to make this short, but I'm getting together with an old friend tonight for drinks. Ericka, I just had a wild thought. Harry is divorced and a great guy. Is Amanda currently seeing anyone?"

"No. What are you thinking?"

"I was thinking of inviting Harry to Seattle if you think Amanda would be okay with the idea."

"Wow, that might work. I think Amanda would be fine with it."

"We both graduated from Harvard with a degree in Business Management, so Harry is educated, traveled the world, and I must say he's aged like a fine wine. Oh, he's from New Orleans."

"I think you may have just given me the one reason you should invite him."

"The fact he graduated from Harvard or the that he's well-traveled?'

"None of the above," I laughed. "It's the fact Harry is from New Orleans. Amanda was born and raised in Georgia. She's Southern to the bone."

"Great. Seattle will be interesting."

"Sweetheart, I'll see you in Portland this week. Text me your schedule. Go back to sleep," Liam laughed.

"See you soon."

Tossing my cell phone on the bed, I was breathless as I lounged back on the bed. There was no doubt. I was falling helplessly in love with this man.

The following day, Amanda and I went our separate ways. She flew back to San Fransico, and I was on my way to Portland. I couldn't wait to see Liam. Later, I would see Amanda in Seattle. She was in for the surprise of her life.

Chapter Five

Arriving in Portland after a short drive across Highway Twenty-Six, it was still early in the afternoon. Walking into the downtown Marriott, I approached the reception desk, where the concierge greeted me.

"Welcome to Portland, Mrs. Reed. We are happy to have you staying with us. You are in room 611 on the sixth floor. I hope your room exceeds your expectations. If there is anything I can do for you during your visit, please let me know."

"Thank you."

I was met with sheer luxury as I unlocked the door. The room was spacious and modern. Large windows draped with elegant damask curtains exposed city views. My publisher, Kate, was now picking up the tab for my lodging and meals during the marketing campaign. As always, she ensured I was given the VIP treatment. Entering the room, I was stunned. Sitting on the credenza, a floral arrangement containing two dozen long stem roses and a bottle of Dom Perignon Vintage awaited me. Walking over to inhale the delightful floral fragrance, I assumed the flowers and champagne were from Kate. An enormous smile lit up my face as I picked up the card.

Sweetheart, welcome to Portland. I can't wait to see you, Liam.

Totally in shock at his romantic gesture, tingles of excitement raced throughout my body. Taking a seat on the sofa, I lounged back, hugging a pillow close to my chest. I was still reeling with exhilaration. Looking down at my watch, I had just a moment to call Liam before meeting my agent, Cynthia, for dinner to go over the schedule. Liam answered on the first ring.

"Hello."

"Oh, Liam, the roses are gorgeous. Thank you."

"I'm pleased to know they made it to your room. But, unfortunately, the florist couldn't assure me they would be delivered before you arrived."

"Well, I received the beautiful bouquet and the Dom Perignon. Thank you again. We'll open it together."

"I've checked your schedule against mine, and I can be there tomorrow night. Why don't I pick you up after the Barnes and Noble signing?"

"Sounds wonderful. Sorry, I have to run. I'm meeting my agent, Cynthia, for dinner this evening. We have to go over any last-minute changes. I can't wait to see you."

"See you tomorrow. Good luck with your book signing."

"Thanks."

Taking a few minutes to catch my breath, I couldn't fathom that a man I hardly knew would go to such lengths to see me. How did I get so lucky?

Hurriedly, changing from my casual clothes into clothing more appropriate for a business meeting, I made sure Fritz was comfortable before leaving. Then, locking the door, I raced toward the elevator. Pushing the button for the lobby, I hoped my ride was waiting. Cynthia had requested an Uber to pick me up. She had scheduled a quick meeting at the Barnes and Noble Book Store before dinner to discuss the arrangements regarding the book signing.

After confirming the details were set at the book store, Cynthia had the Uber driver drop us at La Parrilla, her favorite Mexican restaurant. The décor was stunning as we walked inside. Decorated in bold colors with rustic furnishings and accented with Talavera pottery, the interior easily reflected Mexico's old-world charm. Seated near the expansive windows in the front, we both ordered margaritas along with the house specialties. We feasted on rice, beans, mini chimichangas, and a shared order of nachos.

Discussing the marketing campaign over margaritas, I was relieved to know that we had a driver. It appeared my publisher had everything preordered and arranged to promote my latest book, *Left at the Altar,* a story of love and revenge. We would also be promoting my current project for presale orders. My book sales had skyrocketed over the past two years, maintaining their rank among the top ten bestselling categories. I was indeed blessed at my age to have an enormous fan base, and hopefully, tomorrow's book signing would be a huge success.

Arriving back at the hotel, I sat on the sofa, tucking my feet under me as I checked my cell for missed calls or texts. Glancing at my phone, it indicated I had one missed call from Amanda. Noting the time on my watch, it was still early, and knowing Amanda, she was still awake. I decided to give her a quick call.

"Hello."

"Hey. I just saw your missed call. What's up?"

"Nothing. I'm just checking in to see how things are going in Portland. You must be excited about the book signing. I wish I could be there, but Hazel has an appointment at the vet, and I had to reschedule my dental appointment for tomorrow."

"No problem. I knew you had things to do when you got back. How was the flight?"

"Uneventful, as usual. Why is it I always get seated next to young children and not a handsome unattached CEO returning to the Bay Area."

"Well, you never know, things could change."

"Not unless you know something that I don't," Amanda laughed.

"Well, there's always Seattle," I teased, thinking of Harry. "I had quite the surprise this afternoon when I arrived at the hotel," I added.

"Oh, yeah, let me guess, there was a tall, dark, sexy man waiting for you in your room."

"Amanda, get serious. There was a stunning floral arrangement of two dozen long stem roses and a bottle of Dom Perignon sitting on the credenza when I walked in."

"From who?"

"Who do you think?"

"Your publisher?"

"No. Liam."

"Really. That's interesting."

"Can you even believe it? My entire room is filled with the heavenly scent of roses, and Liam will be at the book signing tomorrow evening. I can't wait to see him."

"Ericka, I didn't think you were seeing him again until Seattle. Aren't things moving a little fast? You're beginning to sound like a giddy teenager again, and for heaven's sake, you're in your seventies."

"Amanda, we've had this conversation. I'm seeing him tomorrow. I suggested we meet for dinner after the event at Barnes and Noble. End of discussion."

"I'll say no more. You're a grown woman and the captain of your ship. Let's just hope it isn't the Titanic. We all know how that story ended."

"Thanks for your vote of confidence. We'll talk tomorrow."

"Have a great book signing. Talk to you later."

Getting dressed for bed, I felt for Amanda. I knew the problem of meeting eligible men who had the attributes she wanted. I could only pray that Harry might fill that niche and be the one guy who might sweep her off her feet. Pulling the covers up to my chin, I fell asleep, excited at the possibilities of seeing Liam.

Waking the following day to the sound of my alarm, I jumped in the shower and afterward ordered room service. Starting the day with a good breakfast was always a great idea, and I didn't relish the idea of going out. I would be dealing with the public tonight, and even though I loved my fans, I was always exhausted by the end. Lounging on the sofa, still wearing my bathrobe, I waited for room service to arrive.

After enjoying a leisurely breakfast, I finally dressed in a pair of sweats and picked up my laptop. Writing the following chapters would be the perfect distraction to fill the hours before I left for the local Barnes and Noble. Completely involved in my writing, the sound of an incoming text from Liam suddenly broke my concentration.

Best wishes for a fabulous book signing. See you soon. Liam

Amanda might be right. Reading Liam's text, I felt warm, tingly, and excited. Perhaps, I was acting like a giddy teenager. They say you're only as young as you feel, and at this moment, I definitely didn't feel old.

Putting my writing aside for the moment, I walked over to the closet. I needed to decide on what to wear for the event. I wanted something which looked professional yet at the same time appeared elegant. Deciding on a pair of black dress pants, I chose a white long sleeve silk blouse with a matching blazer. Accessorizing with a floral chiffon scarf would soften the look and give it a feminine touch. Finally, adding black heels and jewelry would complete my ensemble for the evening. I would be appropriately dressed for the book signing and later dinner with Liam. Having decided on apparel, I once again focused on writing. I wanted to give my publisher an update that reflected substantial progress.

Totally immersed in my characters' lives and their involvement in the story, I wrote nonstop for the remainder of the afternoon. Finally interrupted by the sound of the alarm on my phone, I noticed the time. With less than two hours remaining, it allowed just enough time to order room service, enjoy a glass of wine, and dress before I once again met the Uber driver. Ordering a turkey sandwich on rye bread with a side salad, I only wanted to stave off the feeling of hunger. I knew Liam was an epicurean at heart, and dinner would be incredible even though he hadn't mentioned a choice of restaurants. The possibilities of the evening excited me. I wasn't sure which excited me more, the book signing or dinner with Liam. I highly suspected it was the latter.

Hurriedly finishing the sandwich and salad, I quickly dressed for the evening, allowing myself a few minutes to enjoy another glass of wine before I left. These events always made me nervous. Even though I was an accomplished author, having published dozens of books, I always felt slightly undeserving of all the attention and requests for my autograph. Out of all the faces I would see tonight, there was only one face that would have my undivided attention. Only one man would make me weak in the knees, flushed with excitement, and I couldn't wait to see him.

Quickly grabbing my roller tote, I locked the door and walked over to the elevator. Exiting the hotel, the Uber driver was on time and waiting. Arriving at Barnes and Noble, I was early. However, Cynthia and the store manager were there to greet me. The manager prepared a long table near the front of the store where I would sit to sign books. It held my latest releases and freebies, including bookmarks, pens, and candies. Behind the table were large elegant posters depicting the covers of my recent books. The degree of attention focused on me tonight and my books could easily make any author feel like a celebrity. Comfortably seated yet nervous, a long line was forming near the entrance. If this was any indication, the turnout appeared massive. Focusing my attention on each person who approached the table, I graciously signed my books, bookmarks, and most anything I was asked to autograph. Truly humbled by the generous compliments coming from my readers, my heart was filled with gratitude. I had the incredible privilege of meeting so many of my fans.

After hours of signing, exhaustion was setting in, and my smile slowly waned. Suddenly, as if by magic, my entire demeanor changed, and I recovered my smile, recognizing a debonair handsome profile enter the book store. Instantly straightening my posture to get a better look, one glance at Liam took my breath away. Watching as he patiently waited his turn to approach the table, I was utterly mesmerized. Dressed to perfection in a dark suit and tie, he exuded an air of confidence as he walked over and picked up my latest book. Staring into the depths of his dreamy blue eyes, I was utterly lost.

"Aww, Mrs. Reed, we meet again," he winked with a smile. "I would love your autograph. Would you please sign a copy for me?"

"Of course, Mr. Lachkowski," I paused, absolutely captivated by his appearance. "And to whom should I sign it," I teased.

"Liam," he laughed. "I've made reservations for dinner at ten this evening," he added. "What time will you be free?"

"In about a half-hour," I smiled. "Don't leave the store. There's a coffee bar in the back."

"Sweetheart, I have no intention of leaving," he whispered.

Finally, after accommodating those who remained in line, I gathered my belongings and searched for Liam. Walking to the back of the store, I could see him sitting in a chair reading a book as he sipped a cup of coffee.

"Hey, you, what are you reading?" I smiled inquisitively.

"Oh, a book by my favorite author, Ericka Reed. She's a phenomenal writer."

"So I've heard," I laughed.

"We have reservations at the Acropolis. Do you like Greek food?"

"Yes. Definitely."

"I'm parked out front. Are you ready to leave?"

"Yes. It was fun."

"Great," Liam smiled, extending his arm.

Looping my arm through Liam's, I leaned against his broad shoulders as we exited the book store. Then, walking out to the parking, Liam opened my door, helping me inside.

"It's only a short drive back into town. I hope you're hungry."

"I'm famished. I only had a turkey sandwich earlier at the hotel."

"Well, I think you'll appreciate the culinary excellence of this restaurant."

Arriving at the Acropolis, Liam escorted me inside. It wasn't busy for a weekday. Approaching the maître d', he ushered us to a private table. Following Liam, he reached down, grasping my hand. Pulling out my chair, we were seated in a reserved area. The restaurant's décor gave you the impression of eating outdoors under the brilliance of the night sky at the Acropolis. It was romantic. Returning to our table, the waiter took our drink order.

"Have you ever had shots of ouzo?" Liam questioned with a smile.

"I have, but it was many years ago."

"Well. Care to join me?"

"Yes. Why not," I laughed, up for the challenge.

"Two shots of ouzo, please."

"Yes, sir," the waiter stated.

Picking up the menu, I was famished, but I waited on Liam to make a few suggestions.

"Why don't we start with Mezethakia. It's a combination appetizer plate featuring spanakopita, keftedes, Kalamata olives, feta cheese, tomatoes, cucumbers, pita bread, and tzatziki sauce."

"Wow. That sounds like an entire meal."

"Just wait till you taste the Mousaka. It's delicious. Layers of potato, eggplant, and ground beef, topped with bechamel sauce."

As the waiter brought out the ouzo, I began to rethink my decision. I wasn't sure it was a good idea on an empty stomach. Finally, however, I was determined to try it.

"Here's to a great night in Portland," Liam grinned, tossing back the shot of ouzo.

"Ditto," I laughed, downing it in one swallow. Choking on the drink, I quickly reached for my glass of water.

"Sweetheart, that looked brutal," Liam laughed.

"Geez, that's strong," I gasped, chasing it with a sip of water.

"Well, I think we should order before someone gets tipsy."

Gaining the attention of the waiter, Liam ordered the appetizer. Returning with the Mezethakia, the waiter took pride in suggesting house favorites from their dinner menu. Still, Liam graciously interjected and ordered our entrees. After sampling everything on the appetizer tray, I hardly had room for the main course. However, I thoroughly enjoyed the Greek foods' robust flavors.

"Ericka, the book signing appeared to go well. You have a lot of loyal fans who love your work."

"Yes. I'm very blessed."

Ordering a bottle of pinot grigio, the waiter soon returned with the wine. It had been a long day, and the wine offered a chance to unwind. However, as much as I loved signing books, I always found it stressful. Liam poured us each a glass, and all too soon, I lost track of my good senses as I enjoyed too many glasses of wine during our dinner conversation. Unfortunately, it wasn't long before I was beginning to feel its effects.

"Would you care for dessert, Baklava?" Liam inquired.

"I'm sorry. I don't think I have room for dessert."

"Well, why don't I place an order to go. You can enjoy it in the morning with coffee."

"Thanks. That's really sweet of you," I smiled.

After another glass of wine and more talk regarding our upcoming trip to Seattle, I was beginning to feel extremely relaxed and drowsy. Noticing my increasing yawns, Liam smiled.

"I better get you back to your hotel."

"Yes. I think that would be a wise decision," I sighed.

After paying for dinner, Liam pulled back my chair. Unexpectedly, I felt dizzy as the room began to spin wildly out of control. Utterly embarrassed by my inability to stand, much less walk, Liam scooped me into his arms. Carrying me to the car, I felt genuinely grateful the restaurant had been practically deserted. I couldn't remember a time when I had consumed too much alcohol. Unquestionably, it was the combination of not having a lot to eat before downing the ouzo and then allowing myself to enjoy several glasses of wine. However, I was sure there was a price to be paid later, coming in the form of a severe headache.

My condition had somewhat improved as we arrived back at the hotel. However, I remained extremely dizzy and still heavily under the influence of the drinks. At least, I could walk with the assistance of Liam's strong arms. Deciding he should see me to my room, he helped me into the elevator. Taking my key, he unlocked the door. Once again, I wondered what I had done to deserve such a kind-hearted man. Unconditionally, he took care of me without asking, and I was falling helplessly in love.

"Wait. Please don't leave," I insisted.

"Sweetheart, I'm not sure you realize what you're saying. You've had an awful lot to drink tonight, and I feel entirely responsible."

"Liam, I know what I'm saying. I've never been more sure of anything in my life."

Suddenly, my vision narrowed as everything faded to utter darkness. Before passing out, the last thing I remembered was Liam catching me in his strong arms.

Waking the following day, I found myself in bed with the covers up to my head. I was nauseous and suffering from a debilitating headache. Not surprising. I noticed that my shoes and jacket had been removed as I attempted to sit up. On the bedside table, Liam had left a water bottle, aspirin, and a note.

Sweetheart, you passed out, not sure if you remember. I've left a bottle of water and aspirin. Please call me in the morning, Liam.

Reading the note, I smiled. My only recollection from the previous evening was the book signing and going to dinner with Liam, not much else. How could I have allowed this to happen? Clearly, he would never want to see me again after such stupidity. Wiping tears from my eyes, I didn't know which hurt worse, my head or the thought of never seeing Liam again. What had I done?

Sitting up in bed, I swallowed two aspirin and downed the entire bottle of water. Reaching for Fritz, I pulled him close. I needed to apologize to Liam. Picking up my cell phone, I started to call when I heard a light knock at the door. Grabbing my robe, I slowly made my way over to the door. I felt like I had been run over by a truck. A huge smile crossed my face. Unbelievably, Liam was standing at the door with breakfast and a carton of orange juice.

"How's my girl?" he smiled, setting the food on the credenza as he pulled me into his arms.

"Liam, can you ever forgive me?" I cried, snuggled in the warmth of his embrace.

"Honey, I don't think you're the first woman in the history of the world to pass out from consuming too much alcohol. But, it's okay," he laughed, running his fingers softly through my hair.

Without any hesitation or inhibitions, I lovingly caressed his face, kissing him ever so gently. Not surprisingly, Liam took our kiss to the next level. Pulling me closer, he returned my kiss with intense passion. Feeling weak in my knees and like I might faint for the second time, I allowed myself to be totally consumed by the intensity of his kiss.

Forget the giddy teenager. I was a woman falling madly in love for the second time in my life.

"Wow, sweetheart, that was nice," Liam smiled. "Did you wake up with a terrible headache? I hope you found the water and aspirin."

"Yes on both accounts. I woke up with the worst headache of my life, and I found the water with aspirin. Thank you."

"I feel entirely responsible for what happened? I should never have let you toss back a shot of ouzo and help me finish a bottle of wine. I'm sorry," Liam apologized.

"Liam, I take full responsibility for my actions. Trust me. You're not to blame. Now, what did you bring? I'm starving."

Walking over to the credenza, Liam had stopped by a local Denny's and picked up an order to go. Of course, there was no way he knew about my addiction to waffles. Simply another sign this man was supposed to be in my life. Taking our food over to the sofa, it felt natural and comfortable to enjoy an early morning breakfast with this amazing man. Allowing my mind to wander, I entertained thoughts of a new life for the first time since Bob passed.

For the remainder of the week, I focused my attention on my commitment to completing the marketing campaign in Portland. In between book signings, Liam and I spent every moment together. Long walks with Fritz, romantic dinners, and endless hours of conversation.

Friday night arrived all too soon. Liam had to return to Canada, and I was on my way to Spokane, Washington, the campaign's next stop. Kissing him goodnight at the door, my eyes moistened. We wouldn't see each other again until Seattle.

"Sweetheart, thanks for the incredible week," Liam winked with a smile.

His kiss sent shivers of excitement racing throughout my body as he drew me into a tight embrace.

"See you in Seattle," Liam softly whispered, turning to leave.

Seconds had scarcely passed since he left, and yet, I momentarily leaned against the door, still captivated by his passionate kiss. I couldn't wait to see him again. Only one thing stood between us. Spokane.

Leaving Portland, I said goodbye to an unbelievable week with Liam. I was on my way to Spokane, and afterward, Seattle, which held the hopes of a new beginning.

Chapter Six

I decided to push through the grueling five and half hours it took to drive over to Spokane. I had Kate rent a small condo on the outskirts of the city. Fritz needed a place to play and be less confined. Scheduled to speak at a women's bereavement group the following morning, I picked up fast food, unpacked the car, and went to bed early. Getting enough rest was paramount to feeling alert and on my game the next day.

Arriving at the apartment complex, it was farther from downtown Spokane than I would have liked. In addition, there were no signs of nearby restaurants or shopping centers. Thankfully, I would only be staying for a week, and it did come with a large backyard for Fritz.

I was exhausted from the long drive, getting everything inside and unpacked. Taking Fritz upstairs, I pulled back the brocade duvet and climbed into bed. As I was about to turn off the light, my cell phone buzzed with an incoming call. Glancing at the screen, my face lit up like a Christmas tree. I swear that man could make me smile, even under the worst of circumstances which today was only a long drive.

"Hello," I answered in a soft voice.

"Hey, sweetheart, I'm calling to make sure my girl made it to Spokane."

"Yes. It was a tiring drive. I arrived about two hours ago."

"Great. I wish I were there."

"Oh, Liam, I wish you were here too. You have no idea. I miss you."

"Would you like me to fly in on Friday evening and drive you to Seattle?"

"That would be wonderful."

"I'll rearrange my schedule and see you on Friday. Get some rest. We'll talk tomorrow.

"Thanks, Liam. Goodnight."

I placed my cell phone on the nightstand and turned off the light. Liam's calls were always short and to the point, unlike my conversations with Amanda. We could ramble on for hours. Still, he had given me the best reason ever to get through this hectic week. I had numerous speaking engagements and two additional book signings. Thoughts of Liam ravished my mind as I tried to sleep. Finally, falling asleep from sheer exhaustion, I slept soundly, not waking until my alarm buzzed the next morning.

Waking up, I raced to the shower. I had to be at the First Presbyterian Church before 9:00 a.m. Cynthia had arranged a meet and greet before the meeting started. I had been invited to speak to the ladies of the church regarding my experiences as a widow. Unfortunately, becoming a widow didn't come with a handbook. Amanda and I were living proof. Learning from other women's experiences was often the only guidance a woman received outside of family and friends.

Quickly dressing for the event, I chose to be relatively modest in my choice of attire. Selecting a short sleeve floral wrap dress, flats, and a shawl for the cool morning would have to carry me through the day. I wouldn't have time to return to the condo and change. I was also the key speaker at a luncheon later that morning. Cynthia had arranged for me to speak at a women's book club. She had tightened up my schedule to the degree that I was almost racing between events.

My phone buzzed as I ran down to the kitchen for a much-needed cup of coffee. Amanda's name flashed across the screen. I didn't have long to talk.

"Hey."

"If I remember correctly, you must be in Spokane," Amanda quizzed.

"Yes. I arrived last night. I desperately needed a yard for Fritz, so Kate rented a condo. After being cooped up in the hotel for a week, he needed outdoor space."

"Sorry, I didn't call the last few days. Bob's cousin, Eva, dropped in unexpectedly. She had business in San Francisco."

"Oh, the cousin who was hoping you would buy the farmhouse?"

"Yes."

"Did she ever find a buyer?"

"No."

"Well, that's not surprising. That place was deplorable. Amanda, I hate to cut this short, but I have to be downtown before 9:00 a.m. The condo is located on the outskirts of town, and I'm uncertain about the traffic. I can't be late for my first event. I'll call you later this evening."

"Okay, not a problem. I want to hear all the sappy details regarding Liam," Amanda laughed.

"That's not funny. We'll talk later this evening."

After ensuring that Fritz would have everything he needed for the day, I locked the door and hurried out to the car. Unfamiliar with downtown Spokane, I set the GPS for directions. I was lucky, the traffic wasn't as bad as I had imagined, and I managed to be on time.

Met by the pastor's wife, Charolette, she introduced the members of their group. I felt an instant camaraderie with the women in attendance. Unfortunately, we had all lost a spouse or significant other and faced the stark realities of rebuilding our lives. Taking the podium after a brief introduction from Charolette, I often felt unworthy of the accolades. The facts were accurate. I was a nationally well-known author with an extensive fan base. However, today, I more aptly identified with all the women in front of me—a widow. We shared a bond, widowhood.

"Good morning. I'm Ericka Reed. It was an honor to receive a call from Charolette inviting me to join you. I speak to you today, not as an

author or someone with vast knowledge on the subject of losing a spouse or significant other. Like so many of you, I simply stand before you as a widow.

We can all sum up our reasons for being here today in one simple word, widow. According to webster's dictionary, the word widow simply means a woman who has lost her spouse by death and has not remarried. Yet, this one word signifies so much more, loss, grief, despair, loneliness. The most significant reality is that it's life-changing. No one signs up to become a widow. It is a title that is often thrust upon us unannounced, or we come to it after weeks, months, and even years of caring for a critically ill spouse. My experience was the latter. As most of you know, I lost my husband, Bob, last year in April. Before his passing, I spent three years totally engaged in my role as a loving, compassionate caregiver. During that time, my life was basically put on hold. Unfortunately, after his passing, I was out of a job. I felt lost and abandoned. We step into widowhood, often unprepared for what awaits us. There are no rules or handbooks to help us through the process. We simply rely on the kindness of family or friends or a unique group of women, such as yourselves, gathered here this morning.

I don't claim to be an expert on becoming a widow, and I'm not here to offer vast knowledge on what is expected once you've been given this title. It's, at best, a personal journey for each of us. However, I can relate to waking up in the middle of the night and reaching over to my husband's side of the bed only to discover it's empty and cold. I can relate to having my hot water heater go out in the middle of the night and experiencing a cold shower the following morning. If Bob were alive, he would have easily fixed it. We all share similar experiences and emotions. Crying can quickly become a favorite pastime if we let it. Yet, each of you possesses an inner strength, the ability to move forward with your life. The fact that you are here today is proof.

I often credit my best friend, Amanda, for my survival. We've been fortunate to be neighbors for many years. However, Amanda also lost her husband, Bob, only eighteen short months after my Bob passed. Yes. We both had husbands named Bob, and the similarities they shared are simply too numerous to mention. We saw each other through the worst days of our lives. I hope that each of you has an Amanda or a family member who is willing to give you a shoulder to lean on as you navigate the process of starting over. Don't hesitate to pick up the phone and reach out to those around you for help because it is only with help from others that you will gain the support you need to make it through these difficult times.

Thank you for inviting me here today. It's been a pleasure."

After my brief speech, Charolette had arranged for a local church member, a psychologist, to answer pertinent questions that I felt were not in my field of expertise.

Once again, I raced to my next event. I didn't want to be late. Note to self, ensure Cynthia allows more time between speaking engagements, especially in cities where I'm unfamiliar. Walking in, I was greeted by Linda, the president of the Chic Lits Book Club of Spokane. These women were seriously addicted to reading romance novels of every subgenre Contemporary, Historical, Inspirational, Speculative, and Young Adult. Unbelievably, I recognized a few faces, having previously met them at Book Trade Fairs in San Francisco and Los Angeles. Their current reading project was my book, *Left at the Altar*.

Enjoying the luncheon before the start of the meeting, it offered a delicious assortment of cold cuts, tri-tip, turkey, or ham, along with various salads. It also allowed me time to socialize, make new acquaintances, and sign copies of my book. I much preferred this meeting to the previous one. Not that I didn't easily relate to those women, the truth was that I did in more ways than one. However, this group's focus was my specialty. They supported me through the purchase of my books and reviews. Reviews have always been the life's blood of any author.

Introduced by Linda, I couldn't wait to discuss my love of writing and my newest release.

"Good afternoon. I'm Ericka Reed. I must say it's a pleasure to see so many of you again. There's nothing I enjoy more than talking about books, specifically romance novels, except perhaps writing them. Thank you for inviting me and selecting 'Left at the Altar' as your book selection for this month. I appreciate your kind comments and reviews. Before I get into the book and my reasons for writing this particular story, I always like to give a tiny bit of info regarding what brought me to this day. It's been said that a child's mind from birth to approximately age six is like a sponge, soaking

up vast amounts of information from their environment. They absorb everything around them effortlessly, continuously, and indiscriminately. Some of my earliest memories were spent sitting on my mother's lap as she read books to me. I can't say she was an educated person, but somehow she knew the importance of reading to her children, to me. I was fascinated and drawn into many different worlds, including Bible stories, fairy tales, and books that rhymed. She opened my mind to the world of books. To this very day, I contribute my success to my mother. Without knowing, she instilled a passion inside me which later in life evolved to writing. So, read to your children. It's important.

'Left at the Altar' was a joy to write and written from personal experience, as you might guess. Thankfully, not mine. As most of you know, I lost my dear husband last year after fifty years of marriage. However, this book is loosely based on a dear friend of mine. We were roommates while attending UC Berkeley. Unfortunately, she passed several years ago from breast cancer. If she were alive today, I think she would be pleased with the book and the somewhat fictional account of her life. To keep the summation brief, she met 'the one,' the man of her dreams, while attending Berkeley. He was everything she had hoped for in a life's partner, handsome, rich, and one day destined to join his father's law firm. However, for reasons no one ever knew, she was surprisingly left at the altar. He was a no-show on their wedding day. She was totally devastated. However, as you've read, the story has a happy ending. She married his best man. Truly a match made in heaven. They were married for almost forty years before she passed. By the way, her name was April, and I miss her to this day.

If you have any further questions regarding this book or others that I have written, I will be available for another hour. I would be happy to sign copies and answer any questions you might have. Thank you for inviting me and allowing me to share this incredible story."

Signing a few more books before I left, I was exhausted and ready to return to the condo and slip into my comfortable sweats for the evening. Saying my goodbyes and expressing my thanks to the Chic Lits Book Club members, I walked out to the parking lot. Quickly checking my phone for missed texts or calls before I started the car, I had a text message from Liam and a missed call from Amanda. I would later return Amanda's call when I had time to talk. First, however, I hurriedly read Liam's text.

Hey, sweetheart, thinking of you. I know your speaking engagements were a huge success. Miss you. Catch you later.

My heart simply melted. Did this man even realize what he was doing to me? He quickly became my first thought in the morning and my last thought at night.

Driving back to the condo, I stopped for grocery supplies, wine, and treats for Fritz. He deserved special treatment after being left alone for the entire day. I considered the wine my treat for the evening. Soaking in a warm bath with a glass of wine and later calling Liam when I got into bed would hopefully be all I needed to get a good night's sleep.

Fritz greeted me as I unlocked the door. I decided to take him for a short walk. Hurriedly, finding his leash, we both needed a little exercise before dinner, which tonight would be a store-bought frozen pizza.

Bringing Fritz inside and putting away his leash, I walked into the tiny kitchen to bake the pizza. It wasn't a gourmet dinner but would easily suffice for the evening. Hearing my phone buzz, I rushed over, thinking it was Liam. However, I smiled, seeing Amanda's name scroll across the screen. I knew she was hungry for details regarding Liam and wouldn't stop until she heard every word.

"Hey."

"Why haven't you returned my call," Amanda scolded.

"Well, for starters, I just got back to the condo, walked Fritz, and put a frozen pizza into the oven."

"How did the speaking engagements turn out?"

"Fabulous as always. I had the opportunity to meet a lot of amazing women today, at the bereavement group and later the book club."

"Okay, spill, what's the latest with Lachowski?"

"He does have a first name, you know."

"Details. Please."

"We had a wonderful week in Portland. He came to my first book signing and afterward took me out to dinner at a phenomenal Greek restaurant, the Acropolis. Unfortunately, the worst of it was that I had a shot of ouzo and then one too many glasses of wine. Amanda, I literally couldn't walk out of the restaurant, and he carried me to the car. Can you even believe it?"

"Dear Lord Ericka, are you telling me you got plastered?"

"Yes, and that's not the worst of it. Liam was kind enough to see me to my hotel room, where unbelievably, I passed out. He carried me to bed, removed my shoes, jacket and put me under the warm covers. Oh, and then he left a note with aspirin and water on the nightstand."

"Oh my gosh. You've got to be kidding."

"Amanda, unfortunately, it happened. The following day, I woke with the worst headache. But it gets better. I was just about to call him to apologize for my awkward behavior when I heard a light knock at the door. It was Liam. He brought me breakfast and orange juice."

"Wow. That's unbelievable."

"No. The unbelievable part was we kissed. Amanda, his kiss was intense and passionate. I swear it knocked me off my feet. It left me weak in the knees, and for a brief second, I thought I might pass out again."

"Dang girl, does he have a friend?"

"Well, funny that you should ask. I had planned to keep it a secret. But the fact is that Liam does have a close friend, Harry. You'll be meeting him next week in Seattle. Amanda, he's from New Orleans, wealthy, traveled the world, and graduated from Harvard. I haven't seen a photo, but Liam's exact words stated Harry had aged like a fine wine. And, we know how much you like wine," I giggled.

"Geez, Ericka, for heaven's sake, please tell me he's single and unattached."

"Divorced."

"Wow. You've definitely made my night. Well, this puts a new spin on being in Seattle. I've got to shop for new clothes and color my hair. Is there anything else you can tell me about this incredible man?"

"No. However, knowing you, I'm sure you'll find out everything there is to know about him. I've got to run. The oven timer just buzzed, and I'm starving. We'll talk later. See you soon."

"Okie Dokie. Here's to Seattle," Amanda shrieked.

Deciding to open the wine, I poured myself a glass, grabbed several slices of pizza, and walked into the living room. Lounging back on the sofa with Fritz, the wine was quickly doing its job of releasing the tensions of the day.

After stuffing myself with pepperoni pizza, I went upstairs and turned on the warm water in the bathtub. Soaking in a relaxing bath with my glass of wine was a fitting end to a good day. Stepping out of the tub before I shriveled into a prune, I grabbed a large fluffy towel, dried off, and put on cozy pajamas.

Pulling back the covers, I slipped into bed and pulled Fritz close. Next, reaching for my cell phone, there was only one voice I wanted to hear before I went to sleep. So, I called Liam.

"Hey, beautiful. How's my girl?" Liam answered.

"Fine. I received your text. How are you?"

"I'm good. However, things would be much better if we were together. I can't wait to see you Friday evening if you're still okay with me driving you to Seattle."

"Are you kidding? I wish we were leaving tonight."

"How was your day?"

"It was amazing. I met a lot of remarkable women."

"Not as remarkable as the one I'm speaking with," Liam laughed.

"Wow. Thanks. I'm flattered."

"No need. I am just giving credit where it's due. You've spoken at two events today. I only wish I were there. The women were lucky to have you, and I'm sure your speeches were inspiring and captivating."

"Sounds like I might have another member of my fan club."

"Sweetheart, I've been a fan since the moment I met you."

"Geez, Liam, you're making me blush."

"Get some sleep. We'll talk tomorrow."

"Good night."

Ending the call, I placed my phone on the nightstand and pulled the covers over my head. How was sleep even possible after talking with Liam? He possessed an intangible magnetism. The man was undeniably becoming the air that I breathed.

The following week, I had three book signings at various book stores. Barnes and Noble and two smaller privately owned book retailers. As

Friday arrived, I was finally beginning to familiarize myself with the city streets of Spokane, where I was scheduled for the last event.

Arriving at Page Turners Book Store in downtown Spokane, I was thrilled to meet an avid group of fans as I entered the store. I never tired of discussing my books or upcoming projects. The owner, John Weber, graciously advertised my arrival weeks in advance and selected my books to be displayed in their large storefront window overlooking the busy streets. However, as excited as I was to meet my adoring fans, one face in the crowd would be distinguishable from the rest and demand my absolute attention. The fact that Liam easily stood out in any group was indisputable. He exuded an air of confidence and masculinity. I continuously scanned the crowds during the event, eager to catch a glimpse of him as he walked into the book store.

As I took my place behind the table, it held stacks of my latest novels. All were available for autographing with purchase, as well as my usual freebies, including bookmarks, pens, and chocolates. The number of fans who supported me was impressive. The line wrapped the entire length of the store and spilled outside onto the sidewalk. John arranged for a photographer to attend the event. Trying to be photogenic while signing autographs and carrying on lengthy conversations with fans was difficult. Later, the event photos would advertise the book store and be publicized in the local newspaper.

Finally, with only thirty minutes remaining, the line of people desiring autographs slowly diminished. My fingers were numb.

Suddenly scanning the entrance, I gasped, instantly recognizing his prominent profile. Staring at his extraordinary, sexy physique, I was mesmerized, unable to take my eyes off him as he slowly made his way through the line. Finally, approaching the table, he picked up a book for my signature.

"Aww, Mrs. Reed, I'm a huge fan," Liam winked with a smile.

"Of course you are," I whispered teasingly, hoping no one overheard my comment.

"I'll be waiting."

"I shouldn't be long. But, Sir, I forgot to sign your book," I laughed.

"Later," he grinned.

Blushing from the heat of our brief encounter, I was a puddle of emotions. I needed this event to be over this very moment. However, maintaining a professional demeanor wouldn't be easy, even for the short few remaining minutes.

Finally, starting to pick up items that remained on the table, I turned around to discover Liam hurriedly packing what few things were left.

"Let's get out of here," he whispered.

"You were reading my mind," I laughed.

"I took a taxi from the airport. Where are you parked?"

"Oh, just outside the back door."

Taking what few items were left, Liam carried the small box containing the freebies to my car and stowed it in the trunk.

"I'll drive," he grinned.

"Awesome, I hate this traffic, and it's taken me a week to get familiar with these roads."

Arriving back at the condo, I was in unfamiliar territory. Did I allow Liam to stay or ask that he get a place for the night? So, uncertain, I simply chose to play it by ear. I would let the evening take its course.

"Would you like to stay in or go out for dinner? I'm good at taking almost anything and making a meal with it?" Liam smiled.

"Well," I paused. "I appreciate the offer of going out, but it's been a really long week. Would you mind if we stayed in?"

"Sweetheart, it's completely your call. Do you mind if I see what there is to work with?"

"The kitchen is yours."

Opening the fridge, he laughed. "Well, there's not much. How do you feel about frozen waffles and bacon."

"Are you kidding? I love waffles. I stocked up the other night at the grocery store."

"Geez, that's obvious," Liam chuckled. "Ericka, seriously, you have enough waffles to feed a college fraternity."

Getting out the toaster, I toasted the waffles while Liam fried up slices of bacon. Grabbing plates and silverware for two instead of one, I turned around to admire Liam standing at the stove. Tears moistened my eyes as I stared at his sexy physique. I wasn't eating alone. He was cooking for me in my kitchen, and whether it was a rented condo or wherever, it meant we had taken our relationship to the next level. Despite the fact he had offered to take me out for dinner, we were no longer bound to eat in public. We now shared a familiarity that connected us. We were comfortable together. The scene unfolding in front of me gave me goosebumps. It was the essence of the word 'family.' I missed having that one special person to share my days, nights, go to bed with, wake up with, and spend time together in the kitchen. As tears ran down my face, I discreetly wiped my eyes.

There was no way I wanted him to see the effect he was having on me. The evening was still young, and not knowing where this might lead, I didn't want to become a blubbering idiot watching him cook. For heaven's sake, I wrote romance novels. Though it was all fiction, everything about us was real, too real. Tonight reminded me of a scene in my favorite movie, Jerry Maguire. Laurel says to Dorothy, *'Don't cry at the beginning of a date. Cry at the end, like I do.'* I could do this. I could keep my emotions in check while enjoying a man's company in my personal surroundings without losing it.

"The bacon is done. Are the waffles ready?" Liam asked, snapping me back from my emotional state.

"Yes," I replied from the cramped dining area.

After setting the table, I returned to the kitchen for the waffles as Liam brought in a dish filled with tasty bacon.

"Coffee or milk?" he questioned.

"Milk for me, please. I'm afraid coffee would only keep me awake."

"Well, I could think of ways to deal with insomnia," Liam winked mischievously.

Oh, dear God, did he actually just go there. Trying to pretend that I hadn't heard those words come out of his mouth, I sat down at the table, unsure at this point if I could even swallow a morsel. However, I knew Liam liked teasing me. It was simply a joke.

After eating and putting the dishes away, Liam opened a bottle of wine. Then, taking the bottle and our glasses to the living room, we removed our shoes and lounged back together on the sofa.

"Would you prefer to listen to music or watch a movie?" I asked.

"Definitely music. I'm sorry, I don't indulge in a lot of television these days."

"My kind of guy," I smiled, staring into the depths of his gorgeous blue eyes.

"So, Ericka, what type of things do you enjoy when you're not busy promoting your books?"

"Well, I'm afraid you're going to find my life dull and boring. I've always enjoyed long road trips and, when at home, quiet evenings either, reading or writing."

"I see nothing wrong with that."

"What recreational activities do you indulge in?" I questioned, sipping my wine.

"Well, I love golf, swimming, and hiking."

"That's impressive."

"Not really. A person of any age needs to remain active."

"Good point," I smiled.

Deciding to put on soft background music, I chose Sinatra and Nat King Cole, my favorites.

As Sinatra's voice filled the living room, Liam smiled.

"Great choice. I've always loved Sinatra."

"So, Liam, I'm curious, what was it that you retired from?" I inquired, finishing my drink.

"Umm, did I say that I was retired? I own a small business in Canada. It, unfortunately, necessitates that I travel internationally more often than I would like."

Why did I think there was more to his answer than he cared to elaborate? I was good at reading people, yet something didn't add up. His answers always seemed elusive.

Returning to the kitchen for another bottle of chardonnay, Liam removed the cork and refilled our glasses. Relaxing after my second refill, I snuggled into his arms. For the first time since Bob passed, another man made me feel safe and comfortable. Pulling me into his embrace, he softly kissed the nape of my neck.

"Sweetheart, do you remember anything about the evening I carried you to the car and later into your hotel room?" Liam whispered. "You asked me to stay the night. In fact, you insisted, just before you passed out. Ericka, I'm going to be honest with you, and I hope that what I'm about to say doesn't scare you. I've fallen madly in love with you. I've been single for too many years to count. Remember when I said we were in the 'homestretch' of our lives? Well, I don't want to wait. Sweetheart, unfortunately, time is no longer on our side. I want to spend what years I have left with you, cherishing you, spoiling you beyond your wildest dreams. You don't have to say anything. Think about it."

"Oh my God, Liam, for once in my life, I don't have to think about it. I felt an unexplainable connection the first time we met. Call it fate or karma, I believe we were destined to meet that night. Liam, I do love you. You have no idea. Honestly, I never thought I would fall in love again. How did I get so lucky?" I cried.

Gently wiping away my tears, he drew my face to his kissing me with an intense passion. I felt entirely breathless as my heart stopped beating. I ceased to exist as I melted into his embrace. Tears flowed down my face becoming emotional. Liam lovingly kissed each one.

"I just have one question," he grinned mischievously. "Where's the bedroom?"

"Upstairs."

Scooping me into his arms, Liam carried me upstairs. Turning out the light, the night I was about to experience was only written about in my books. Nights like this only existed between the pages of a romance novel. They didn't happen to a woman my age and certainly not most widows. Yet, making love to Liam felt right. Somehow the stars had aligned to bring him into my life. For a brief moment, reflecting over the bottle of Aramis, I knew. It was a connection made in heaven.

The following morning feeling the closeness of Liam's warm body wrapped around me, tears filled my eyes. I knew that my bed was no longer empty or cold. It once again contained someone who simply owned my heart. Wiping the tears from my eyes with the back of his hand, Liam smiled.

"Sweetheart, if you continue to cry, I'm going to have to buy stock in Kleenex."

Later that day, we were on our way to Seattle. I couldn't wait to see Amanda. I knew she would be happy for us, and I couldn't wait to introduce her to Harry. Our lives were about to change in ways we never expected.

Chapter Seven

Arriving in Seattle, gray clouds swirled ominously overhead. However, the weather couldn't dampen my spirits. Checking into the Fairmont Olympic Hotel, an impressive four-star hotel, Liam had reserved a suite for us and separate suites for Amanda and Harry. They were both holding reservations for late arrival.

Opening the door to the Cascade Suite, it was sheer opulence. Neutral tones and rich oak furnishings highlighted the spacious well-defined living area and oversized bathroom. The décor was on a scale that easily signified the hotel's four-star rating. As the doorman set our luggage inside, Liam walked over, giving the young man a generous tip.

"Sweetheart, you'll find this hotel offers everything you might need. I've stayed here often on business trips."

"Liam, honestly, it's beyond anything I would have expected. It's incredibly kind of you to cover Amanda's room. However, she is going to flip out to discover she has a separate suite."

"Amanda is your best friend. It's the least I can do."

"Thank you. You're very generous," I replied, giving Liam a quick kiss.

Taking the kiss further, Liam pulled me tight against his chest. The passion in his kiss melted me to my core, making me weak in the knees.

"Wow, sweetheart, that was nice," Liam smiled. "Why don't I take you to dinner? I'm afraid if we continue, we might not leave the hotel."

"Sounds wonderful. Should I change clothes?"

"No. You're absolutely perfect. I have a friend who owns a family-style Italian restaurant, Sapori D'Italia. If you're ready, we should go. I've arranged for a car service for the weekend. I find it more accessible and conducive to the four of us enjoying our stay in Seattle. The driver is waiting to take us."

"Wow, you certainly know how to impress a lady," I grinned.

"Oh, sweetheart, it has nothing to do with trying to impress you or anyone. We have to talk later," he laughed.

A black Lincoln town car waited for us as we walked out to the front entrance of the hotel.

"Good evening, Mr. Lachowski," the driver stated, opening our door.

"Good evening. Sapori D'Italia, please."

Sapori D'Italia was uniquely tucked away between tall buildings in Seattle's University District. Stepping out of the car, Liam reached down, grasping my hand. Then, entwining his fingers through mine, he led me inside. The restaurant was cozy. It glowed with the ambiance of lit candles that centered the bright red-checkered tablecloths.

"Good evening, Mr. Lachowski. Your table is ready," the maître d' smiled, showing us to a table in the back which offered privacy. "Giovanni is unavailable to welcome you this evening. Please accept a bottle of our best wine as his way of apology."

"Thanks, Dominic."

"Sir, I'll return shortly with your wine and to take your selection for this evening."

"Liam, I think we need to talk."

I was totally confused at this point. How was it that everyone knew him?"

"Sweetheart, I know. Let's eat first," he laughed. "Trust me. I'm not a Mafia Don if those are your thoughts," he added with a smile.

Dominic returned with a bottle of wine and two glasses.

"Sir, would you like to taste the Barolo before I fill the glasses."

"No. That won't be necessary. Thanks."

Toasting to our first night in Seattle, my hands were shaking. What was it that I didn't know about Liam? I had always suspected he was hiding details of his life. What had I gotten myself into? God forbid, he was nefarious. How could I have allowed myself to fall in love with anyone without first knowing everything about them? Lord, help me if Amanda was right on her warnings regarding Liam and that I had allowed myself to be smitten with him. However, smitten didn't cover it. I was in love with him. Downing, several glasses of wine, to calm my nerves was my only recourse. Why did I feel like I was drowning in my stupidity?

"May I offer a suggestion for dinner?" Liam questioned.

"Of course. Don't you always," I frowned, being obstinate.

"Ericka, relax. I promise it's not anything despicable."

"We would like to order the grilled lamb chops with marble potatoes, spring onion, Swiss chard, roasted garlic aioli, with olive salsina. You'll love the grilled lamb. It's by far my favorite item on the menu."

Quickly downing my entire glass of wine, I asked for another. At this rate, I might not even remember dinner once again, much less any discussion that Liam would have regarding if he was retired or working. Which at this point, both seemed debatable.

"Sir, may I have another?" I teased, asking for a refill. I needed all the liquid courage I could muster, not knowing where this conversation was going and fearing the worst.

"Ericka, you're silly. Seriously, three glasses of wine on an empty stomach. Honey, this might not bode well for you. If your past history is any indication," he frowned, refilling my wine. "You're now cut off until you have dinner, or I might have to carry you out once again."

"Liam, I'm a grown woman, in case you haven't noticed. I don't need anyone telling me how many glasses of wine I can have," I replied, feeling obstinate, giddy, and light-headed.

"Oh, sweetheart, trust me, I've noticed. I should carry you out of here right now, but I'll indulge your fantasy of being a world-class drinker."

The waiter returned with our meals which typically would have been delicious, except I was already feeling slightly intoxicated and nauseous. However, I knew that I should try to sample a few bites. Tasting a small piece of the lamb, I was afraid that it might not stay down. However, looking over at Liam, he seemed to be having no difficulties as he cut into his grilled chop. Watching as he finished eating, he hadn't commented on the fact that everything remained on my plate.

"Ericka, I was hoping to discuss a few details of my life with you over dinner, but now I question if this is the right time or place. Honestly, I'm not sure you will even remember."

"Oh, Liam Lachowski, you're not getting off the hook this easy. You brought me here to discuss something over dinner. So I suggest you get on with it. But, unfortunately, I'm not feeling so well."

"Geez, Babe," Liam paused, pensively staring at me with his smoldering blue eyes. "I wonder why that could possibly be?" he teased.

Just one look into his gorgeous blue eyes, and I was utterly lost. Maybe I could live with a serial killer, bank robber, corporate criminal. I had steeled myself with enough alcohol to face whatever he was about to say. The wine would soften the blow.

"Ericka, I know you questioned my background. What career path I had chosen, if I was retired or even employed. You know I graduated with a degree from Harvard, and I told you that I owned a small company in Canada. Well, some of that might not exactly be true."

Oh, dear God, this is it. This is where he says he's an ax murderer.

"Sweetheart, remember the night in the condo, and I said I wanted to cherish you and spoil you beyond your wildest dreams. Well, I can do that," Liam smiled, reaching across the table to grasp my hand.

"What? I'm not sure that I'm following you."

"Ericka, it's not a small company that I own. I own an entire conglomerate. I have more money than I could spend in several lifetimes. I'm worth more than the Canadian budget as a whole. You'll never have to worry about any financial aspect of your life ever."

Oh my God, what reality was I in? What paradigm shift had just occurred? The past few minutes had felt like a roller coaster of emotions, and I was about to be sick. Then, suddenly feeling my few bites of dinner making a reappearance, I felt a wave of nausea overtaking me.

"Excuse me, I'm going to be sick," I hastily remarked, bolting for the bathroom.

Running for the ladies room, I hurried into a stall, closing the door only seconds before I threw up the wine and the few morsels of food I had eaten. Wiping the remains from my mouth, I walked out to the sink. Dousing my face with cold water, I looked in the mirror. Was it true? Was Liam a billionaire? Make that a multi-billionaire? Staring at my reflection, a smile slowly crossed my face.

Suddenly hearing a knock on the bathroom door, I quickly ran my fingers through my hair to give it some semblance of normalcy and grabbed a mint from my purse.

"Ericka, are you alright?" Liam questioned. "Sweetheart, open the door, or I'm coming in. Do you hear me?"

Opening the door, my knees buckled, and I literally fell into his arms. Scooping me up, once again, he carried me out to the waiting car. Wrapping my arms around him, I giggled.

"You find this funny," Liam grinned with a sexy upturned lip.

"Yes, very," I smiled.

Helping me inside the car, Liam pulled me close. Gently pulling back my hair, he ran his fingers softly through my short curls, kissing me tenderly on the nape of my neck.

"Geez, I think it's back to frozen waffles for you," he whispered in my ear. "Dining out has become a slight problem," he laughed.

"Oh, Liam Lachowski, I love you."

"Ericka Reed, you're going to be trouble."

Arriving back at the hotel, I still felt wobbly but revived enough to walk in on my own. Taking the elevator up to our suite, Liam pulled me into his arms.

As he unlocked the door to our suite, I followed him inside and sat down on the sofa. Looking down at my cell phone, I had several texts and missed calls from Amanda. I knew she would arrive soon, so I needed to return her missed calls. She answered immediately, somewhat confused.

"Ericka, I'm sure there's been a huge mistake. I was given a suite when I checked into the hotel. The hotel said it was compliments of Mr. Lachowski. Can you even believe it, an entire suite," Amanda exclaimed.

"Yes. I know, it's fine. We have a lot to talk about. Can we possibly chat tomorrow? I'm sure you're drained from the flight, and I'm rather tired myself."

"Of course. We'll talk tomorrow. Get some rest. Oh, please, thank Liam."

"I will. Enjoy."

Liam had graciously paid someone to walk Fritz during our stay. However, checking his food and water supply, I found they had also been refilled. Knowing that Fritz was taken care of, I walked into the bedroom. Unexpectedly, I gasped. Catching sight of Liam as he removed his white dress shirt, I froze in my tracks. Even for a man of his age, his sculpted muscular physique was exemplary. The words eye candy were utterly inadequate to describe the gorgeous man standing before me. A huge smile washed over Liam's face as he noticed my reaction.

"Sorry, I didn't know you were changing?" I blushed.

"Sweetheart, were you checking me out?" Liam teased, putting on a more casual tee shirt.

"Maybe?"

"Well?" he laughed, walking over to kiss me. "Like what you see, love?"

"Liam, you're the sexiest man ever, and you're wealthy," I mused.

"Guess that makes you one lucky girl."

"Liam, I loved you before I knew you had money. I didn't fall in love with you because you were rich. It doesn't take money to make me happy."

"Oh, sweetheart, that last comment is ridiculous," Liam paused with a laugh. "It's going to be fun reminding you of that statement for the rest of your life. I love you and your undeniable innocence. Why don't you change into something more comfortable and meet me in the living room? I need a drink."

Wow. I needed to talk to Amanda. We were overdue for a long conversation, and I couldn't wait to see her tomorrow. I changed into my comfortable pajamas and wrapped myself in a luxurious cotton bathrobe. I walked out to the living room to join Liam. Note to self, shop for lingerie.

"Would you care to join me?" Liam questioned, pouring himself a glass of scotch. "I won't have far to carry you," he laughed.

"Definitely, and that's not funny," I mentioned, walking over to the credenza. "I'll have a glass of white zinfandel. Do these suites always come with fully stocked bars?" I questioned.

"Well, let's just say they know what I like," Liam chuckled, handing me a glass of wine. "Bring your wine over to the sofa, and let's get comfortable."

Following Liam over to the sofa, I curled up next to him, sipping my wine. The soft relaxing music of Frank Sinatra filled the room. He was quickly becoming aware of things I loved, even my choice of music.

"I heard from Harry. He's arriving tomorrow."

"Oh, I thought he was coming in tonight?"

"He was, but his plans changed at the last minute."

"So," I paused, taking a sip of wine. "What are the odds that Harry and Amanda will hit it off?"

"Well, sweetheart, I don't claim to be a matchmaker, but I think they're good. Harry is a product of the South, born and raised, and as you've said, Amanda is Southern to the bone. So I think there's an excellent chance."

"I'm excited. Amanda's life has been complicated, and I would love to see her find happiness again. She's spent years sacrificing herself, caring for an extremely sick husband. Now that Bob has passed, Amanda said she feels she's out of a job, abandoned, and lonely. Liam, she's my best friend, and more than anything, I want her to be happy," I explained, wiping my moist eyes.

"Honey, I hear you. I know you care for Amanda. Trust me," Liam smiled, kissing my temple. "Harry is a great catch. We've been business partners for years. He's smart, has a great personality, richer than sin, and as you girls might say, he's the total package. Now, why are you crying? Geez, I forgot how emotional females could be. Sweetheart, let me ease those worries. You've had a rather bizarre day," Liam winked wickedly, savoring the last of his scotch.

Scooping me into his arms, Liam carried me into the bedroom. Turning out the light, our nights could easily be summed up with two words, total ecstasy. Falling asleep wrapped in Liam's arms after a night of passion and waking up cuddled into the warmth of his embrace was quickly becoming my favorite place to be. He not only warmed my bed, but he also warmed my heart.

Hearing the buzz of Liam's phone early the next morning, he immediately answered. Naturally, I hoped it signified a call from Harry. As Liam answered the call on speaker, I wasn't to be disappointed, and I was privy to the guys' conversation.

"Hey, I got in late. I was hoping we could meet for breakfast."

"Sounds good. Why don't we meet downstairs in about an hour?"

"Great. Perhaps, you could invite Amanda to join us."

"Sure. See you soon."

Ending the call, Liam smiled, giving me a quick kiss.

"Well, as I'm sure you heard, it sounds like Harry is anxious to meet Amanda. So why don't you give her a quick call and let her know we're all meeting for breakfast."

"Sounds good."

After calling Amanda, I jumped in the shower. I had only just turned on the warm water when suddenly, I felt Liam's strong arms encircle my waist.

"Conserving water," he whispered. "Shampoo?"

"You're silly," I laughed.

As the refreshing water cascaded over us, this was all new territory for me. Tears welled within my eyes, knowing that once again, I had someone to share my life with. I hoped Amanda would be so lucky.

Stepping out of the shower and quickly getting dressed, it was almost time to meet Harry and Amanda downstairs for breakfast. Deciding to dress casually, I was anxiously hoping and praying their meeting would result in their wanting to see each other again. It was Amanda's birthday, and Harry was the perfect gift.

Entering the elevator for the short ride down to the hotel lobby, I was nervous.

"Today is Amanda's birthday," I smiled, staring at Liam.

"Well, that makes today even more special. I can't think of a better present than Harry escorting Amanda to all the tourist spots in Seattle. Why don't I call and make reservations for dinner tonight? Harry and I always enjoy eating at the Harbor House in Seattle. I think Amanda would love it. It's located on the wharf, and the menu and ambiance are impeccable. She does like seafood, right?"

"Of course."

"Great. I'll make reservations for 8:00 p.m. this evening. That will give us enough time to enjoy the sights of the city and still have time to return to the hotel and dress for dinner."

"Liam, thank you. Thank you for making Amanda's day special and for taking such good care of me."

"Sweetheart, I love you. You both deserve the best. It's the least I can do for Amanda, especially since it's her birthday. Now, let's see if they've both made their way downstairs and into the restaurant. I'm starving."

Walking into the restaurant, Liam immediately walked over to meet Harry. He was just as Liam had described. Tall, thin, and very handsome for a man of his age. It was evident he kept in shape. His physique clearly defined his efforts at keeping fit. His salt and pepper hair gave him a distinguished air. Wearing jeans with a buttoned-down shirt and a leather jacket, I knew Amanda wouldn't be disappointed.

Looking around, Amanda was nowhere to be seen. I prayed she hadn't decided to cancel at the last minute without letting me know. I knew she was excited to meet Harry, but I also understood her hesitation. Following a hunch, I decided to check the ladies room.

"Wow, if I didn't know better, I would think you were nervous," I laughed, entering the bathroom to find Amanda applying lipstick.

"Ericka, I am nervous. This is all happening so fast. I'm not sure I'm ready to meet anyone. Perhaps, it's too soon."

"Geez, Amanda, I'm not asking you to sleep with him. Get a grip. It's just a casual date. I just got a glimpse of him talking with Liam.

Trust me, he's extremely handsome, not to mention richer than sin, and you'll regret this if you don't get out there right now and allow Liam to introduce you. Amanda, I know how you feel, but our Bobs have left the building. They're not coming back. Now, stop being silly and put your lipstick away. You look gorgeous. For heaven's sakes, it's your birthday. Come on, the guys are waiting, and Liam is starving," I giggled.

"Alright, give me a moment. I hope Bob understands that you forced me into this."

"I somehow think Bob would want your happiness. I love you. Now, let's go. I promised you an unforgettable birthday in Seattle, and I don't see it happening inside the ladies room."

Walking out, the men turned to face us as we approached the table. Sensing Amanda's hesitation, I was relieved as Harry's handsome smile instantly broke the ice between them.

"Harry, this is Amanda Collins, Ericka's friend, and I might add, it's her birthday," Liam grinned.

"Well, Amanda, it's nice to meet you finally. Liam has told me a lot about you. Happy Birthday."

"Thank you. I hope it was all good," Amanda smiled.

"Nothing, but Liam is a man of his word. He said you were from Atlanta. I was born and raised in New Orleans. As Southerners, we have a lot in common, don't you agree?" Harry questioned with a grin.

"Definitely. There's no place like home," Amanda laughed.

"Shall we order? I'm starved," Liam suggested pulling out my chair.

Following suit, Harry pulled out Amanda's chair as the waiter brought out menus and glasses of water.

"I think a round of mimosas is in order," Harry suggested. "After all, it's someone's birthday," he winked with a smile staring at Amanda.

"Yes," I agreed, relieved the earlier tension I witnessed in Amanda had disappeared.

I knew there would be instant chemistry between them, knowing they were both born and raised in the South. Amanda, just like myself, had been lonely far too long, and Harry was just what she needed to get her life back on track. Becoming a widow meant lonely days, days that merely became an ordeal to make it to 12:01 a.m. It was a constant joke between us, which meant holding on to make it through another day. Looking at my best friend, I saw a sparkle in her eyes. Discreetly wiping my moistened eyes, I was thrilled that she now had the hope of having someone in her future, and Harry was the perfect guy.

After consuming a hearty breakfast, Liam suggested our itinerary. We would start our day at the Pike Place Fish Market near the wharf, the Seattle Great Wheel at Pier 57, the Space Needle, and the Chihuly Garden and Glass, an exhibit in the Seattle Center directly next to the Space Needle showcasing the studio glass of Dale Chihuly. After enjoying our conversation over our last round of coffee, it was time to start the day. Liam had arranged for a limo to make our day more enjoyable.

As the limousine parked in front of the Pike Place Fish Market, we hurriedly made our way inside as a light rain began to fall. Watching as Harry held Amanda's hand, pulling her into the shelter of the market, I smiled. It was already obvious they were instantly attracted to each other. Making our way to check out the flower arrangements, Harry purchased a beautiful bouquet of sunflowers for Amanda.

"Buddy, you're setting the bar high," Liam teased, watching as Harry paid for his purchase.

"Well, you're not getting off that easy," I laughed. "Flowers are nice, but I have my eyes on a pair of boots I saw in a store near the market."

"Geez, sweetheart, I hope you brought your wallet," Liam grinned humorously. I knew he would gladly buy me whatever my heart desired—watching him smile melted my heart.

Holding onto Harry, Amanda appeared a natural fit. They held hands while making their way through the crowds visiting the market.

Deciding to check out the local seafood, Liam stopped at one of the fishmongers. Being silly, he challenged me to catch a fish.

"Hey, if you can catch a fish without dropping it, those boots are yours."

"Come on, Ericka, you can do it," Amanda laughed. "You want the boots, right?"

"Okay, you've got a deal," I agreed. Forgetting about the weight of the slippery fish, the stench, or the fact my clothes would smell, I accepted Liam's dare.

Liam laughed, watching as I stood back with my feet apart. I firmly positioned myself for the best chance of catching the slippery fish. I was determined to give it my best shot.

"Are you ready?" the fishmonger yelled.

"Ready."

Hurling the fish in my direction, I fought with all my might to hold onto the slippery creature before it quickly slipped from my grasp.

"Darn it," I yelled, disappointed at my inability to win the challenge.

Looking around, Liam, Amanda, and Harry were laughing hilariously.

"You're not sitting next to me," Amanda giggled. "You smell like fish."

Walking over, Liam pulled me into his arms.

"Sweetheart, I like your tenacity. You can sit next to me anytime," he whispered. "By the way, those boots are yours. Let's buy you some clean clothes."

Purchasing a tee shirt and pair of jeans, I hurriedly changed in the restroom. Afterward, we leisurely strolled along the market, checking out all the vendors. We spent over an hour browsing through unique homemade crafts. Finally, we decided to walk down to a local coffee shop. Of course, we were stopping beforehand to purchase my boots. It appeared Amanda also decided new boots were in order. Taking her pricey possession to the counter to make the purchase, I smiled, watching as Harry refused to let her pay.

"I'll take those. It's your birthday. So, I can't let you pay," Harry smiled.

Utterly speechless, Amanda was caught off guard by his sudden act of kindness.

Enjoying a hot cup of coffee in one of Seattle's famous coffee shops, we laughed over my fish escapade. Devouring warm cinnamon rolls, we watched the rain turn into a downpour. We were having fun, and the weather never became a deterrent. We were fortunate enough to have the luxury of a limo waiting outside.

"Let's move this party to our next location," Harry smiled. Reaching for Amanda's hand, he hurriedly covered her with his jacket, protecting her from the rain as he led her outside and into the waiting car.

"Don't worry. I won't melt," I laughed as Liam took my hand.

"Oh sweetheart, I wouldn't allow it," he winked with a smile.

Once inside the limo, Liam pulled me into his arms. Noticing Amanda as she snuggled closer inside Harry's muscular embrace, it appeared his decision to purchase her boots was working in his favor. Smart man.

Our day was off to a fun start.

"Next stop, the Seattle Great Wheel at Pier 57," Harry grinned.

As the limo slowly parked in front of the pier, the guys assisted us out of the car and onto the curb. Harry and Liam walked ahead to purchase tickets giving Amanda and me a moment.

"So, what do you think?" I whispered.

"Think?" Amanda quizzed. "Think of what?"

"Harry, you silly goof. What do you think of Harry?"

"Oh, Harry. He's incredible. I'd say he was made to order if that was at all possible?" Amanda blushed.

"Do you see yourself going out with him again in the future?"

"Are you kidding? You saw the beautiful sunflowers and the boots. He's from New Orleans, a true Southern gentleman. Yes, my answer is a definite yes. Without hesitation, I would go out with him again if he asked."

"Well, then, tonight it is. Liam has reservations for the four of us at the Harbor House to celebrate your birthday."

"Aren't we overplaying that fact just a little?"

"Are you kidding? Amanda, it's totally working in your favor. You deserve to be treated like a queen for the day. I know you're uncomfortable with all the attention, but please, just go with it. I think Harry likes you."

"Okay. But, when did trusting you ever turn out to be such a great idea?" Amanda laughed.

Oh, don't go there, girlfriend. Trust me on this one. You can thank me later."

Quickly ending our conversation before the guys returned, I knew despite Amanda's playful resistance to all the attention, she was already smitten with Harry.

"Okay, we're all set," Harry smiled, flashing the tickets.

"Geez. It looks really high. I'm not sure," Amanda hesitated.

Giving Amanda one of my stern warning glances, I was going to drag her onto that wheel if I had to carry her on. I wasn't going to standby as her best friend and watch her blow her chances with Harry.

"Oh, come on. Be a good sport. I promise you'll be fine," Harry insisted. "You're with me, and you're in safe hands."

"The views from the top are phenomenal," Liam added, giving her reassurance.

"Amanda, it moves so slow that you'll hardly know your moving. Trust me, this is a lame ride, but it looks fun. Some of the pods have a bar. So we can get a drink."

"Alright, but only if I can get a drink first."

"No problem. I can easily take care of that," Harry offered.

Amanda's fears abated later, entering the glass-enclosed pod for a slow ride to the top with a drink in hand. Harry was the true essence of a Southern gentleman. He stood behind her with his arms tightly encircling her waist and lovingly held her for the duration of the entire ride. Watching as they took in the incredible vistas, it was apparent Amanda's apprehensions had easily been replaced by the safety and warmth of Harry's embrace. My best friend was falling in love, and I couldn't be happier. Caught up in the excitement of the moment, I kissed Liam.

"Wow, sweetheart. Don't stop," Liam whispered into my ear.

"We're in public. We should control ourselves," I countered.

"Ericka, look around. It's just the four of us," he smiled, pulling me farther into his arms.

How did I ever get so lucky to find love for the second time? And the best part was the fact Amanda might have someone to share her life with, a true Southerner. Watching as Amanda relaxed, laying her head against Harry's chest, they were the perfect fit.

"So, what do you think of those two?" I asked, taking a glance at Harry and Amanda. "Think there's a chance of them becoming romantically involved?"

"Well, I've known Harry for a long time. He doesn't usually attach himself to women so quickly. I'd say there's a good chance. Perhaps, he's been waiting all these years for the right person to come along," Liam smiled. "A true Southern Belle."

"What about us? Where do you see our relationship going?" I whispered, snuggling inside the warmth of his arms.

"Sweetheart, if you're fishing for answers, that's easy. I love you. I'm not ever letting you go. You were mine the day I first saw you," Liam winked with a seductive smile.

Trying desperately to hold back a flood of emotions, I discretely wiped my eyes. My life before meeting Liam had been trying at best. After losing Bob, life had given me such difficult moments that dying along with him would have seemed a far better fate. Just like the discovery of the bottle of Aramis and the fact it vanished, after meeting Liam, I knew he was in my life for a reason. Now, I was more determined than ever to hold onto him with every ounce of my being. My life had taken on a new significance because of the incredible man who held me in his arms.

"I love you too," I whispered.

As the giant wheel slowly came to a stop, the time spent inside the pod had been cathartic and reassuring. But then, it was time for a new adventure.

"Okay, gang, where do we go from here?" Harry playfully jested.

"Next stop on tour is the Space Needle," Liam laughed.

Amanda frowned. "Really? I don't like heights. Why did I think this was the worst of it?"

"Hey, you survived. I promise nothing will happen. I've got you," Harry grinned.

"Well, I think another drink is in order."

"That can be arranged."

It appeared the rain had stopped momentarily as the guys reached for our hands, leading us towards the waiting limo. Once inside, Harry grabbed glasses and popped the cork on a bottle of Moet & Chandon Champagne, filling each glass. Finally, it was time for a toast.

"Here's to Amanda. Happy Birthday, gorgeous," Harry grinned.

"Here's to a day filled with adventure and a spectacular year ahead," I added. "I love you."

"Yes. Happy Birthday," Liam smiled.

"Thank you. I can't ever remember having such a fun birthday," Amanda blushed. "However, the wheel was a little intimidating."

"No worries, sweetheart. Drink up. I've got you."

Arriving at the Space Needle, it appeared the liquid courage was working. Amanda took one look skyward at the impressive structure and smiled.

"Okay. Let's do this."

"That's my girl," Harry teased.

Harry reached for Amanda's hand as the limo parked, helping her out of the car.

"Why don't you two go ahead. We'll catch up in a few minutes," Liam suggested.

"Is everything alright?" Harry questioned.

"Yes. I have to make a quick phone call."

"Hey buddy, we promised no business today. Remember?"

"Ericka and I will meet up with you in a few minutes. I promise."

Watching as Amanda and Harry disappeared, Liam turned to face me.

"I forgot to order a cake for tonight."

"That's it? The reason you had them give us a few minutes. I was scared something might be wrong."

"Sweetheart, we can't have dinner tonight without a cake. It's a celebration, and I know the perfect bakery. They can deliver a cake to the restaurant. What is Amanda's favorite type of cake and her favorite flowers?"

"Well, to be honest, she loves pink roses, and she's always been partial to vanilla with fresh strawberries."

"Sounds delicious. Just give me a moment while I take care of this."

"No wonder I've fallen in love with you. You're so thoughtful and generous."

"Done. I ordered a vanilla cake filled with fresh strawberries and covered in pink roses. It will be delivered to the Harbor House in time for dinner this evening."

"Liam, thank you," I smiled.

"Not a problem."

Reaching for my hand, Liam helped me out of the car. Racing towards the Space Needle, trying to stay ahead of the oncoming downpour, we had hoped to reach the safety of the lobby without getting soaked. However, that was not to be the case. The heavens opened, releasing a deluge before we made it halfway. We were drenched from head to toe.

"Oh my God," I laughed. "We're completely soaked."

Panicked by the sudden downpour, I froze. It felt like a firehose had been aimed in our direction.

"Liam, I'm drenched. I can't go inside looking like this."

"Sweetheart, I swear, you've never looked more gorgeous."

Unexpectedly, our lips met. We were standing in a torrential rainstorm, kissing as if the world was on fire. Oblivious to everything around us, time simply stood still. Coming back down to earth, we laughed.

"What now?" I asked in sheer desperation as sheets of rain pelted us.

"We make a run for the limo," Liam laughed, grabbing my hand.

Racing towards the car, we were stunned by our misfortune to be caught in such a predicament. Gently, pulling my wet hair away from my face, Liam once again softly kissed me.

"I'm so sorry. I had no idea that might happen,' Liam apologized.

As our eyes met, we burst into laughter. Then, hurriedly reaching for his cell phone, which thankfully was still working, it was Harry.

"So that you know, I captured your little fiasco on my phone. I must say that's one for the books."

"Where are you?"

"At the top of the Space Needle. Where you were supposed to be before you were caught in that monsoon, I've got Amanda. Why don't you have the limo take you back to the hotel? We'll catch up later this evening. I think you need a change of clothes. See you later, buddy."

Reaching the hotel, we were met with numerous stares. Oblivious to the awkward glares around us, we made our way up the elevator and to our suite. Liam pulled me into his arms to keep the exposure of my wet, now somewhat transparent clothes at a minimum. I was helplessly lost, captivated by the brilliance of his dreamy blue eyes. I simply melted into his embrace, feeling loved, protected, and safe. Our unexpected encounter in the rain had connected us in an unexplainable way.

"Let's get you out of those wet clothes," Liam laughed, unlocking the door.

"Ditto," I smiled.

Walking into the bathroom, I quickly shed my drenched clothes. Stepping inside the shower, I turned on the warm water. It felt revitalizing, easily staving off the chills from being soaked. Reaching for the shampoo, I lathered my hair with suds. Suddenly feeling the warmth of strong hands massaging my shoulder, I turned to face Liam.

"Saving water," he grinned with a mischievous wink.

I was falling hard for the handsome man who now shared my shower. Gently rubbing suds over his buffed chest, the shower quickly became steamy, and it had nothing to do with the hot water. How lucky could one girl get, I thought. My life had drastically changed, and I wouldn't change a thing.

Wrapping me in the fluffy softness of a large towel, Liam scooped me into his arms and carried me into the bedroom. For the rest of the afternoon, the world simply failed to exist. The fact we were in Seattle, that it was Amanda's birthday, or even that she was with Harry escaped me. Instead, for the first time since losing Bob, I felt alive, breathless in the arms of another man. Feeling a single tear escape my eyes, I finally allowed myself to move on with my life. No longer would the worries of being alone, depression, or the word 'widow' confine the embodiment of my being. Liam had entered my world and brought with him unexplainable happiness. Turning to face the love of my life, I smiled.

Hearing the buzz of Liam's cell phone brought us back into reality.

Reaching for his phone, he sat up in bed. Liam's phone was on speaker, and I heard some of their conversation.

"Hey, Amanda and I are at the hotel. We had an unbelievable afternoon. What did you guys do after leaving the Space Needle? Never mind. Knowing you, don't answer that," Harry laughed. "We'll meet you both in the lobby at 7:00 p.m. for dinner. Behave, buddy. See you in a few."

"See you at 7:00 p.m. Oh, and Harry, I'm not the one you should worry about. I hope Amanda knows what she's getting herself into with you. She's Ericka's best friend, need I have to remind you. So keep it checked, buddy."

"I'm always a gentleman."

"Right, man. See you later."

Pulling the duvet up to cover my chest, I sat up.

"What was that about? You two sound like a couple of ditzy boy scouts."

"Harry was letting us know they had arrived at the hotel. We'll meet them in the lobby at 7:00 p.m."

"Did he mention Amanda?"

"Just the fact they had a wonderful afternoon."

"Did he say what they did?"

"No, but I'm sure you'll hear all about it from Amanda later this evening."

"Now. Where were we?" Liam winked, pulling me into his arms."

Later that night, after making sure Fritz was taken for a short walk, we dressed and once again entered the elevator for the short ride down to the lobby. As the elevator doors opened, I instantly caught sight of Amanda with her arms around Harry. She was dressed to perfection in a black sequined halter gown. She was the personification of beauty, wearing her hair swept up in an elegant chignon with dazzling diamond earrings. Standing next to Harry, whose choice of attire was a trendy three-piece suit, they easily replicated the figurines on top of a wedding cake. I could only wonder if this was a sign of things to come."

"Wow, Amanda, you look exquisite," I smiled.

"My thoughts exactly," Harry grinned.

"Well, it is, after all, my birthday, and you don't look so bad yourself," Amanda responded.

I felt her equal in the fashion department, wearing a black silk pantsuit with brilliant rhinestone heels and my short hair in curls. Liam chose a sophisticated black suit that fit him like a glove, giving hints of his well-defined muscular physique. He was the definition of eye candy, and he was mine.

"Well, if everyone is ready, the limo is waiting," Liam stated, taking my hand.

After everyone was comfortably seated, Harry again popped the cork on a bottle of Moet and Chandon.

"I believe the occasion calls for another toast. So here's to the most gorgeous woman in Seattle. Happy Birthday."

"Let's make that two of the most beautiful women in Seattle, shall we? Happy Birthday, Amanda," Liam grinned with a wink, kissing me lightly on the cheek.

"Happy Birthday to my best friend. I love you."

The evening was off to a great start. I couldn't wait to arrive at the wharf and the famous Harbor House Restaurant. Even though Liam and Harry were considered wealthy entrepreneurs in the business world, they reflected the traits of true gentlemen. Liam exuded confidence which earned him the respect of everyone he met. His tenacity and boldness had enticed me the moment I first saw him approach my table.

Arriving at the wharf, the limo slowly stopped, parking at the entrance. As our door was opened, Liam took my hand and graciously helped me exit the car. Watching as Harry grasped Amanda's hand, the sparkle in his eyes indicated their involvement was quickly evolving into a romantic relationship. I couldn't have been happier for them. Amanda and I had traveled the same path of heartbreak, losing our husbands, and more than ever, she also deserved a second chance at happiness.

Entering the restaurant, a delicious aroma of baked bread and cooked to perfection steak and seafood infused the air as the maitre d' escorted us to a private room near the back. A wall of windows exposed the sparkling waters of Elliot Bay and numerous ferry boats, which shuffled people back and forth from the islands surrounding

Puget Sound. We were privileged to dine in private while enjoying the spectacular nighttime vistas. The restaurant had an old-world charm. Floor-to-ceiling windows surrounded tables, eloquently set with red damask linens and centered with tiny lamps. Exquisite chandeliers scattered throughout the tall recessed ceilings added to the undeniable ambiance.

Approaching our table, the waiter placed menus and crystal water glasses on the table. Discreetly reaching into my evening purse for reading glasses, I was helpless without them. Noticing my dilemma, Liam smiled.

"Ericka, may I offer a few suggestions from the menu?"

"Of course."

"We'd like the Dungeness Crab and Lobster Bisque to start. As far as our entrée selection, we would like the Alaskan Black Cod, oven-roasted, with Sake Kasu marinade, green onions with chef's choice of starch, and seasoned vegetables. Also a bottle of Dom Perignon Champagne 2006."

"I'll make it easy for you tonight," Harry grinned, looking up at the waiter. If this gorgeous young lady approves, we'll have the same. However, we would also like Plateau de fruits de mer cooked."

"Okay, except I don't speak French, and I think I would like to know what I ordered," Amanda hesitated with a laugh."

"It's simply a platter of cooked seafood, shrimp, mussels, crab, oysters, and clams served on ice. It's your birthday, and we're simply covering all the bases. Hopefully, you like seafood?" Harry added.

"I do. I must say it sounds delicious."

"Will there be anything else, sir?" the waiter smiled.

"I believe that's it, provided the young ladies save room for dessert."

Looking at Liam, I smiled. I knew Amanda would love the cake he chose. So tonight was not only the celebration of my best friend's birthday but the fitting end to a perfect day.

The waiter returned to fill our water glasses and brought the chilled Dom Perignon. The night was off to a great start as the waiter poured us each a glass of sparkling bubbly. The service was impeccable, and our conversation flowed effortlessly after a few sips of champagne.

"Liam, thank you for the upgrade in accommodations and for providing such great care for Hazel. The young man who took care of Hazel was the best. He even took her for a walk between rain showers. Thank you so much."

"You're welcome. If there's anything you need, please don't hesitate to call room service."

"Or, call me," Harry boldly interjected.

"Geez, buddy," Liam laughed.

Amanda blushed, and I laughed, knowing Harry was looking for any excuse to see her. They had only spent one day together, and already their relationship was moving at warp speed.

"Did you enjoy your afternoon?" I questioned, trying to alleviate Amanda's embarrassment.

"Yes. Harry is a great tour guide. We took the Beneath the Streets Underground History Tour. It was fascinating and a great place to escape the rain. A knowledgeable guide walked us through numerous underground tunnels. During the tour, we discovered the history of Pioneer Square from a rare below-ground perspective. I highly recommend it."

"Maybe, the next time I visit Seattle, I'll check it out."

"I can't believe you and Liam were caught in the rain and had to return to the hotel. Harry showed me the video, and I must say, it was hilarious. I had gone to the ladies room, and I wondered why you never came."

"We had no choice. Liam and I were completely drenched and needed a change of clothes. The weather was terrible, so we decided to stay in for the afternoon."

"Umm, weather? Right?" Harry laughed.

"Dessert, anyone?" Liam winked at me with a smile changing the conversation.

Motioning for the waiter, Liam gave the cue to bring the cake. Within minutes, the gorgeous two-tier cake covered in pink roses made its appearance. Glowing with candles, the cake was the highlight of the evening.

"Happy Birthday," we said in unison.

"Oh my gosh!" Amanda cried. "It's beautiful. Seriously, I never expected anything like this, especially a cake. Thank you."

"You more than deserve it, and I think you'll love it. It's your favorite, vanilla layers with fresh strawberries," I smiled. "Liam put in a special order."

"Liam, thank you," Amanda smiled, giving him a huge hug. "And, you knew my favorite roses. It's exquisite. Thank you."

"Well, I had a bit of help thanks to Ericka."

"Ericka, what can I say. You never cease to surprise me. Thank you," Amanda smiled, giving me a gigantic hug.

"Okay, I might not have been involved with the cake, but I did play the role of tour guide," Harry chimed in.

"Harry, what can I say? Thanks to you, it was an unforgettable birthday. Today was the best, despite the weather. Thank you," Amanda beamed, embracing the handsome man beside her.

As the waiter returned with extra plates and silverware, it was time to cut the cake.

"Make a wish," I announced.

Watching as Amanda blew out the candles, my eyes moistened. I knew her wish was sitting next to her. It was Harry. The past two years had been brutal for Amanda. I knew the lonely nights, the empty side of the bed, the tsunami of emotions at hearing the favorite song you shared, the endless worries of responsibilities that were previously shared, and thoughts of wanting to give up. Still, knowing it wasn't an option, the connotations were endless. I wished her more happiness than she could ever know. Discreetly wiping my eyes, it appeared Liam had noticed.

"Sweetheart, are you okay?" he whispered, kissing me on the cheek.

"Yes. It's been an eventful day. I just need a good night's sleep."

"No worries. I can help with that," Liam winked wickedly.

After enjoying too many slices of cake, the evening came to an end. Once again, we were on our way back to the hotel. Snuggled inside the safety of Liam's strong arms, I knew that whoever had brought this wonderful man into my life, be it God, Bob, or fate, had saved my life. I was finally able to breathe again and experience joy even in the midst of a sudden rainstorm in Seattle.

Feeling drowsy, as we entered the elevator for the short ride up to our suite, I barely noticed Amanda and Harry draped around each other as they stepped out of the elevator. Finally, it appeared her wish was coming true.

The following day, Liam hired a private tour guide. The weather was finally cooperative, and we spent the day at Mt. Rainier. We experienced the majestic beauty of the mountain, the tallest in the lower forty-eight states, and a narrated journey past lakes and waterfalls. The vistas were breathtaking, stopping for photos at Christine Falls, the Nisqually River, and Narada Falls.

As with all good things, our weekend finally came to an end. Liam was called back to Vancouver on business. Harry had a personal issue to deal with, which meant his return to Vancouver. Amanda was flying back to San Francisco. Once again, my agent unexpectedly called to confirm she had secured more book signings in Seattle. It appeared I was left behind. However, I promised Liam to join him in Vancouver the following weekend.

Seattle had been unforgettable. I discovered that Liam wasn't an ax murderer but an extremely wealthy entrepreneur. The fact he took such great care of me and covered Amanda's hotel expenses was a trait that many men sorely lacked. I was falling head over heels in love with him. Saying our goodbyes at the airport wasn't easy. After ensuring that Amanda was safely at her terminal, I continued with Liam and Harry.

"Well, sweetheart, Seattle was wonderful. Sorry, I'm missing your book signings, but I can't wait to see you this weekend. Talk to you tonight. I love you," Liam winked with a smile stepping onto the curb with his luggage.

"Liam, I love you too. I'll miss you. See you this weekend," I replied, trying to hide my tears.

"Don't worry. I'll make sure he behaves," Harry grinned. "It was nice meeting you, and especially Amanda. Perhaps, I'll see you this weekend."

"Don't count on it," Liam laughed, giving me one last kiss.

Returning to the hotel, I took the elevator up to our suite. Unlocking the door, I hesitated. Slowly walking inside, it still held the memories of the wonderful weekend we shared. The scent of Liam's cologne lingered in the air with hints of bergamot and sandalwood. Picking up Fritz, I grabbed his leash. He was overdue for some fresh air and a nice long walk. Afterward, I would pour my emotions into my manuscript. The deadline was quickly approaching, and I needed to finish before the weekend.

After writing for hours, I took a break. Reclining on the sofa, with Fritz snuggled into my arms, thoughts of Liam and our weekend in Seattle consumed me. I couldn't wait to see him. Vancouver now represented more than the end of my road trip. It held the promise of a new beginning. Life was good.

Chapter Eight

Driving carefully in a shower of rain, I was still an hour away from Vancouver. Yet, I began to feel my heart racing with excitement. Thoughts of seeing Liam were consuming me. Noting an incoming call on the screen, I answered hands-free with the press of a button. The sound of his voice sent tingles of excitement throughout my entire body.

"Hello."

"Hey, sweetheart, I was calling to get your estimated time of arrival."

"I'm about an hour away."

"Great. My flight got in early. Why don't you meet me at the apartment? I've made dinner reservations at 7:00 p.m."

"Sounds good. It's raining, but the traffic is light. It might be sooner."

"Not a problem. Drive safe. See you soon, love you."

"Love you too."

Arriving at the Marina Towers, it was accurately named and impressively located near the downtown waterfront. The afternoon sun brilliantly reflected off the modern high-rise glass structure as I slowly entered the underground parking garage. Again, luck was on my side. Surprisingly, I discovered a vacant spot in guest parking. Before leaving the car, I reached for my purse and quickly checked my makeup and hair in the mirror. Afterward, locking the car, I walked over to the elevator. Stepping inside, I pushed the access code for the thirty-ninth floor. As the elevator doors opened, I smiled, hearing a familiar voice.

"Hey, sweetheart, you're early. How was the drive?" Liam inquired, giving me a quick passionate kiss.

"Not bad, except for the rain. Traffic was light."

Suddenly met with the affectionate kisses of Liam's black lab. She was adorable. Even Fritz found her friendly.

"You never mentioned her name," I smiled, leaning down to give her a quick rub behind her ears.

"It's Ebony."

"Well, that's certainly original," I laughed. "Wow, you never mentioned that you lived in a penthouse."

"Babe, it's just an apartment. However, I do own the floor above. It's perhaps a little larger than average and with better views. That's all," Liam laughed. "Where's your luggage?"

"This place is huge. Oh, I left my luggage in the trunk of the car."

"Not a problem. We'll deal with it later. Come inside, and let me show you around."

The interior was extremely modern as I walked inside. White marble floors reflected the afternoon sun as it streamed in from tall, floor-to-ceiling windows. White leather sofas were conveniently centered between an oversized glass and chrome coffee table. The penthouse easily reflected its owner was a single male. Even at Liam's age, it screamed, 'bachelor pad.' I laughed, knowing it desperately needed a woman's touch. Perhaps, if things progressed between us, I might, with his approval, get the opportunity to redecorate.

"You seem amused. Let me show you the kitchen. Maybe that's more in line with your taste."

"Oh, Liam, you're funny. I love you but has no one ever mentioned that your apartment might appear a little 'sterile' for lack of a better word?" I laughed.

"Wow, that hurts," Liam chuckled, pretending to be stunned. "I'll show you the kitchen," he smiled, taking my hand. "Perhaps you can pretend to love it."

Looking around the kitchen, it was stylishly executed.

"Geez, Liam, what's not to love? The kitchen is gorgeous."

"Finally, the lady approves," he smiled.

The kitchen's décor, even though still modern with white cabinets and black granite, felt inviting. It was beautiful. The kitchen cabinets had intricate etched glass doors and were lit from within, giving the kitchen a soft ambiance. State-of-the-art appliances clearly made it a chef's dream.

"Let me show you my favorite part of the penthouse and the reason I purchased it."

Taking my hand, Liam led me back into the living room. Next, walking over to the wall of windows, he slid back enormous glass pocket doors which exposed the living area to the outside. Instantly, we were met with a warm breeze as we stepped onto the patio that wrapped the penthouse's entire circumference.

"Sweetheart, this is what I call a million-dollar view," Liam continued.

"Totally," I smiled, taking in the panoramic vistas. The views revealed massive skyscrapers, multimillion-dollar yachts, and people out for a walk along the seawall that surrounded the harbor's shimmering waters. "It's spectacular."

Glancing at his watch, Liam panicked.

"Sweetheart, our dinner reservations are for 7:00 p.m., and the limo is waiting. I'm sorry not to offer you time to rest, shower, or change before dinner. However, I must say you look stunning, and I wouldn't change a thing. Are you okay with leaving now?"

"Yes. Of course."

After ensuring the dogs would be fine and locking up, Liam grasped my hand as we bolted for the elevator. Reaching the entrance of the apartment building, we were met by Liam's driver.

"Good evening, sir," the chauffeur grinned, opening our door.

"Good evening, Patrick. We're dining at Berlusconi's this evening."

"No problem. Traffic is light. I'll have you there within ten minutes."

"Thanks."

Snuggling into Liam's arms, I settled in for the short ride.

"If I remember correctly, I believe you love Italian cuisine?"

"Yes. You remembered."

"Awesome. I'm sure you will like Berlusconi's. It's a well-known establishment in Vancouver."

"Liam, I never doubt you. You have impeccable taste."

"Did you say impeccable taste?" Liam laughed.

"Well, let me clarify that statement. I meant you have impeccable taste in restaurants," I smiled.

"Thanks, I suppose," Liam grinned.

Arriving at the restaurant, Patrick parked in front. Opening our car door, he smiled.

"Have a good evening, sir."

Entering Berlusconi's was visually stunning. The walls were covered in a rich red damask material accented with scrolled lit sconces, tall mirrors, and highlighted portraits of Michelangelo and Caravaggio added to its ambiance. In addition, the savory aroma of warm bread, along with a noticeable hint of garlic, spices, cooked tomatoes, and sausage, infused the air.

"Good evening, Mr. Lachkowski. It's wonderful to see you again. Your table is ready. This way, sir."

Once again, following the maitre d' to a private room, Liam always had the respect of those around him. I was hungry and ready to indulge in my favorite cuisine. Presented with the menu, I already knew the entrée I craved without reading the selections.

"I suppose you have an entrée in mind, knowing your love of Italian cuisine."

"Of course. I would simply like the lasagna and afterward, tiramisu for dessert."

"Geez, sweetheart, for someone who relates to impeccable taste, isn't that rather boring?" Liam chuckled.

"Liam, I refuse to be teased when it comes to my favorite foods."

"Duly noted. Lasagna and tiramisu it is," Liam winked with a smile.

I wasn't the least bit envious as I watched Liam enjoy his entrée.

He savored every bite of the Tuscan Tomato Bread Soup with steamed mussels and Spinach and Ricotta Gnudi with tomato-butter sauce. Some things were better-left simple, I mused.

After finishing our entrées and dessert, Liam reached for my hand, giving me a questionable stare.

"Sweetheart, how are you with spur-of-the-moment ideas?"

"Well, I'm not sure. Why?"

"Let me ask you this, do you trust me?"

"Yes. Of course."

"Great. We're leaving. No more questions. Patrick is waiting for us."

"What's going on?"

"No more questions."

Once inside the limo, Liam reached for a blindfold. Not knowing what I had gotten myself into, I played along.

"May I place this over your eyes? It's not for long, I promise," he grinned.

"I suppose. But, your surprise better not be weird or kinky," I warned.

"Ericka, I assure you it's definitely neither weird nor kinky. Trust me."

As the limo drove away from the restaurant, my curiosity heightened. I did trust Liam, but I was also nervous. Spontaneity wasn't usually my idea of fun. During our fifty years of marriage, I couldn't remember Bob and I doing anything remotely like this. But, on the other hand, maybe it was time to live life boldly. As the limo slowly came to a stop, I held my breath.

"Sweetheart, I'm going to help you out of the car. Then I'll remove the blindfold."

Feeling a slight breeze as I stepped out of the limo, I had no idea where we were or what to expect.

"Ready?" Liam asked.

"Yes."

Dropping the blindfold, I gasped. I was standing in front of a luxurious Lear Jet.

"Wow, Liam, what does this mean? Why are we here, and why is there a jet?"

"Ericka, it means we're on an overnight flight to Paris. I read your books. You do have your passport, right?"

"Yes," I cried as my legs buckled.

Catching me before I passed out, Liam carried me on board.

"Good evening, sir. It's nice to see you again. Is there anything I can bring you before we're airborne?" Stacy inquired, welcoming us on board. She was a loyal employee. But, like Patrick, she kept things discreet.

"Yes, a glass of champagne for my companion. I'll have my usual, a double shot of bourbon, Michter's. Later, we'll retire to the back. First, however, we would like breakfast before arriving in Paris."

"Yes, of course. I'll get your drinks."

"Liam, I'm speechless," I remarked, still reeling with dizziness as we were seated. Wiping my eyes, I glanced around the cabin. "I've never seen the inside of a Lear Jet, much less traveled on one. It's sheer luxury."

"Well, sweetheart, I truly hope you enjoy the flight," Liam smiled with a wink. "You're with me now, and I spend a lot of time in the air. It will soon become your second home."

"Pinch me. This can't be real. It only happens between the pages of my books."

"Babe, I assure you it's real. Perhaps this will help," Liam grinned, pulling me into his arms, kissing me with such passion my toes curled.

"Liam," I panicked. "Where's my luggage? I have absolutely nothing to wear. What about Ebony and Fritz?"

"Babe, no clothes work for me," he laughed mischievously. "Your luggage is back at the penthouse. My housekeeper, Elena, will take great care of Fritz and Ebony."

"Liam, that's not funny. I don't have any clothes."

"Ericka, I've heard Paris has the latest fashions. I don't see that as a problem. Does this help," Liam smiled, revealing an American Express Black Card. "The last time I was in Paris, it was widely accepted," he added with a laugh.

"Thanks, but I can't take your money."

"Oh, sweetheart, this is going to be fun. You're so naive. Remember what I told you at Sapori D' Italia, our first evening in Seattle? I'm a man of my word, and I intend to spoil you beyond your wildest dreams," Liam winked.

I blushed utterly speechless for the second time since boarding the aircraft. Unexpectedly, since meeting Liam, my entire world had shifted once again. I was a widow without a husband, simply trying to hang on to my sanity. I had written numerous romantic books, fictionalized romantic rendezvous, and created phenomenal characters like Liam. However, it was entirely fantasy. None of it was real. Yet, here I sat next to an incredibly handsome man, on a Lear Jet, and unbelievably on a night flight to Paris. Wiping away tears, I cried softly, thinking perhaps Bob had some involvement. Was it possible for him to change the course of my life?

"Babe, please, no more tears. I love you. Trust me, your safe with me," Liam smiled, kissing me on the cheek. "I think you're tired, and I'm sure the evening has been a little overwhelming."

"A little?" I managed to laugh.

Stacy smiled, returning with the champagne and bourbon as the plane reached its cruising altitude.

"Thanks, Stacy. I believe we will take our drinks to the back of the aircraft."

Reaching for my hand and taking our drinks, Liam ushered me toward the rear of the cabin. My breath hitched as Liam opened the door. It contained a queen size bed and shower.

"Wow, this has to be a dream," I smiled once again, feeling faint. I wasn't sure I would survive the flight. Two luxurious white robes were lying on the bed.

"Ericka, you look tired. Why don't we change into the robes and finish our drinks? I'm sure you'll feel more relaxed."

"But," I paused, totally embarrassed. "I have no clothes."

"Babe, you're in my private cabin. Clothes aren't a requirement," Liam winked mischievously. "Now, don't be silly. It's a long flight over the pond. You need to sleep."

Gently unzipping my dress, Liam removed my outer garments,

wrapping me in the softness of the luxurious fabric. Next, pulling back the blue duvet, he lifted me under the warmth of the covers.

"Drink up," he smiled, handing me the glass of champagne as he dimmed the lights.

Watching as he shed his outer garments, he dismissed the idea of a robe. Downing his bourbon, he joined me in bed. Taking my empty glass, he sat it on the nightstand.

"Is sleep a requirement?" I giggled, rolling over to face him.

"I like the way you think."

Pulling me into the warmth of his arms, I sought the safety of his embrace. The hint of bourbon on his lips and the hypnotic fragrance of his cologne was an irresistible aphrodisiac. For the duration of the flight, we simply made love like two giddy teenagers on a first date. We had barely drifted off to sleep when Liam's alarm woke us.

"Wow, did this really happen?" I asked, pulling the covers up to my chest as I sat up in bed. "Did we just make love for hours while flying over the Atlantic Ocean?"

"Sweetheart, you don't actually expect me to answer that, do you?" Liam laughed.

"Babe, I don't have anything to wear, and my dress is wrinkled."

"Open the closet door."

"Really? Why?"

"Trust me."

Opening the closet, I gasped, seeing its contents. An elegant black dress with matching heels instantly caught my attention. Taking the garment from the hanger, it held a designer tag, Versace.

"Liam, it's my size. It's Versace."

"I know. You'll find new undergarments in the drawer below."

"I can't believe this is happening. It's all surreal," I answered. "How can I ever repay you for everything?" I cried.

"Oh, I'm sure I can think of a few ways," he winked with a sexy smile.

Sitting at the edge of the bed, I was simply overwhelmed. He gently wiped the tears from my face as he pulled me into his arms.

"Well, for starters, we have to get your emotions in check. I can't have you crying all over Paris. First, people will think I'm abusing you. And second, we're going shopping. I believe I've seen those tags in Paris. If not?" Liam laughed, "We'll fly to Rome."

"Liam, it doesn't take designer labels to make me happy. I love you."

"Sweetheart, I love you too. But, we've got to hurry. I've asked Stacy to serve breakfast before we land. So, there's just enough time for you to shower and dress before breakfast is served in the forward cabin."

Enjoying coffee along with a full complement of waffles, sausage, and eggs as the sun rose over the Atlantic Ocean was completely foreign to me. It was hard to imagine the lives of people who lived this extravagantly, yet here I sat.

"Sweetheart, is this your first time in Paris?" Liam inquired, taking a sip of coffee.

"No. Bob and I honeymooned in Paris over fifty years ago. Unfortunately, our lives got hectic after the boys came along, and we never made an effort to return. Sadly, time ran out."

"Well, you haven't seen Paris until you've seen it with me. No disrespect to your deceased husband. I have an apartment close to the Champs-Elysees, and I've made reservations at several of my favorite restaurants. However, first things first, we need to add to your wardrobe."

"Sir, we're less than thirty minutes out from the airport. Is there anything else I can bring you before we land?" Stacy questioned, approaching our seats.

"No. Thanks. We're fine."

Stepping off the plane at Charles de Gaulle Airport shortly after sunrise, I was excited to be back in Paris. Liam, as usual, had arranged for a limo to be waiting. Quickly the car sped away, taking us into the heart of the city.

As we entered the third-floor walk-up, the building's old-world charm was quaint and impressive. Gorgeous red geraniums flowed over the wrought iron terraces which lined each level. Reaching Liam's floor, he opened the door. Suddenly, taking a reserved stance, he waited.

"Well, give it your best shot. I can take it. Sterile or impeccable?" Liam laughed.

"Truly impeccable, " I countered with a smile.

The apartment was breathtaking and visually stunning. There was no comparison to the penthouse in Vancouver. It lacked nothing, not even the touches that a woman might bring.

Walking further inside, I felt compelled to touch everything. An elegant floral carpet centered the room as Victorian sofas sat across from each other, encapsulating an oversized scrolled mahogany coffee table. European art stylishly covered every square inch of the walls. However, the room's main focal point was an ornate baroque fireplace tucked into a corner of the room and tall narrow doors that opened onto the terrace.

"Liam, it's gorgeous."

"So, I nailed it?" he questioned with a smile.

"Without a doubt."

"Well, I can't take the credit, but I'll be sure to pass it along to my interior decorator. Allow me to show you the bedroom," Liam grinned, pulling me into an adjoining room.

It was beautiful. A massive four-poster mahogany bed sat against one wall, and an ornate matching credenza sat against the opposite wall. The large bed was exquisitely covered with a blue country toile duvet. The duvet eloquently coordinated with toile drapes encasing the tall glass doors. Walking over, Liam opened the doors allowing a warm breeze to flow in from the outside terrace. The slight noise of traffic from the street below, along with the hustle of tourists, and locals let you know you were in the midst of a thriving city.

"I hope you're comfortable here?"

"As long as you're with me."

"So, sweetheart, my next question is, would you prefer to stay in and rest for today, shop, or take a tour of the city?"

"Liam, if I'm completely honest, staying in sounds amazing. I still feel a bit disoriented due to the long flight and, of course, the time change. Could we possibly relax for today? I know that I need to shop for clothes, but I'm exhausted."

"Babe, say no more. I understand. Reaching into his closet, he pulled out his bathrobe. Why don't you change? I'm going to dash downstairs to the local market. I won't be long, I promise. The kitchen needs to be restocked, and perhaps, I'll cook tonight."

"Thanks. Take your time. I'll just be here admiring your impeccable apartment."

"You're hilarious. I'll be right back."

Liam's robe hung loosely around my body as I walked into the living room. Feeling tired, I relaxed on the sofa. Within minutes, sleep consumed me. I slept peacefully until I heard Liam unlocking the door. Glancing up, as he entered the apartment, he looked like a pack mule weighted down with shopping bags.

"You look like you bought out the store," I laughed. "Let me help you. Give me some of those bags," I insisted.

"Well, I haven't stayed here for over a month, and the kitchen shelves are depleted. Plus, there were a lot of needed items like cheese, wine, fruit, and fresh vegetables. So how does pizza sound for tonight?"

"Can I reserve the right to tell you after I try it?" I teased.

"Really. That's your answer?" Liam scoffed, quickly putting the refrigerated items inside the tiny fridge. "Oh, girl, you're going to regret that," he grinned.

Walking over, he scooped me into his arms.

"One last chance. Do you want to take back your answer?" he laughed.

"No. Not a chance," I replied amusingly.

"Your choice. Now you'll have to suffer the consequences of doubting my culinary skills."

Carrying me into the bedroom, Liam gently laid me on the bed.

"Just a moment."

Closing the doors, Liam used a remote device to lower the blackout shades and access soft romantic music.

"Where were we? Oh, that's right. We were here," he smiled, kissing me with such an intensity it took my breath. The passion which ignited between us was searing. I simply failed to exist, melting into his arms.

"Oh my God," I gasped as Liam pulled back the duvet. I loved this man.

In the darkness of the room, Liam gently slipped me under the covers. I could only envision him as he undressed. Sinking into the extreme softness of the mattress, I felt his strong arms pulling me closer as he slid into bed. The world simply faded away as I snuggled into the warmth of his body. I felt loved and safe. There was no place I'd rather be than wrapped in his arms. Paris could wait. For the rest of the day, we never left the bedroom. Making love to the point of exhaustion, we fell asleep, not waking until the following day.

Waking to the sound of Liam's alarm, sleeping in had allowed us to adjust to the vast time difference. Opening the blackout shades, the brilliance of the morning sun bathed the room in a soft glow. Our first day had been perfect. Now it was time to see Paris.

"Wow, sweetheart," Liam smiled, giving me a quick kiss. "Last night was one for the books," he added with a sexy wink sitting up in bed.

"Don't worry. You won't be reading those scenes in one of my books," I giggled.

"Thank God. Why don't you jump in the shower? I'll cook breakfast. Later, I have a city to show you."

"I can't wait."

Stepping out of the warm shower, I reached for Liam's robe. The aromas coming from the other room were scrumptious. Hurriedly wrapping my damp hair in a towel, I strolled into the kitchen.

Observing Liam's shirtless physique as he effortlessly flipped pancakes, wearing sweat pants, I smiled. Admiring my sexy guy, even at his age, he could easily grace the cover of GQ Magazine. Walking over, I put my arms around him, giving him a quick kiss.

"Definitely, my idea of the perfect breakfast," I remarked. "A sexy, shirtless man making pancakes."

"Coffee?" he asked with a grin.

"Of course."

"Sorry, not exactly the latest in fashion," I frowned, securing my robe.

"Babe, you could be wearing a burlap sack, and you'd still be sexier than hell," Liam winked with a wicked smile.

"Geez. Who are you? Where did you come from, and what did I ever do to deserve you?"

"Sweetheart, we were fated to meet. Have a seat," he grinned, placing a stack of pancakes smothered in warm maple syrup and butter, with sausage on the table.

"You're joining me, right?"

"Absolutely, but we have to hurry. I've arranged for George to pick us up in less than an hour. So we have a huge day ahead."

Hearing a light knock at the door, Liam smiled. "Sorry. I've got to get this. Enjoy your pancakes."

Watching curiously, he opened the door. An attractive young girl stepped inside laden with shopping bags.

"Great. Thanks, Simone. I was worried you wouldn't make it on time," Liam remarked, taking the elegant shopping bags. "Please let Brian know that I'm only here for a few days, but I plan to come into the office before I leave. Thanks again," he mentioned seeing the young girl out.

"Who was she?" I questioned, looking up from the kitchen table.

"Oh, Simone Chastain, my personal assistant. Harry and I have an office on Rue de Rivoli, and I called her this morning."

"What's in all the shopping bags?"

"Well, why don't you come over and take a look?" Liam grinned.

"I'm certain I didn't order anything."

"Awww, but I did."

Curiosity getting the best of me, I walked over to the sofa. I knew Liam had been up to something. He had made several phone calls when we first woke up.

Opening the first shopping bag, it was stylishly tied with ribbons and stuffed with gorgeous tissue paper. Removing the curled ribbons, I gasped. It contained clothes—things I desperately needed. Pulling out several pairs of designer jeans, I smiled. Reaching further into the bag, I discovered stylish blouses, cashmere sweaters, and even a leather jacket sporting a Gucci tag.

"Oh my gosh, Liam, these are expensive. I can't take these."

"Oh, but you can. Open the next bag," he insisted.

Opening the next bag, it contained several boxes. Holding my breath, I removed the lid from the first box revealing leather boots that matched the jacket from the first bag.

"Liam, there are Gucci tags on these boots and the jacket. They must have cost a small fortune. Are you crazy?" I laughed.

"Well, I'm taking the fifth on that statement," he laughed. "Hurry, we don't have much time before George arrives. Just pick an outfit. Anything you decide will look spectacular on you, I promise."

Quickly opening the other boxes, there were flats and a pair of running shoes.

"Really? Running shoes?"

"We'll talk about those later. Keep going. I have to say the next bag is my favorite," Liam smiled.

Hurriedly opening the next bag, I blushed. It contained a sexy black negligee, more lingerie than any woman could ever hope to have, and the most exquisite undergarments I had ever seen.

"Wow, Babe, I'm completely speechless. Honestly, I don't know what to say. Thank you!"

"Sweetheart, you don't have to say anything. I love you. Now, pick something. We have to leave soon."

Grabbing the bags, I quickly escaped into the bedroom with my treasures. Choosing a pair of denim jeans, a silk blouse with a coordinated cashmere sweater, and the flats, I hurriedly dressed. I was finally ready for the day after styling my short hair and applying a light touch of my favorite red lipstick and makeup.

"Wow. You look amazing. Maybe we should forget Paris and stay in for the day."

"Not a chance. You purchased all these beautiful designer clothes. Trust me. I'm wearing them today."

"Ericka, I feel an apology is in order. I had planned to take you shopping so that you could personally select your clothes, but I realized time would be an issue today, so I asked Simone to shop for you. I hope that's alright. I promise before we leave to let you shop until you drop, as the ladies say."

"Thanks, but that's not necessary. The clothes Simone purchased are gorgeous and the right size. Thank you."

Entering the limo, Liam had planned our entire day, with our first stop being the Eiffel Tower. George had been instructed to bring a picnic basket filled with wine, cheese, crackers, along with enough baguette sandwiches and condiments to last the entire day. I was excited to revisit Paris.

Arriving at our first stop, the Eiffel Tower, the massive steel structure appeared intimidating. It was hard to imagine the engineering required to erect such a structural masterpiece. As awe-inspiring as it was to be standing under the giant behemoth which was built to highlight the Paris World's Fair in 1889, thoughts of Bob and my first visit flooded my mind.

Exiting the limo, memories of my honeymoon with Bob and our time in Paris consumed me. Trying hard not to let my emotions overwhelm me was difficult. As newlyweds, I had just graduated from college, and Bob had taken leave before being transferred to Southeast Asia. We were crazy in love, and not having been abroad, Paris, the city of love, seemed the perfect place for our honeymoon. We were young, carefree, and energetic. However, it seemed like only yesterday that Bob and I were here. We had taken one of the last tours of the day. Reaching the top, a vast sea of lights expanded beneath us. It was magical and breathtaking. Now, I was back and a widow. Wiping my eyes, I tried to remain stoic.

"Ericka, are you okay?"

"Memories can be a little daunting," I smiled. "As I told you, Bob and I spent our honeymoon in Paris."

"Sweetheart, I'm sorry. I had no idea when I decided to bring you to Paris that you had spent your honeymoon here. But, Babe, trust me, I'm not trying to replace your memories. We can leave."

"No. I want to take the elevator to the top. I've only seen the view at night. I would love to experience it during the daytime."

"Okay. If you're sure."

"I'm sure."

Reaching for my hand, Liam led me inside to purchase our tickets. Making our way through the crowd of people, we finally had our tickets and were on our way toward the stairs and later the elevator. Reaching the Panoramic Observatory, a warm breeze greeted us. Taking in the city bridges, the Arc de Triomphe and Notre Dame were spectacular. However, I didn't want Liam to feel he was only holding second place in my heart after Bob.

On the contrary, I was now falling in love with him more than ever. Liam shared so many traits that I missed in Bob, fun, spontaneity, sexiness, and thoughtfulness. Wrapping my arms around him, I snuggled into his embrace, still reeling with emotions as I gazed at the vastness of the city spread out before us. Once again, my eyes moistened.

"Liam, I love you," I whispered. "I simply adore you. Trust me when I say this, you're not holding second place in my heart. I loved Bob with all my being, but that was another lifetime. The day we met at the restaurant, I was drowning in a sea of loneliness and despair. Losing a spouse and becoming a widow comes with a lot of unwanted baggage. You've shown me what it's like to live again, love again, and wake each morning embracing a new day. Liam, you've simply owned my heart since we first met, and I never want to live without you."

"Sweetheart, that sounds like a proposal. Marry me," Liam asked suddenly without any reservations. "I promise to make you happy for the rest of your life."

"Liam, you can't be serious."

"Oh sweetheart, I've never been more serious in my entire life. Marry me. Let's take our relationship to the next level. I love you, and I know that you love me. Life is short. Let's get married. Maybe this will help," Liam winked, pulling me into his arms with a lengthy, passionate kiss. The intensity of his kiss sent quivers of excitement racing throughout my body, from my head to my toes. Coming up for air, I smiled.

"*Yes.*"

"Babe, what was that? I'm not sure I heard you?" Liam laughed.

"Yes. Liam Lachowski, I'll marry you!" I exclaimed.

"She said, '*yes.*'" Liam grinned at the young couple standing next to us.

Overjoyed by the fact someone had proposed at the top of the Eiffel Tower during their visit, they beamed with approval.

"Congratulations," they remarked with a huge smile.

"Thank you," Liam grinned.

"Sweetheart, you've just made me the luckiest guy on earth. I promise you'll never lack for anything," Liam grinned, kissing me once again, leaving me breathless.

I, too, felt like the luckiest woman on earth. I couldn't wait to call Amanda. However, I knew she would think I'd finally lost my mind. She had no idea that I was in Paris.

"Let's get down from here. I'm finding the best jeweler in Paris." Liam winked.

Taking one last glance at the extraordinary views, I felt like the world had just been laid at my feet, and I was ecstatic. Unbelievably, I had gone to the top of the Eiffel Tower as a widow, letting my emotions and memories consume me. In only minutes I returned to the bottom of the tower, engaged with all the hopes and promises of a new future. A future that now included Liam.

"Oh my God, did that really just happen?" I laughed, staring at Liam as we returned to the main entrance.

"Yes. You're not having second thoughts?" he questioned with a look of concern.

"No. Relax. I love you, Liam Lachowski, for better or worse."

"Whew. For a brief second, I thought you had changed your mind. You certainly know how to give a man a heart attack," Liam grinned.

"Liam, I want to get married on the beach in Hawaii."

"Well, for someone who just got engaged, you're certainly not wasting any time."

"Why should we wait? I remember you once said that we were in the home stretch of our lives."

"I did. Hawaii it is."

As we entered the limo, thoughts of seeing Paris didn't seem as significant. Instead, starting our lives together took precedence.

"George, there seems to have been a change in our plans. Please take us to Rue de Faubourg Saint-Honore, Cartier's showroom. I believe the young woman is missing an important accessory."

"Certainly, sir."

"She's agreed to become my wife."

"Congratulations, madame."

"Thanks, George," I smiled. "Liam, really, it doesn't have to be an expensive ring," I whispered.

"Oh, but sweetheart, it does. It's the last time that I will ever purchase an engagement ring, and you deserve the best. So excuse me for one second," he smiled, reaching for his cell phone.

Easily overhearing Liam's phone conversation, he made an unplanned appointment with a jeweler.

"Okay. We're all set," he announced.

I had no idea of the significance of his statement until we entered the Cartier's showroom. Walking in, we were met at the entry and immediately ushered to a private room. I was speechless for the next hour as trays of exquisite diamonds were placed in front of me for my perusal. Finally deciding on a round four-carat, flawless solitaire diamond, the ring wasn't ostentatious. It was perfect and epitomized our commitment. I was overjoyed, walking out of Cartiers with the new addition brilliantly sparkling on my left ring finger. Maybe happy endings didn't just happen in my books.

"Sweetheart, I believe that makes us officially engaged," Liam grinned.

"Liam, thank you. It's exquisite. However, I'm in love with you, not the ring."

"Babe, I believe I'm the one who should be thanking you for saying *yes. I* almost forgot we have a picnic basket filled with snacks. However, I think a proper dinner is more appropriate, and I know the perfect place. Which would you prefer?"

"Picnic. I know you have the best restaurants on speed dial, but I'm not ready to share you with the world, at least not today."

"Wow. I like the sound of that. I have an idea."

"George, please take us to the Vespa rental near the left bank of the Seine."

"Vespas?" I panicked. "Liam, I'm not sure about this?"

"Ericka, no worries, you're riding with me."

"And, that's supposed to make me feel safe." I laughed.

Arriving at the scooter rental, Liam rented a blue Vespa. Then, quickly putting on matching blue helmets and securing the picnic basket, we were off. Weaving in and out of traffic, we soon reached our destination, the Jardin des Tuileries. The beautiful gardens with their symmetrical gravel paths and gorgeous rows of trees offered spectacular views of the Louvre Museum, the Eiffel Tower, the Musee d'Orsay, and the Champs-Elysees. It was truly the most romantic place to enjoy a picnic in Paris. Spreading a red checkered cloth on a grassy clearing, it was perfect. Feeling the sun's warmth and a slightly cooler breeze, the weather and the magnificent views of Paris were breathtaking.

"So, what do you think? Perfect place for a picnic?" Liam smiled.

"Yes. It's perfect," I agreed, giving him a quick kiss.

Watching as children rambunctiously chased their labrador puppy, I snuggled into Liam's arms once again, sensing the closeness of family.

Opening the basket filled with savory baguette sandwiches and cheese, Liam popped the cork on the bottle of wine. Filling two glasses, we relaxed back on the checkered cloth. Once again, I felt like I was living out a scene from my books. Looking down at my brilliant new accessory, I smiled.

"Wow. Is this truly happening?"

"Sweetheart, I can assure you it's entirely real," Liam grinned, pulling me into his arms. "You can have all the money in the world, but without someone special to share it with, it means nothing. My life got a major upgrade the day I met you."

"Liam, those are the sweetest words. When I started my journey and left Marin, I never thought it would end in a proposal. I love you. I can't wait to call Amanda."

"Well, today is about us. We can announce it to the world once we're back."

Interrupted by the buzz of Liam's cell phone, it was a reminder we were still connected to the outside world.

"I'm sorry. It's the New York office. I've got to take the call."

After a short phone conversation, it was apparent something was wrong.

"Is everything alright?"

"Unfortunately, a small problem has come up, and I've got to be in New York tomorrow morning. It seems I'm the only one who can take care of this. Sweetheart, I'm so sorry. It means we'll have to leave tonight."

"It's okay. I understand." Staring pensively into his gorgeous blue eyes, I knew that regardless of whatever came our way, we were together. I wasn't alone.

"I promise to make up for the unexpected interruption."

"Liam, I believe we're engaged and in a committed relationship. So no worries," I smiled.

After enjoying the remainder of the day, once again, I hesitantly hopped on the Vespa behind Liam for the ride back to the rental office, where we met George.

Entering the limo for the ride back to the apartment, I couldn't believe how fast things had transpired. Amanda was going to be surprised. I couldn't wait to tell her. Heck, I was still in shock, but I wouldn't change a thing.

Reaching the apartment building, Liam grasped my hand, pulling me up the steps. Quickly unlocking the door, he scooped me into his arms.

"Now, at last, I can thank you properly," he winked mischievously. "We have a couple of hours before we leave, and I know just how to fill them."

Carrying me into the bedroom, I reached for the new black negligee.

"Sweetheart, trust me, it isn't necessary," Liam grinned. Removing my cashmere sweater, he slowly unbuttoned my blouse, slipping me beneath the warm duvet. Then, lowering the shades, he undressed and slid into bed beside me. For the next few hours, we simply shut out the world.

Hearing Liam's alarm on his cell phone, we both knew our time in Paris had abruptly come to an end.

"Ericka, we've got to pack," Liam lovingly whispered. "We have to be at the airport in less than an hour. I've arranged for our departure at midnight." Gently pulling my hair away from my face, he quickly kissed my cheek. "Sorry."

Hurriedly throwing our clothes back into our suitcases, we had just enough time to reach the airport for our on-time departure. Once again, Liam had his private jet and crew expecting our arrival. Saying our goodbyes to George, we quickly ascended the steps to the Lear Jet.

"Good evening, sir. I hope your time in Paris was enjoyable," Stacy questioned with a warm greeting.

Stacy gasped before Liam could respond, noticing the sparkling diamond on my left hand.

"Wow. Congratulations."

"Thank you," I smiled.

"We'll have two mimosas with dinner before we retire to the back of the aircraft."

"I can offer you a choice of salmon or beef tenderloin with balsamic cranberry compote."

"I'll defer to my fiance."

"Oh, the beef tenderloin. It sounds amazing."

Taking a seat next to Liam, the idea of flying on a private jet for once didn't seem pretentious. Quickly returning with our drinks, Liam handed me a fluted glass.

"I think the occasion calls for a toast," he winked.

"I agree."

"Here's to the future Mrs. Lachowski. Thank God you said *yes*.

"To us," I smiled.

Watching below as the lights of Paris gradually faded away into the darkness, I was leaving with new memories. Staring at the brilliance of my engagement ring, I felt the excitement of once again being in love.

After enjoying our mimosas and a fabulous meal, I leaned into Liam's arms, feeling relaxed from the drink.

"I think it's time to retire."

Leaving our seats, Liam gently ushered me toward the back of the Lear Jet, closing the door.

"Now, where were we before we were suddenly interrupted by my alarm," he winked playfully.

For the remaining hours, we were in the air time stood still. The fact we were at forty-six thousand feet over the Atlantic Ocean never entered my mind. Wrapped in the strong embrace of Liam's arms, he simply owned my heart and my thoughts.

It appeared my life was moving at warp speed as we arrived in New York. Checking into the Ritz Carlton, our suite was sheer luxury and came with a stunning panorama of Central Park. During our short stay in the city which never sleeps, I played the role of tourist. I shopped during the day while Liam worked long hours at his office, taking care of an urgent business matter. We dined in the finest restaurants at night and were fortunate to get tickets to a broadway play, *Wicked,* with Idina Menzel. I was quickly becoming acquainted with Liam's lifestyle and all it entailed.

Leaving New York, we were soon on our way to Vancouver, where I planned to pick up Fritz and my car for the drive back home. It was hard leaving Liam. However, he made arrangements to visit me in Marin later and plans for a jaunt to Las Vegas to celebrate our engagement and my birthday. At last, I was finally looking forward to returning to Marin and seeing Amanda. We had a lot of catching up to do.

Now, the only thing remaining between home and finally seeing Amanda was roughly a nine hundred fifty-mile drive or two grueling eight-hour days. But, despite the long drive, it would give me a chance once again to reflect on my life and envision all the new changes my engagement to Liam would bring.

Reaching Marin, Fritz, and I were excited to be home. However, catching the brilliance of my new diamond, I knew my life would never be the same, and I wouldn't change a thing. The following morning, I called Amanda. Our conversation was long overdue.

Chapter Nine

Picking up my cell phone, I called my best friend. Thankfully, Amanda answered on the first ring.

"Girlfriend, we need to talk. Are you busy?"

"No. Where in the world have you been? I've been trying to reach you for days."

"Well, I was a bit busy. Why don't you come over? We have a lot of catching up to do."

"Actually, I just took a peach cobbler out of the oven. Why don't you walk over, and I'll brew us a pot of coffee."

"Sounds tasty. I'll be right there."

I knew the conversation we were about to have wouldn't be easy. I loved Amanda. However, I knew that sometimes we didn't agree. I could only pray that she might understand and give Liam and me her blessings. Greeted by Hazel as I walked in, the scrumptious aroma of the warm cobbler infused the air.

"I'm in the kitchen," Amanda answered, hearing me enter the house. "Grab two coffee cups while I dish up the peach cobbler. The coffee is almost ready."

"Wow. It smells delicious. You know how much I love it when you bake."

"Thanks. It's been a while, but it's my usual recipe. Have a seat."

I reached for the cups and sat down at the kitchen table waiting pensively for her to notice my ring. Amanda was huge at overreacting, so I braced myself. However, I didn't have long to wait as she sat our dishes of cobbler on the table.

"Oh my God, Ericka," Amanda screamed. "What have you done? I can't believe it. Bob is probably turning over in his grave as we speak. Don't tell me? Liam, right?"

"Yes. Sit down. You're being overdramatic as usual. You knew we were in a serious relationship. We've just taken the next step."

"Do the boys know?"

"Yes. I called Keith and Greg while I was in New York."

"How did they take the news of your engagement?"

"Initially, I think they were a bit shocked. However, they only want my happiness and are looking forward to meeting Liam."

"Well, I, for one, don't get it. I think this calls for something a lot stronger than coffee," Amanda scoffed, reaching for a bottle of white peach margarita and two glasses.

"Amanda, calm down. Honestly, you're overreacting."

After consuming two margaritas, we both sat back in our seats, taking a deep breath. Then, sitting in silence, Amanda simply stared at me from across the table.

"Alright. I'm over the initial shock. Let's just enjoy the cobbler and then tell me everything, everything," Amanda reiterated.

"Fine. By the way, it's delicious," I smiled, tasting the yummy dessert. I was relieved that Amanda appeared to be coming to terms with the fact I was engaged.

"Thanks. I'm sorry. I was a bit overwhelmed at seeing that huge diamond on your left hand," Amanda apologized.

"Amanda, I love you like a sister, no need for an apology," I replied, taking a sip of coffee. "The ring is from Cartier's in Paris. Isn't it gorgeous?"

"Wow. It's stunning. Ericka, I do want your happiness, but don't you think it's a bit soon after losing Bob?"

"Amanda, Bob's been passed almost two years."

"I know. It's hard imagining you married to someone other than Bob."

"Amanda, do you remember the hardships we endured while taking care of our Bobs?" I asked while refilling our coffee.

"Don't remind me. I'll never forget the numerous hospital trips. On one trip to the emergency room, I spent almost forty hours waiting for Bob to be moved into a room. Do you remember the holidays they both unbelievably broke their shoulders and how hard it was for them to recover?"

"Yes. We spent years caring for them. There were so many times I felt like giving up."

"I know. Bob hated being in a nursing home even when it was temporary."

"Well, if you remember, we couldn't even find a nursing home that would take Bob. Unfortunately, he required a one-on-one attendant, and no convalescent home provides that type of care. Geez, Amanda, we've been to hell and back. Don't you think it's time we deserved a little happiness in our lives?"

"Yes, I suppose," Amanda wept. Memories consumed her as tears gently rolled down her face.

"I've fallen in love with Liam. It wasn't planned, as you know. I left Marin on a journey that unexpectedly changed my life," I cried softly, reaching across the table to grasp Amanda's hand.

"Amanda, no one truly knows the long nights and days we've been through except other widows who've walked in our shoes. No one could ever prepare us for what we endured on a twenty-four-hour basis. I had no help outside of my immediate family until hospice finally assisted me during Bob's last months. Honestly, I don't know how you survived. Your son was living in Guadalajara, and you were on your own for years before finally hiring someone to help during your Bob's final days."

"Ericka, you have to remember that even though we loved them, our guys weren't perfect. I loved Bob, but he could be challenging at times. He much preferred to be at home rather than mixing socially at events or with other people. I always had to carry the conversation when we were out together."

"You're right. My Bob had a quick temper and could be rather difficult at times. But, we both deserve another chance at happiness, another chance at finding love. I'm happy for you. Liam is a lucky man. So, fill me in. Where were you, and how did he propose?" Amanda smiled, wiping her face as she took a slow sip of coffee.

"Well, this is where the unbelievable part starts. Liam flew me to Paris," I grinned.

"Wow. Paris. Really? That's so romantic."

"The romantic part was the fact he read my books, all of them. He knew my fantasies. Remember how I've written scenes in which my main character, a sophisticated, rich, handsome, man surprisingly takes the love of his life on an overnight flight to Paris. Well, Liam took me to a well-known Italian restaurant in Vancouver. You know my love for Italian cuisine. Afterward, he said he had a surprise and asked that I wear a blindfold leaving the restaurant. Well, I did trust him, so I played along, not knowing what he had planned. Amanda, when he finally removed the blindfold, I was standing in front of a Lear Jet. He then informed me that he had scheduled a night flight to Paris on his private plane. Can you even imagine? I was speechless," I smiled.

"Wow. That's the most romantic thing I've ever heard. It gives me goosebumps."

"Well, it gets even better. I guess you could say that I'm now an official member of the mile-high club."

"What?" Amanda chided. "Ericka, you didn't?"

"Yes. As a matter of fact, we did, in the private stateroom on board his jet at forty thousand feet over the Atlantic Ocean. I had not packed any clothes, and before we arrived in Paris, he told me to open his closet. Guess what it contained?"

"Oh dear Lord, I have no idea."

"A Versace dress, heels, and undergarments."

"You've got to be kidding?" Amanda gasped.

"Honestly, I almost fainted. Later, we ate breakfast before arriving in Paris, where George, Liam's limo driver, met us. He whisked us away to Liam's apartment. Amanda his apartment was stunning and located near the Champs Elysees. I felt like I was in a dream. The following day, we went to the Eiffel Tower. Remember me telling you that Bob and I spent our honeymoon in Paris. Well, the memories of being at the Eiffel Tower with Bob consumed me, and I became a little emotional. When we reached the top, Liam explained that he wasn't trying to replace my memories. However, it was the strangest thing. I knew that he wasn't, and I began explaining how much he meant to me, and suddenly out of nowhere, he proposed. Amanda, it was hotter than any scene I've ever written and way more romantic. Can you even envision it?"

"Honestly, I'm trying, and you're a darn good writer."

"Well, as you can see," I smiled, flashing my exquisite ring. "I said, '*yes.*'"

"Ericka, I'm so happy for you. Really, I am. So, when's the wedding?"

"We haven't set a date. However, I want to get married on the beach in Hawaii at sunset."

"You would. I've read it in your books," Amanda laughed.

"Unfortunately, Liam was unexpectedly called back to his office in New York. We had to leave that evening. We were only in Paris for a short time."

"Well, I must say, it might have been short, but it was eventful. You look happy."

"I am. Now, tell me what happened after you left Seattle?"

"Harry surprised me the next day. He booked a flight to San Francisco."

"What? Are you kidding?"

"No. I met him at the airport, and we spent a lovely day in the city. Oh, Ericka, I really like him. We have so many things in common. His Southern roots, for one, the fact we share the same sense of humor and love the same movies. I miss him."

"I can fix that. Liam is flying in tomorrow. We're going to Vegas for a week to celebrate our engagement and my birthday. Why don't you both join us? I will ask Liam to invite Harry. It would be a blast, just like Seattle except thankfully minus the rain?"

"Wow. You would do that?"

"Yes, of course. Start packing. We're going to have a little Vegas fun."

"Great. I can't wait."

"Well, I've got to run. Oh, I've arranged for someone to watch Fritz, and I'm sure they'll be more than happy to watch Hazel. I'll call you later tonight. Thanks for the cobbler. It was amazing."

"I almost forgot. Congratulations," Amanda smiled.

"Thanks. Talk to you tonight."

There was never a doubt that Harry would accept Liam's invitation. The four of us were Vegas-bound the following afternoon.

Chapter Ten

Our mantra boarding the plane in San Francisco was the familiar saying, *'what happens in Vegas, stays in Vegas.'* We were in the mood to party, and Vegas was the perfect place.

"Geez, I've never flown on a private plane," Amanda laughed as Harry ushered her to a seat.

"Well, sweetheart, it's the only way to fly," Harry smiled.

"Good evening, Mr. Lachowski. Welcome aboard. Can I get drinks for you, Harry, and the ladies?"

"Yes. Thanks. I believe the occasion calls for champagne."

"I'll be right back with those. Hey Harry, I haven't seen you in a while," Stacy mentioned.

"Oh, hey, Stacy. This is my friend, Amanda. Amanda, this is Stacy. She takes care of us while we're in the air."

"Nice to meet you," Amanda smiled. "Wow. It must be nice," Amanda added with a whisper.

"What? Stacy or the jet?" Harry teased.

"Really. Harry, the plane, your lifestyle?" Amanda inquired, feeling slightly intimidated.

"Sweetheart, it's just transportation, and Stacy is one of several flight attendants hired by our company. She's nice, but you're the one that I have my eye on," he winked. "After all, you're seated next to me."

Overhearing their conversation, I laughed.

"Amanda, relax. You'll soon get used to the extravagant lifestyle of these guys. Trust me. Enjoy the ride. We'll be in Vegas soon."

"Champagne. Just what our girls need," Liam laughed. "Thanks, Stacy."

Sipping champagne on a Lear Jet wasn't the norm for Amanda or me, but I knew we would quickly adapt.

"Here's to one hell of a week in Vegas," Harry toasted.

"I'll drink to that," Liam grinned.

"So, where are we staying? I forgot to ask?" Harry inquired, taking a sip of his drink.

"The Bellagio. It appears to be Ericka's favorite hotel, and it's her birthday."

"You're truly spoiling me."

"Oh, sweetheart, this is going to be fun. Must I keep reminding you of the promise I made to you in Seattle? I've made enough money in my life to live comfortably, and now that you've agreed to marry me, well, let's just say, your wish is my command," Liam grinned with a wink.

"Wow. That sounds like one hell of a commitment," Harry laughed. "Here's to Ericka and Liam."

"Thanks, buddy. Somehow, I get the feeling that you might be next."

"Well, things do happen in Vegas," Harry grinned, giving Amanda a quick kiss.

We touched down on the runway at McCarran International Airport in Las Vegas an hour later. The evening was still young. Parking near a private terminal, a limo was waiting.

"Good evening, sir," Charles smiled. "It's only 7:00 p.m. You've arrived early."

"Yes. Thank you, Charles," Liam grinned. "We have reservations at the Bellagio."

As the limo approached Las Vegas Boulevard, my heart raced with excitement. I had fond memories of Vegas and the Bellagio.

Parking under the hotel entrance, Charles opened our door, where we were instantly met with the concierge.

"Welcome back, Mr. Lachowski. It's nice to have you staying with us again."

"Geez, Liam, does everyone know you? And, you frequent this hotel?" I whispered.

"Sweetheart, I've simply stayed here on occasions. Does that help?"

"I'm afraid not. We'll have this discussion later."

"Ericka, I've reserved the Bellagio several times for training seminars, and our company has held various corporate meetings here over the years. So, I promise you; it's nothing sinister," Liam laughed.

"I love this hotel," Amanda smiled. "Especially the fountains."

"I've reserved the President's Suite for Ericka and myself. Harry, I reserved the Chairman's Suite for you and Amanda. Why don't we check into our rooms and freshen up a bit from the flight? We have dinner reservations at 8:00 p.m. at Spago. So we can meet for dinner."

"Sounds like a plan, buddy. See you at 8:00 p.m."

Liam grasped my hand as I followed him through the exquisite lobby of the hotel. I had stayed at the Bellagio on numerous occasions, but not once had I ever stayed in the President's Suite. However, my life with Liam had just received a considerable upgrade.

Walking across a suspended walkway above a tranquil pool, we had arrived. Liam scooped me into his arms as he opened the door to the President's Suite. Carrying me inside, I gasped. The spacious room reflected the ultimate in indulgence. It featured a solarium, an indoor garden with a fountain, fireplace, and a spectacular bar. I was a bit overwhelmed, noting that it contained two master bedrooms.

"Does it meet with the approval of the future Mrs. Lachowski?"

"Without a doubt. Liam, it's breathtaking."

"You want to know my favorite part of the suite, besides the fact you're here. It's the conference room."

"Of course," I smiled. "Let's hope you don't receive any urgent calls from your office."

"Sweetheart, I'm off the clock and completely unavailable. No worries."

Walking over to the bar, Liam poured himself a glass of bourbon. "Would you care for a drink? Champagne or wine?"

"Champagne. I might as well keep the party going?" I laughed.

"My kind of girl."

"Why don't we take our drinks into the living room and enjoy the gorgeous sunset. It's brilliant this evening."

"You're right. It's beautiful."

Lounging back on the sofa, I snuggled into the warmth of Liam's arms. "You know this suite was big enough to have included Harry and Amanda."

"Excuse me?" Liam laughed. "Sweetheart, that would never happen."

After a few sips of champagne, I began to feel drowsy. Resting my head on Liam's shoulders, sleep quickly overtook my body. Removing my shoes, Liam covered me with a blanket and allowed me to sleep until it was time for dinner.

"Ericka, I hate to wake you," Liam lovingly whispered. "It's almost 7:30 p.m. You have just enough time to shower and change for dinner. We're meeting Harry and Amanda at Spago at 8:00 p.m."

"Thanks. I'll hurry."

"Sweetheart, I took the liberty of adding to your Versace collection. So you'll find a new dress waiting for you in the bedroom."

"Oh my God, you didn't. How can I ever thank you?"

"Babe, that's not a problem. I'm sure I can think of a way later tonight," Liam winked with a mischievous grin.

Walking out of the bedroom in a short, red Versace dress, I felt like a diva and not someone merely going to dinner.

"Wow, sweetheart, you look stunning. Maybe we should cancel and eat in tonight?"

"Not a chance. You've no doubt spent a lot on this gorgeous dress, and I'm going to wear it to dinner proudly. However, I feel it might be too short for someone my age."

"You look stunning. You'll make one hell of an entry. If you're ready, we should make our way down to the restaurant," Liam winked, taking my hand.

Walking beside Liam, eloquently dressed in a stylish black suit, he exuded sex appeal and charm. Entering the elevator, I found myself staring at the handsome man who would soon become my husband. He was perfect, and once again, I felt like the luckiest woman alive.

Entering the posh restaurant, the maitre d' escorted us to our table. Harry and Amanda had already ordered drinks.

"Wow. Glad you two could make it. You're only twenty minutes late," Harry scoffed.

"Thanks, buddy, but who's keeping track of time. It's Vegas."

"Well, some of us might be ready to order. I'm starved."

"Did you like the President's Suite?" Amanda inquired.

"Yes. It's simply beyond words. It's amazing. How was your room? What did you do when you arrived?"

"Don't answer that," Harry interjected.

"Really. Which part?" Liam laughed. "How was your room, or let me guess, what did you do when you arrived?" he grinned.

"Geez, buddy, you're the one celebrating an engagement. I can only imagine what you did."

"Ericka took a nap, and I enjoyed a bourbon on the rocks and watched sports."

"Right. And donkeys can fly," Harry roared.

"If you're done with your snide remarks, I think we're ready to order. I thought you were starving."

Harry and Amanda decided on the seafood tower as the waiter approached our table. Liam and I ordered a bottle of Dom Perignon Champagne 1996 P2 Rose with an entrée of the grilled prime flat. Afterward, we all enjoyed the spiked lemon dessert while watching the famous Bellagio fountains. It appeared the evening was off to a slow, relaxing start despite being in Vegas.

"Wow, that was a quiet dinner. Everyone must be tired. Why don't we call it an early evening? We have a huge day tomorrow," Liam suggested.

"Speak for yourself, buddy. Amanda and I are going to take a stroll along the strip."

"Well, suit yourself, but stay out of trouble. I don't feel like bailing you out of jail later tonight."

"Not happening. It's past your bedtime, old man," Harry grinned.

"Perhaps," Liam laughed wickedly. "I believe someone owes me a thank you," Liam leaned over, whispering into my ear. "See you, kids, early tomorrow. I've booked a helicopter flight in the morning. Champagne brunch in the Grand Canyon. Oh, Amanda, please keep him out of trouble."

"I'll do my best, but I can't make any promises. Ericka, call me later."

"Will do. Enjoy your evening."

"Thanks."

I was breathless as Liam opened the door to our suite. Tears streamed down my face taking in the beauty of the scene in front of me. Lit candles covered every square inch of the expansive room. Exquisite floral bouquets of red roses infused the air with their incredible fragrance, and rose petals were strewn across the floor, creating a path that led to the master suite.

"Wow. It's beautiful," I cried. "Oh, Liam, I never expected this, never."

"Sweetheart, I know. I never expected anyone as beautiful as you would ever enter my life," he smiled, reaching for my hand. "Thank you for agreeing to become my wife." Suddenly feeling faint, Liam scooped me into his arms and carried me into the bedroom. A huge heart made of rose petals covered the bed.

"Wow. The bed is gorgeous. How did you do this?"

"I had help. Trust me, staying in the President's Suite comes with perks," Liam smiled.

"I'm speechless. Thank you."

"Umm…I believe someone promised to thank me," Liam winked, pushing the petals off the bed. "Open the closet."

Walking over to the closet door, I slowly opened it. Hanging on a soft hanger was a white satin negligee and matching robe.

"Why don't you change. I'll get the champagne and strawberries."

"Geez, you don't miss a thing. I love strawberries." I couldn't imagine what Amanda was doing at that moment, but I knew it could never rival the experience I was having. Thank God Liam had other plans.

For the entire night, once more, we simply shut out the world.

Waking the following day at the sound of Liam's alarm, I wasn't ready to start the day.

"Can't we just sleep in?" I lazily suggested.

"I'm afraid not. We have a helicopter reserved for 10:00 a.m."

Liam drew back the blackout curtains flooding the room with the brilliance of the morning sun. Rubbing my eyes as they attempted to adjust to the brightness was a futile attempt. A hot shower was my only option. Grabbing my robe, I walked into the bathroom.

"How is it possible that you can function on such few hours of sleep yet wake up early and be so cheerful and alert?" I asked loudly from the bathroom.

"Years of practice. I guess. It took a lot of long hours and hard work to build Everet International, named after my grandfather."

"Well, if New York was any indication, I'd say you're still putting in a lot of long hours."

"Sweetheart, I plan to cut back on my work schedule once we're married."

"Is that a promise?" I yelled from the shower, lathering shampoo through my hair.

"Yes. It's a promise," Liam whispered, stepping inside the shower gently kissing the nape of my neck.

"Geez. I had no idea you were in the bathroom," I laughed.

"Well, you take forever in the shower. We're running out of time, and I'm here to help," Liam grinned, massaging my shoulders.

"Mr. Lachowski, if you continue with those hands of yours, we may be later than you think," I teased.

"Wow, babe, it might be worth it."

"Not today. Amanda is excited about seeing the Grand Canyon, and neither of us has ever flown in a helicopter," I mentioned stepping out of the shower.

"Are you referring to an EcoStar 130?"

"How do you know so much about helicopters?"

"Oh, work. We use them a lot for short commutes."

Hurriedly getting dressed, we decided to layer our clothes and pick outerwear suitable for hiking. Finally, we were on our way down to meet Amanda and Harry.

Watching as Amanda approached the lobby, she looked tired.

"Wow, you look worn out?" I laughed.

"We didn't get back to the hotel until almost 3:00 a.m."

"For heaven's sake, what did you do?" I asked, looping my arm through Amanda's as we made our way through the lobby of the Bellagio

"Oh, we had an amazing night. We started at the Skyfall Lounge at Mandalay Bay. It's located on the 64th floor, and the views from the open-air terrace were phenomenal. We enjoyed a few drinks, then Harry and I took a taxi to Freemont Street. Unfortunately for me, but lucky for him, I watched him play poker at the Golden Nugget for almost two hours. He walked away with over ten grand. Can you even believe it? But, Ericka, I swear everyone knew Harry, from the bartenders to the card dealers. I think Liam and Harry have frequented Vegas a few more times than we know," Amanda giggled.

"I agree. I think these guys are a little too familiar with Vegas, but let's face it, they're fun to be with and, more than that, easy to fall in love with," I laughed, glimpsing my sparkling diamond.

"Ericka, I think I've fallen in love with Harry."

"What? Are you serious?"

"Yes. I know it might seem sudden, and I feel bad about our conversation that day in my kitchen when I found out you were engaged. I suppose I truly didn't understand. But Ericka, I get it. I know it happened rather quickly for you and Liam. Who's to say it couldn't happen for Harry and me. Time isn't exactly on our side anymore, and he makes me happy. Ericka, honestly, I love him, and I think he feels the same. You're being awfully quiet. What are your thoughts? You know that I love you like a sister and your opinion matters to me."

"Oh, Amanda, if you truly love him, you have my blessings. I would never stand in the way of your way happiness. Unbelievable. We might be taking another walk down the aisle. We'll talk more tonight. I think Liam is in a hurry to get to the airport."

"Hey, girls, get a move on. I've reserved a helicopter, and we're going to be late," Liam remarked.

Entering the limo, we were driven out to McCarran International. The limo slowly parked next to a sleek red helicopter. However, it seemed odd there was no pilot insight. Perhaps, he was running a little late himself. A gentle breeze felt refreshing as we stepped out of the car and made our way across the tarmac.

"Are you girls ready to enjoy your ride out to the Grand Canyon?" Liam grinned.

"Yes. But where's the pilot? He must be running late," I laughed.

"Oh, but he's not," Liam grinned with a wink opening the door to help us inside.

Still unaware of who would fly us to the canyon, Amanda and I took our seats. Harry stepped inside, gave us a pair of headsets, and ensured we were safely strapped in.

"Aren't you going?" I asked Liam, who remained on the tarmac.

"Of course," he laughed, taking the pilot's seat at the controls.

"What?" I gasped. "You're the pilot?" I asked in total disbelief. "Liam, are you sure you know what you're doing?"

"Oh, he's been flying these things since he was in the Marines," Harry laughed. "Don't worry, I've flown with him too many times to count, and he's never crashed, not even once."

"Wow, and that's supposed to make us feel safe?" Amanda questioned with a quizzical frown.

"Liam, you never told me you were a pilot," I asked, still dumbfounded at his abilities.

"Sweetheart, relax. I promise to get you to the canyon in one piece. Now sit back and enjoy the flight. I'll point out some interesting places."

"Wow, are you even believing this?" Amanda laughed.

"No."

Lifting off the ground, the views of Vegas were incredible. I had never seen the strip from this perspective, and I could only imagine how it might look after dark. Hopefully, Liam could take us up at night. Flying out of the valley towards Boulder City, we approached Hoover Dam. It was breathtaking. I had visited the dam on numerous occasions when the kids were growing up. Still, I never saw it from above in a helicopter. The views of Lake Mead and the magnificent structure of the dam were spectacular.

Turning to take a quick glimpse at Liam, my heart melted. My future husband was at the controls. There were so many amazing things that I didn't know about this brilliant, knowledgeable man. Relaxing into the comfort of my seat, I no longer doubted his abilities to keep us safe.

"Don't panic," Liam announced. "We're at the western rim of the canyon. I'm going to descend about 3,200 feet. We're landing on a remote plateau overlooking the Colorado River."

The views were breathtaking as Liam descended into the canyon. The striation of colors embedded in the walls was almost beyond description. The cliffs and gorges were a rainbow of muted earth tones ranging from rusty reds, dusty pinks, blacks, and numerous shades of brown. The river below for eons had carved its way through the canyon. Once again, the views were almost unfathomable.

Harry assisted Amanda and me as we stepped out of the helicopter. Running up to Liam, I smiled.

"So, you fly helicopters," I remarked, giving him a huge hug.

"Of course. Doesn't everyone?" Liam laughed.

"What other things don't I know about you?"

"I suppose that's for you to find out. You are marrying me, right?"

"Oh, Mr. Lachowski, I'm afraid you're stuck with me."

"Great. I think that calls for champagne, at least for you. I'll be having coffee."

Harry brought out the picnic basket filled with fancy Muffaletta sandwiches and loaded Turkish Bread sandwiches along with assorted fruits, cheese, and a bottle of Moet and Chandon Champagne.

"Who's ready to eat?" Harry asked, spreading out a large blanket.

"I'm starved. Liam and I only had coffee earlier this morning."

"Geez, those look delicious," Amanda replied, picking up one of the Muffaletta sandwiches.

"Well, you can thank the Bellagio. I had the butler assigned to our suite pick it up from the kitchen," Liam mentioned popping the cork on the champagne.

Filling three glasses, he smiled.

"Here's to my gorgeous fiance and one hell of a week in Vegas," Liam toasted with his thermos of hot coffee.

"Thanks, Babe."

"So, who's up for a little hiking?" Harry inquired.

"Me," Amanda answered a little too enthusiastically.

"Geez, Amanda, I think the champagne has gone to your head."

"You guys head out. We'll catch up in a few minutes," Liam mentioned.

Watching as Amanda and Harry strolled out of sight on a trail near the river, I laughed.

"I think they're serious. Maybe even in love?"

"Yes. I talked with Harry before we left. He's going to propose to Amanda."

"What?" I screamed. "When?"

"Oh, I'd say within the next hour," Liam laughed, glancing down at his watch. "That is if he doesn't get cold feet."

"Well, I have to confess. Amanda told me earlier today that she had fallen in love with Harry. So I'm truly excited and happy for them."

"Sweetheart, I love it that you are excited for them. But honestly, the only thing that matters to me is us," Liam smiled, giving me a quick passionate kiss.

"How long have you known that Harry was proposing to Amanda?"

"Let's just say that I knew before we flew in yesterday. Harry was smitten with Amanda from the moment he met her. I think their Southern roots connected them. He purchased an engagement ring after returning from their weekend in San Francisco."

"So. You knew that Harry was planning to propose today at the bottom of the Grand Canyon?" I questioned.

"Yes. I suppose you could say that. I was just happy to fly them here."

"Geez, and I thought this trip was your idea and that you wanted to show me the canyons from the air and go hiking," I teased.

"Sweetheart, I definitely wanted to fly you here. I wanted to see your reaction when the pilot was a 'no show,' and I took control of the helicopter. Regarding the hiking, I'm ready when you are," Liam grinned with a sexy wink.

"Liam Lachowski, I love you. Why do you always have the perfect answers and make me feel special."

"Babe, that one is easy. I love you."

Melting into his arms, I was breathless. The fact we were at the bottom of the Grand Canyon or on Mars was inconsequential. I had found the man of my dreams for the second time in my life.

"Let's take a hike," Liam laughed, pulling me up from the blanket.

Walking hand in hand, we leisurely rambled along a narrow trail that led down to the Colorado River. Despite its muddy appearance, it looked like a great place to go river rafting. Stopping for a moment to take in the phenomenal landscape, I glanced upward. The immense height of the canyon walls was daunting.

"Wow. There's so much natural beauty here. I can see why the Grand Canyon is considered part of the seven wonders of the world," I smiled.

"Yes. I've been here numerous times, and it never gets old. I could stay here for hours and simply appreciate the peaceful, tranquil setting."

"I agree. Communing with nature," I added.

We continued hiking along the trails at the bottom of the canyon, taking in its seclusion and unparalleled beauty. Finally, after a short while, I caught sight of Amanda and Harry slowly making their way back towards the helicopter.

"Oh my gosh, I see them. Amanda looks happy."

"I'm sure. Harry spent a small fortune on her ring," Liam laughed.

"Liam, don't be facetious. An engagement isn't about the size of a diamond. It's about two people finding each other and making a lifetime commitment. Unbelievably, Amanda and I have been blessed to find true love not only once but twice. I guess that makes us two incredibly lucky girls. Thank God Harry was your best friend, single, and most importantly Southern bred."

"Sweetheart, call it fate or karma. I believe we were destined to find each other," Liam smiled, pulling me into his arms.

"Maybe," I answered as my eyes moistened, recalling the bottle of Aramis. But, I knew it was neither fate nor karma. Instead, a loving husband's last wish for my continued happiness.

"Brace yourself. Here they come," Liam laughed.

"Oh my God, Ericka, I'm engaged!" Amanda exclaimed. "Just look at this ring! Can you believe it?" Amanda beamed, extending her ring finger. "It's five carats!"

"Wow. That's quite a rock," I laughed, staring at the five-carat pear-shaped diamond. "Congratulations. I'm truly happy for you both."

"You'll need a bodyguard to wear it," Liam laughed. Leaning over, he whispered quietly into my ear. "She may have gotten the bigger ring, but you got the better man."

"Liam Lachowski, you're conceited, but I love you."

"Congratulations, buddy. I was afraid you might have gotten cold feet. So I guess that officially takes you off the market."

"There is one small technicality, the wedding. However, I have an idea. We need to talk later tonight," Harry suggested quietly.

"Sure. If everyone is ready, I suggest we take this party back to Vegas."

Hurriedly, packing our picnic supplies, we boarded the helicopter for the short ride back to Las Vegas. Tonight we were going to a small venue off the strip to see my teen heartthrob from high school, Kyle Westmont, sing a rendition of classic songs from the 1960s. Even though his singing career had never taken off professionally, I had to see him.

Chapter Eleven

Finally, it was showtime. We were on our way to the other side of the valley. I had several things on my to-do list while in Vegas and seeing my old friend, Kyle Westmont, held the top spot. As the limo slowly came to a stop in front of the small lounge, I got goosebumps.

"Geez, I think someone is a little excited," Liam laughed.

"Oh, I hate to tell you, but you might get second billing tonight. Ericka has always had a slight crush on Kyle," Amanda laughed.

"Really. Second billing," Liam whispered. "I think I might be able to change that later tonight."

Walking into the small, obscure lounge was rather daunting. No concierge was waiting to greet us.

Approaching the bar, Liam smiled.

"My girl is here to see her crush, Kyle Westmont."

"Babe, that's not funny," I blushed.

"Down this way to the back, and the theater is on the right," the bartender stated.

Our tickets were taken as we reached the entry, and we were ushered to our seats on the front row.

"Girls, make yourselves comfortable. We'll be right back," Harry laughed. "We need some liquid refreshments."

Watching as Liam and Harry disappeared up the aisle, I laughed. I knew they were doing this for me and Amanda. Given a choice, they would both rather be anywhere than the front row of a Kyle Westmont performance listening to hits of the 60s.

Returning with two beers and two plastic drink glasses which had blinking lights on their stems along with Kyle Westmont written across them, I snickered. The night was off to an exuberant start, and Kyle had not even taken the stage. A short while later, I caught Harry pulling a flask from his suit pocket. I knew it contained something a lot stronger than beer. Taking a closer look, Harry discreetly passed it along to Liam, who without hesitation indulged.

"Can you believe the guys brought a flask?" I laughed, nudging Amanda.

"Whatever it takes to get them through the night."

As the theater lights lowered, I was excited. However, glancing at Liam, he yawned.

"Oh, you're so getting it tonight, Mr. Lachowski," I threatened.

"The best thing I've heard since I've gotten here."

Taking the stage to the light roar of the audience, Kyle opened with a rendition of hits from the 60s. However, after performing only a few songs, I began to realize that his career was a thing of the past. My heart broke for him. I knew people could change, but it was evident the years had not been kind to him. My fondest memories of him from high school were dashed.

Respecting Kyle enough to remain through his entire performance, I couldn't wait to go backstage and get reacquainted.,

"Ericka," Kyle grinned. "Wow. What a pleasant surprise. How long has it been? High School? It's so good to see you," he remarked as we were ushered into his dressing room.

"Yes. It's so good to see you. How's your family?"

"Stephanie and I are divorced. However, the kids are grown, and mom and dad still live in the Bay Area. It's so good to see you. Thank you for coming."

"Oh, I wouldn't have missed it. Once I discovered you were in Vegas, I had to see you," I smiled, knowing in my heart his career was on the decline. "Kyle, this is my fiancee, Liam Lackowski, my friend Amanda and her fiancee, Harry Morgan."

"Nice to meet everyone. I hope you enjoyed the show."

"Yes. As a friend of Ericka's, we wouldn't have missed it," Liam smiled, being completely supportive.

"Nice to meet you," Harry grinned. "Great song selection. Who doesn't love those hits."

"Yes," Amanda smiled.

After the introductions were made and a bit of small talk reminiscing over our high school days, Liam called for the car.

"I have tickets for the High Roller Wheel at 9:00 p.m. if we hurry, we can just make it," Harry stated on our way out of the lounge.

Charles returned immediately to drive us over to the High Roller's Wheel. Once inside the limo, Harry opened a bottle of champagne to get the party back in the right direction.

"Ericka, I know you had high expectations in regards to seeing Kyle perform, and I'm truly sorry, it didn't work out as you expected. However, he seems like a genuinely nice guy," Liam mentioned empathetically.

"Thanks. I'm a bit heartbroken. Kyle was voted in our high school yearbook as being the one person to most likely succeed in life."

"I'm sorry. Unfortunately, as you know, life isn't always kind."

"You're right," I sighed, taking a sip of champagne.

"The evening is still young," Harry mentioned. "Let's not dwell on the past. Instead, I'd like to make a toast to the future Mrs. Harry Morgan."

"I'll drink to that," Liam smiled.

"Yes, to a bright and happy future," I toasted, trying to lighten the mood.

Arriving at the High Roller Wheel, Amanda panicked once again, remembering her Seattle experience.

"I'm not so sure about this. Remember the wheel in Seattle? It was a bit scary."

"Amanda, I've just flown you to the Grand Canyon. Trust me. You were a lot higher than the wheel."

"I know."

"Babe, I'm going to be with you. I didn't put a ring on your finger to risk losing you," Harry smiled, pulling Amanda into his arms.

"I'll be with you too. You've got this," I smiled.

"Alright, but I might need another drink."

"That can be arranged," Harry laughed.

Stepping inside the giant pod as it slowly moved past, we were excited to see the panorama of Vegas at night. With his arms wrapped securely around Amanda, Harry led her to an adjacent bench to sit. As the wheel slowly got higher, I stood embraced in the warmth of Liam's arms watching the spectacular lights of the hotels appear over the vast horizon. The views were breathtaking. Slowly reaching its highest elevation, an announcement stated that we had reached High Roller status. It was a fun experience, and it appeared that Amanda had survived the short ride. Stepping off the wheel with my arms wrapped securely around Liam, we were on our way to the Sky Fall Lounge at the Mandalay Bay for drinks before retiring for the evening.

Finally, after 1:00 a.m., we reached our hotel suite. I was exhausted as I quickly removed my shoes. Then, surprised at the buzz of Liam's phone, he promptly answered the call on speaker.

"Hey, would you guys mind if I came over? I have something I'd like to discuss. It won't take long," Harry inquired.

"Sure, but make it quick."

Within a few short minutes, Harry walked in.

"So, buddy, what's up. You know it's getting late, and some of us are ready for bed."

"Yeah. Just hear me out. I need your opinion, especially Ericka's."

"What's going on?"

"I want to marry Amanda before we leave Las Vegas."

"Why the rush? You just got engaged?"

"I know. But, I think the idea of getting married in Vegas and having our marriage officiated by an Elvis impersonator would be cool and unforgettable. Ericka, do you think Amanda would think it offensive or fun?"

"Seriously, Harry, you're asking me? Don't you think you should be asking Amanda?"

"Of course. I just need to know if you think there's any chance she might consider it?"

"Well, to be honest, you've truly caught me off guard. However, as crazy as it sounds, I think Amanda might just love the idea. I'm not sure she likes spontaneity, but we are in Vegas, and I know she loves you. I think you should ask her?" I laughed.

"Thanks. I know that you and Amanda have been best friends forever, and I wanted to run it past you before I asked."

"Okay, buddy, if you've got what you came for, some of us have other plans for the evening," Liam jested.

"Right. Well, on with it," Harry chuckled, closing the door.

"Geez, sweetheart, want to make it a double wedding?" Liam smiled with a wink.

"Not on your life, Mr. Lachowski. We're getting married on the beach in Hawaii."

Turning out the lights, Liam had other things on his mind that didn't include an Elvis impersonator or wedding chapel.

Waking up the following morning as the sun slowly invaded our room, thoughts of Amanda being married in Vegas consumed me. I had assumed that Liam and I would have married first. Now, she had the bigger ring and was getting married. Rolling over to face Liam, I kissed him awake

"Wow, sweetheart, we could stay in bed today?" Liam teased wickedly, slowly opening his eyes.

"Not a chance. We're in Vegas, and if things went the way I think they might have, I could be shopping with Amanda for her wedding gown."

The words had barely gotten out of my mouth when my cell phone rang. Reaching over to retrieve my phone from the nightstand, it was Amanda.

"Hey, Ericka, why don't ya'll meet us downstairs for breakfast. I've got some exciting news," she exclaimed.

"Well, that just answered my question," I laughed, sitting up in bed. "Amanda wants us to meet them for breakfast, and she sounded excited. Guess they're getting married."

"Great. I suppose we get to stand in as the best man and the maid of honor. This should be interesting," Liam laughed.

"Oh, Liam, it's going to be fun. I can't think of a more memorable way to tie the knot. I'm excited," I smiled, running for the shower.

"Well, my offer still stands. We could make it a twosome."

"You're not getting off that cheap. I want an extravagant beach wedding in Maui at sunset," I replied loudly from the bathroom.

Dressed for the day, we were on our way downstairs to meet the happy couple. Instantly, we saw them at a table near the back, as we entered the restaurant. Amanda looked happy.

"Oh my gosh, you're not going to believe this. Harry and I are getting married on Saturday."

"Geez, let me guess. It involves a wedding chapel and an Elvis impersonator," I laughed.

"How did you know?"

"Maybe, it's the fact Harry came barging in late last night," Liam interjected with a scowl.

"Hey, I didn't just barge in. I called first," Harry countered.

"Whatever, buddy. I suppose you'll be needing a best man."

"Of course."

"And a maid of honor," Amanda smiled, reaching across the table for my hand.

"I'd be delighted," I answered as my eyes moistened.

Noticing my emotions and tears, Liam gently wiped my face.

"Sweetheart, weddings make you cry?" he questioned.

"My best friend is getting married. We've been through so much over the last two years."

"Ericka, be happy. We deserve to be happy," Amanda reiterated as tears welled within her eyes.

"I know."

"Girls, this is supposed to be a happy occasion. So maybe this will help," Harry smiled, handing Amanda his Black Amex Card. "By the way, there's no limit. Hopefully, you can find the perfect wedding gown, and of course, a dress for the maid of honor. So shop till you drop, but remember the wedding is Saturday, so there's no time to place an order or alterations."

"What about the best man?" Liam teased.

"We're renting tuxedos," Harry grinned.

After drying our tears, we enjoyed breakfast and went our separate ways. The guys went to secure the Chapel of the Bells, and the Elvis officiate. We went shopping.

Arriving at the first bridal boutique, we were met by knowledgeable consultants. Taking us to a private room in the back, they brought in dresses that Amanda had explicitly requested. Deciding to try on a cream, heart-shaped trumpet wedding dress with a beaded sash, it looked spectacular. However, after taking a long look in the mirror, Amanda decided it wasn't the one. Trying on several other designs, she was still indecisive. Finally, after two hours of trying on various styles, we decided to move on to the next boutique.

As the limo dropped us at the next bridal shop, we were both hoping to find the one dress which would capture Amanda's heart. Once again, we sipped champagne, as consultants took pride in parading their latest fashions past us. Finally, after an hour, Amanda beamed, noticing a cream, floral tulle wedding dress with removable sleeves. The dress was romantic, emphasizing the corseted, heart-shaped bodice and A-line silhouette. Embroidered with floral appliques cascading down the flowing tulle skirt and glittery layers that added a sparkling dimension, it was visually stunning.

At last, Amanda had her dress, and more importantly, it fit perfectly. No alterations were required. Adding a matching short veil attached to a diamond-encrusted headband, Amanda looked radiant. I smiled, knowing that despite our age, all brides were beautiful. We had been lucky enough in life to find love for the second time.

Now, as maid of honor, it was my turn to find a dress. The process was much easier. Amanda loved the color mauve, and it took less than an hour to find the perfect mauve gown. Choosing an exquisite floor-length chiffon gown with a fitted heart-shaped bodice and tank straps joined by sheer off-the-shoulder straps, the gown was elegant. The design featured an empire waistline and a fashionable open slit. My eyes moistened as I stood in front of the mirror. Soon I would be standing on a gorgeous beach in Hawaii next to the love of my life. I loved Bob more than life itself. However, I knew that he played a significant role in bringing Liam into my life. Wiping my eyes, I smiled. Amanda and I were one step closer to a new beginning.

Adding a few small pieces of jewelry, along with heels, we were set. Watching as Amanda covered the charges with Harry's American Express Card, I gasped. The price of our purchases far exceeded the cost of my new car.

Amanda was ecstatic to meet the guys later that afternoon for dinner at Spago's.

"Well, I guess from the look on your face, you found a dress," Harry smiled.

"Oh, Harry, it's gorgeous. Thank you."

"Yes. Amanda's dress is stunning and fits perfectly," I added, taking a seat as Liam pulled out my chair.

"And, is the maid of honor happy as well?" Liam inquired.

"Totally," I smiled. "Harry, thank you."

"It's the least I can do. After all, Amanda did agree to marry me on Saturday," Harry grinned, seating Amanda at the table with a quick kiss.

"Let's order. I'm starved," Liam mentioned motioning for the head waiter.

It was a night of celebration. Ordering a bottle of champagne, we celebrated the upcoming nuptials of Amanda and Harry. The evening was off to a great start.

"Here's to the happy couple," Liam toasted.

"Yes," I smiled. "Here's to Amanda, my best friend, and Harry. I wish you all the happiness in the world."

Ordering asparagus soup with Parmigiano Reggiano and saffron oil for starters, later we added our entrée, Cote de Boeuf, bone-in rib steaks with vegetables.

"Well, good news. I was able to reserve the chapel on Saturday and a special officiate. So, sweetheart, we're only lacking a marriage license, which we can pick up tomorrow," Harry smiled. "The ceremony is set for 1:00 p.m."

"Wow, it's really happening," I smiled. "Amanda, I could never have imagined you becoming engaged, much less married, while we were in Vegas. Harry is a great guy, and I'm truly happy for you both," I added as tears moistened my face.

"Thanks, Ericka. You know that I love you like a sister. You've also found a great guy, someone who will no doubt make you happy for the rest of your life. Liam, you better take good care of my girl," Amanda replied, wiping her eyes.

"Geez, this conversation is getting rather deep and emotional," Liam grinned. "I think you're both exhausted from shopping. It's been a long day. Harry, I think we should get these girls upstairs."

"No arguments here," Harry smiled, standing to assist Amanda.

Later, reaching our suite, I dressed for bed. Slipping under the covers next to Liam, it was all becoming real, too real. Amanda was getting married, and I would be next. Our lives were about to change drastically. Suddenly becoming emotional, I snuggled into the safety of Liam's arms, releasing a torrent of tears.

"Sweetheart, what's wrong?" Liam questioned, holding me through my emotional outburst.

"I've never felt such happiness. Yet, I'm not sure I deserve it. Oh, Liam, I feel like I'm being pulled between two worlds. I feel like I'm abandoning my old life, the only life I ever knew. The one I shared with Bob, and it feels like cheating on someone who isn't even here. But, on the other hand, is it wrong to be this happy and start over at my age?" I wept.

"Ericka, one simple question. Do you love me?" Liam asked, kissing away my tears.

"Yes. Without a doubt."

"Thank God, because, honestly, I couldn't live without you. I love you. Sweetheart, there's a line from the movie, Love Story, which says, *Love means never having to say you're sorry.* When you truly love someone, no matter what you've gone through in the past, it no longer defines you. Love is unconditional. There's no reason for regrets. Trust me. I promise to keep you safe and, above all else, love you with my entire being. My greatest joy will be to spoil you beyond your wildest dreams. I love you."

"Liam, how did I ever get so lucky. I love you more than you know."

"No more tears. Our best friends are getting married in less than forty-eight hours, and soon we'll be next. I promise you the wedding of your dreams," Liam whispered, kissing me tenderly.

For the rest of the night, I simply belonged to the man who held me in his arms. Passion consumed us, wiping away any doubts.

As the morning sun crept into our room, it found me still wrapped in Liam's arms.

"Wow, sweetheart, what a night," Liam grinned, gently kissing the nape of my neck. "Please tell me that erased any lingering fears in that sweet head of yours," he whispered.

"Yes."

One night with this amazing man, and not only were any lingering doubts erased, but I couldn't wait to say, *"I do."* I had a wedding to plan. However, before I could start making plans, Amanda would take a walk down the aisle.

The following two days went by in a blur as we played the role of tourists in Vegas. Then, finally, Amanda's wedding day arrived. The Chapel of the Bells, along with Elvis, would soon witness the vows of two people I loved.

Stepping inside the limo, Amanda and I were leaving early. Watching as Charlie put our garment bags into the car, we were at last on our way to the chapel.

Chapter Twelve

Arriving at the Chapel of the Bells, Charlie opened our door.

"Amanda, are you nervous?" I asked.

"No. Should I be?"

"No. Definitely not. Harry is a great guy. I'm so happy for you."

"Speaking of the groom, we should hurry. I don't want Harry to see me before the ceremony."

Hurriedly following Charlie, carrying our garment bags, we rushed inside the ornate white chapel. Soft romantic music welcomed us. Taking a quick peek inside the chapel, I was speechless. A hint of fragrance infused the air. Exquisite floral arrangements containing pink roses and peonies elegantly wrapped the tiny chapel. Stained glass windows showcasing pairs of white Turtle Doves reflected the burning candles, giving the sanctuary a dreamy ambiance. There was no hint of Elvis as I looked down the center aisle covered in white satin. I laughed, knowing only Amanda and Harry would have chosen an Elvis impersonator as their officiate.

"Over here," Amanda called. "I found the dressing room."

Following the sound of her voice, I entered the tiny room. It appeared to have everything a bride and bridesmaid would need, including tall floor-to-ceiling mirrors. Unzipping our garment bags, I was already holding back tears. Amanda's dress was gorgeous. I knew Harry would approve. Listening to the velvet voice of Luther Vandross's heart-stopping song, *If Only for One Night*, my eyes moistened. Keeping my emotions in check wasn't going to be easy.

"I need help with my make-up," Amanda giggled, changing into a white, satin robe embellished with the word *Bride*.

"Okay. I suppose that's my job as your bridesmaid," I smiled.

"Ericka, open the closet. You have a robe as well. We'll need them while we apply our make-up. We can't risk getting it on our gowns," she panicked.

"Amanda, stay calm. Breathe. Trust me, we're going to get you dressed," I smiled.

Applying Amanda's make-up first, she was glowing. Thank God we both had made early morning hair and nail appointments. After Amanda was satisfied with her make-up, it only left attaching her veil to the diamond-encrusted headband and dressing in her gorgeous gown. I generously applied a layer of coverage. At my age, I needed all the help I could get. With our make-up done, it was time to dress. Hearing a soft knock at the door, I walked over.

"Flower delivery," the young girl stated, handing me two large boxes.

Excitedly, Amanda rushed over to discover the contents. The boxes contained a gorgeous bridal bouquet of pink roses embellished with silk ribbons and a smaller version consisting of white peonies. We now had our last accessories.

"Wow, these are exquisite," Amanda announced.

"Yes. The flowers are gorgeous. Harry is on top of everything."

Time was running out as I hurried to get dressed. With only thirty minutes left, we had to hurry. Quickly helping Amanda into her wedding dress, I anxiously began the task of buttoning all the tiny buttons on the back. Ensuring none were missed, we attached her veil. Standing in front of the mirror, Amanda was a vision of beauty. Grabbing tissues, we lightly touched our faces, catching tears as they escaped our eyes. Just as I was about to step into my elegant mauve gown, there was another knock at the door.

"What is this, Grand Central Station?" Amanda laughed. "I'm not answering the door in my gown. Can you see who's there?"

"Yes. Just a second while I zip up my dress," I giggled, running for the door half-dressed.

"Delivery for the bride," the young man announced, handing me a tiny blue box.

"Amanda, another box has arrived."

"We have the bouquets. What is it?"

"Umm, I'm not sure. I think it might be from Tiffany's. Not that I've ever received one of their blue boxes," I laughed.

Walking over, Amanda's eyes lit up like a Christmas Tree. Tearing into the tiny box and removing the tissue, Amanda gasped. It revealed exquisite diamond earrings with a note attached.

"Sweetheart, thank you for saying, 'yes.' See you at the altar. Love Harry

"Wow, I love this man," Amanda cried, quickly putting on the earrings.

Reaching for more tissues, I worried we might run out at the rate we were going through them.

"Take these tissues. You're going to need them," I smiled.

With only a few minutes left, we walked over to the large mirrors for a final inspection. My eyes moistened standing next to my best friend. Together we had been to hell and back, but at this moment, Amanda's life was about to change in ways she could never imagine, and I was ecstatic.

"Amanda, you're gorgeous. Harry is a lucky guy. I love you, and I wish you all the happiness in the world. Are you ready to take a walk down the aisle?"

"Yes."

Grabbing our bouquets, I grasped Amanda's hand. Together we walked out of the dressing room toward the double doors which led into the tiny sanctuary. As the doors were opened, my breath hitched as my eyes landed on Liam standing next to Harry. He had never looked more handsome, charming, and sexy wearing a stylish black tuxedo. My heart stopped. I was breathless. I felt like the luckiest girl in the world, and I wasn't the bride.

"See you at the altar," I whispered.

Slowing walking down the aisle to the soft music of Elvis's hit song, *I Can't Help Falling In Love With You*, I silently laughed, staring at the Elvis impersonator.

If there were moments in life that were truly unforgettable, this would surely top the list.

Taking my place next to Elvis, all eyes were on Amanda.

Slowing taking her first step, Amanda entered the chapel. She was an angelic vision. Harry wiped his eyes. No doubt he was having a hard time keeping his reactions in check. At this point, I was having a difficult time trying to keep my emotions under control.

Reaching the altar and Harry, he gently took her hand, giving her a quick kiss.

The Elvis impersonator smiled. Quickly imitating Elvis's famous hip-swiveling, rubber legs shaking, with a quirky upturned lip, it was hilarious. It was comedy at its best, and his timing was perfect. Breaking an air of seriousness that had consumed us, it brought a much-needed sense of joy. Taking a glance at Liam, he smiled.

"I love you," he mouthed inaudibly with a wink.

My knees almost buckled, feeling the love we shared.

"It's my honor this afternoon to unite Amanda Collins and Harry Morgan in the bonds of marriage," Elvis announced. Harry, please take Amanda's left hand and repeat after me. Afterward, please place the ring on Amanda's left hand.

"I Harry, take thee, Amanda, to be my wedded wife, to have and to hold from this day forward, for better or worse, for richer, for poorer, in sickness and in health, to love and to cherish, till death do us part, according to God's holy ordinance, and thereto I pledge thee my faith. I give this ring as a sign of my love," Harry vowed, placing the ring on Amanda's left hand

Amanda, please take Harry's left hand and repeat after me. Afterward, please place the ring on Harry's left hand.

"I Amanda, take thee, Harry, to be my wedded husband, to have and to hold from this day forward, for better or worse, for richer, for poorer, in sickness and in health, to love and to cherish, till death do us part, according

to God's holy ordinance, and thereto I pledge thee my faith. I give this ring as a sign of my love," Amanda vowed, placing the ring on Harry's left hand.

"It's my pleasure to pronounce you, husband and wife. Harry, you may kiss your bride."

As the soft music of Elvis singing, *Love Me Tender* filled the air, Harry pulled Amanda into his arms, kissing her passionately. And, just that quick, my best friend was married for the second time. The lyrics composed by Jimmy Van Housen, *Love is lovelier the second time around,* played in my mind.

Walking over, Liam grabbed me, pulling me into his arms.

"Has anyone told you how beautiful you look this evening?" he whispered.

"No."

"Well, let me be the first," Liam smiled, kissing me passionately. His kiss took my breath, leaving me weak in the knees. Had Liam not held me in his arms, I wouldn't have had the strength to stand. I loved him more than life itself. I couldn't wait to marry him.

Walking over to Harry and Amanda, we offered our congratulations.

Liam smiled. "I've arranged a little surprise. The jet is fueled and waiting to fly you both to Tahiti. So there's no need to check out of your suite or pack. It's all taken care of. Charlie is waiting outside. Enjoy."

"Liam, I don't know what to say. Thank you," Harry grinned.

"Yes. Thank you," Amanda smiled.

"Now, you two get out of here. Enjoy yourselves. I'll see you later in Vancouver."

Watching as Amanda and Harry hurried out of the chapel, I hugged Liam.

"Wow, babe, that was the sweetest thing ever. I love you."

"Now, I finally have you right where I want you, alone," Liam smiled with a sexy wink.

Walking out of the chapel with our arms locked around each other, Liam hailed a cab for the short ride back to the hotel.

Reaching the hotel, we decided to dine in for the evening. I already felt the loss of Amanda. However, I smiled, remembering my first time alone with Liam on the Lear Jet. I could only imagine that Amanda might attain membership in the elite mile-high club after tonight.

Popping the cork from a bottle of Moet & Chandon, Liam filled our glasses with champagne.

"Here's to us," he toasted. "Do you regret not getting married today?"

"Maybe," I smiled.

"Sweetheart, I understand, but I promised you the wedding of your dreams, and I'm a man of my word," Liam grinned. "Why don't I order dinner. Afterward, I think we should enjoy the jacuzzi."

"Sounds romantic."

"That's my girl."

Ordering entrées from a local Italian restaurant didn't take long for the food to arrive. Lobster, smoked bacon, sugar snap peas, truffle cream sauce with spaghetti soon made their appearance. The food smelled heavenly, but I didn't have an appetite. Something was off. I felt down, and it didn't take Liam long to sense my discomfort.

"Sweetheart, you haven't tasted a thing. What's wrong?"

"Honestly, I don't know. Maybe it was the euphoric feeling of their wedding, and afterward, a sense of sadness knowing it wasn't us. We didn't walk away married," I cried unexpectedly in another emotional outburst.

"Oh, Ericka, I love you. It doesn't take a marriage certificate to make me love you more. That's an impossibility," Liam smiled, pulling me into his arms as he kissed away my tears. "Why are you worried? Because we weren't married today?"

"Maybe."

"Sweetheart, you're simply exhausted. It's been a busy week. I have an idea. Let's forget dinner and relax in the jacuzzi with our champagne."

Grabbing two robes, Liam scooped me into his arms, carrying me out to the balcony. Shedding our clothes, we stepped inside the warm swirling water. The lights of Vegas lit up the night sky like a beacon in the darkness.

"Now, doesn't this feel better? Today was hectic," Liam winked, handing me a glass of champagne.

"Yes. I have to admit, it does feel relaxing. You're right. Perhaps, I was just tired."

"I'm sure you're exhausted. I don't know about Amanda, but Harry was a bundle of nerves earlier today," Liam grinned, sipping his champagne. "Don't get me wrong, he loves Amanda, but getting married was a big step for Harry, even if Elvis officiated it," he laughed.

"Liam, I don't want to stay in Vegas. Can we leave?"

"Babe, where did that come from? What's wrong? Is there a reason?"

"No. Not really. I just feel restless. I didn't mean tonight."

"Yes. Of course. We can leave whenever you want. Where would you like to go? Do you want to go back to the Bay Area?"

"No. Honestly, I don't know. I don't mean to be a pain."

"Sweetheart, don't ever say that. I let Harry take the Lear Jet, but I could have one of our planes flown into McCarran or simply charter a jet. How soon do you want to leave?"

"Tomorrow."

"I have an idea. Why don't we fly to Hawaii tomorrow and check out wedding venues? I think if we nailed down our wedding plans, you might feel better. I think someone just needs a little assurance that the promises connected to your diamond are for real."

"Could we?"

"Yes. Babe, spoiling you is going to be fun. Let's go to bed."

Laying next to Liam, I finally smiled. He knew me better than I knew myself. I was anxious to get married, and I did regret the fact we chose not to say our vows today with Amanda and Harry. Turning out the light, I snuggled against the love of my life. Loving Liam was easy. He was simply the air that I breathed.

The following day, Charlie took us to the airport. Finally, we were on our way to Hawaii.

Chapter Thirteen

The following day as we boarded the chartered jet to Hawaii, it almost felt normal to be flying in such luxury.

"Mr. Lachowski, welcome aboard," the young cabin attendant smiled. "If there's anything you need, please let me know. Weather conditions look great, and we should have you and your companion in Honolulu in about six hours. Enjoy your flight."

"Thanks. I'll have a scotch, and the young lady would like a mimosa. I'm sorry. I didn't catch your name."

"Oh, Alana," the young girl blushed.

"Thanks, Alana.

Turning to face me, Liam smiled. "Sweetheart, if you don't mind, I'm going to take care of a little business this morning. I've got to crunch some numbers on a project in Singapore that Harry and I've recently acquired," he added, opening his laptop.

"No problem. I can spend the time writing. I'm just a few chapters short of finishing my current manuscript."

"Great. I promise no work-related issues once we touch down in the islands."

"Oh, Mr. Lachowski, I'm holding you to that. I promise."

The six-hour flight into Honolulu went by in a hurry as Liam and I both kept busy working and enjoying lunch. Dining at 41,000 feet was always an experience. Served an elegant artisan cheese board of Prosciutto Crudo Italiano, Italian salami along with Black Forrest Schinken, with an assortment of fine cheeses, fruits, and crackers, it easily satisfied any epicurean's appetite.

Sir, we're only forty-five minutes out from Honolulu. Is there anything I can bring you before we land?"

"Yes. A coffee with Bailey's for me and another mimosa for my fiancee. Afterward, before landing, two warm towels would be refreshing. Thanks."

"I'll be right back with your drinks and later your towels," Alana smiled.

Arriving in Honolulu, as always, a limo waited for our arrival. Taking a compact mirror from my purse, I quickly checked my make-up and hair as I entered the car. Then, applying my favorite lipstick, I was ready for the day.

"Isn't this when you tell me where we're staying?" I inquired with a smile.

"Really. You're not up for a surprise?" Liam winked.

"Surprise?" I questioned.

"Let's just say I own a little place on the beach."

I decided to play along with his silly game. Getting comfortable, I leaned into Liam's arms. It didn't matter to me if it was a shack on the beach as long as we were together.

"It's not that far. We should arrive in approximately forty minutes if the traffic holds. I promise you won't be disappointed."

"Liam, disappointment isn't a concern. I would be happy in a grass shack on the beach with you."

"Geez, Babe, that's cute," Liam laughed. "Trust me. It isn't a grass shack. However, that could be arranged if you insist."

Watching the gorgeous tropical scenery, Amanda came to mind.

"I haven't heard from Amanda. I hope she's enjoying Tahiti."

"Sweetheart, she's on her honeymoon. So give them some time," Liam winked with a smile.

Finally, as the limo made a sharp right off the highway, I gasped, sitting up.

"Liam, really, a little place on the beach."

Intricate wrought-iron gates suddenly opened, allowing us entry. The limo slowly continued on a narrow winding path surrounded by tall Queen Palms. The expansive grounds leading toward the sprawling Polynesian home were stunning, with tropical plants and lit tiki torches dotting the manicured lawns.

"Babe, this little place of yours is quite impressive."

"Sweetheart, I'm happy it meets with your approval. But, it's just a home, sitting on a beach, which just happens to be in Hawaii," Liam laughed, entertained by my reaction.

"Whatever, Mr. Lachowski. What else don't I know about you?"

"Marry me and find out," he grinned, pulling me into his arms with a sudden passionate kiss.

Slowly the limo parked, stopping underneath a tall wooden portico that showcased traversed timbers. As my door opened, I was met with the relaxing sound of trickling water from a nearby Koi pond and lush tropical greenery. Admiring the oversized carved teak doors leading into the home, I was convinced I could enter with Liam and lock out the world forever. It was paradise.

"Welcome," Liam grinned. "Let me give you a quick tour," he added, taking my hand.

I smiled. The house revealed unparalleled beauty as I walked in through the double doors. My eyes were instantly drawn toward the back of the massive living room. A wall of floor-to-ceiling windows exposed an enclosed lanai with magnificent views of the cobalt blue waters of the Pacific along with a warm, inviting beach.

"Wow. This is incredible. Why did you ever leave?"

"Babe, it's just a house. Thank God I did, or I wouldn't have met you."

"Geez, Liam, why do you always have the perfect answers," I laughed.

"Sir, I put your luggage inside the foyer," the chauffeur interjected.

"Thanks," Liam acknowledged with a tip. "So, sterile or impeccable?" he laughed, turning to face me.

"Impeccable. You're never going to let me forget that remark, are you?"

"Sweetheart, you have an irresistible innocence, and I can't resist teasing you. I'm sorry," Liam winked mischievously. "Want to see the bedroom?"

"Of course," I replied as he grabbed my hand, pulling me down a long hallway.

Entering the master suite, the room was stunning. A kingsize teakwood bed sat midway in the room, facing a panel of glass doors. Drawing back white, sheer curtains exposed a patio with views matching the living room. A baroque teak dresser held an exquisite floral arrangement containing bird of paradise flowers on one side of the room. Their vivid tropical colors accented the room.

"Oh my Lord, Liam, this is stunning."

Picking up a remote, a flat-screen television instantly raised from a cabinet at the end of the bed.

"You don't miss a thing. Do you, Mr. Lachowski?"

"Hopefully not," he winked, playfully pulling me down to the bed.

"I want to see the kitchen," I giggled.

"Later."

It was apparent I wasn't getting a tour of the rest of the house at the moment. Pulling me into his arms with a passionate kiss, thoughts of seeing the house quickly vanished. The house could wait. The world could wait. I was right where I wanted to be, in his bed, in his arms. Reaching for the remote, Liam closed the blackout curtains. Loving Liam consumed me. Hardly coming up for air, we never left his bed. Later, putting on bathrobes, the pangs of hunger finally sent us running for the kitchen.

"Sit," Liam smiled, pulling out a barstool at an oversized granite island.

"How does breakfast sound?" he asked, checking out the contents of the fridge.

"Great, if you're cooking."

"Eggs or pancakes?"

"Both. I'm starving."

Watching as Liam cooked breakfast, his kitchen was a chef's dream. It was visually stunning. Light teak cabinets lit from within reflected a warm glow through etched glass doors. The lights from the surrounding cabinetry softened the black granite counters. The kitchen beautifully reflected the Polynesian décor of the home. State-of-the-art appliances, including a sub-zero fridge, completed the stunning design.

"Mimosa," Liam asked.

"Of course. Always," I smiled.

Popping the cork from a bottle of champagne, he filled two glasses with orange juice. Then, handing me a mimosa, he made a toast.

"Here's to my girl, Hawaii, and finding the perfect wedding venue."

"Here's to us," I toasted.

Sitting down to eat breakfast, I looked at Liam and smiled.

"I hope Amanda's honeymoon is as wonderful as my first day in Hawaii."

"Sweetheart, speaking of our wedding, we should discuss plans for our honeymoon. If you could spend two weeks anywhere in the world, where would it be?"

"Liam, this might sound crazy, but anyplace with you would be perfect."

"Well, you're not getting off that easy. Babe, the world is yours. Would you prefer to spend it on a yacht in the Mediterranian, a villa in the Greek Islands, Monte Carlo, or Bora Bora? Trust me. I'm easy. However, what do you think about Thailand? Phuket, to be exact. The white sandy beaches are world-renowned and exclusive. The photos of the resorts online are impressive. I'm sure you will love it."

"Well, to be honest, I've not thought of Phuket, but it sounds phenomenal."

"Great. Phuket. I'll make all the arrangements once we've settled on a date."

The evening was getting late, yet we had just eaten breakfast and settled on a honeymoon destination.

"Why don't we take the bottle of champagne and walk down to the beach."

"Sounds perfect."

Grabbing a blanket, champagne, and glasses, we walked to the vast stretch of sandy beach behind the rambling single-story home. A refreshing cool breeze wafted in from the ocean as Liam spread out the blanket.

"Wow. I don't think I've ever seen so many stars," I smiled, gazing into the night sky.

A canopy of sparkling brilliance stretched across the vast darkness. Combined with the tranquil sound of waves gently washing ashore, it created a dreamy atmosphere.

"Liam, thank you for bringing me to Hawaii and your beautiful home."

"Ericka, moving into this house, I could never have envisioned a night like this. Finding someone like you has exceeded my wildest expectations, and you make it complete. I love you."

"Liam, my life was at a crossroads before meeting you. I was married fifty years to a man I loved, and then becoming a widow was the worst thing I've ever had to endure. You have no idea. The lonely nights I cried myself to sleep and learning to live single after almost fifty years was the hardest. There were mornings I felt breathless waking up to the stark reality that he was never coming back. There's no handbook to tell you how to cope, and the best intentions of family and friends, even though well-intended, often lacked the emotional support I needed. But, honestly, I'm not sure what would have happened if you had not walked into that restaurant."

"Sweetheart, you are much stronger than you think," Liam answered, giving me a quick kiss. "Bob was here for you for fifty years, and now I'm here to be with you for the rest of your journey. I'm your safe place, your shelter from the storm—no more worries. You give them to me. Babe, I love you, and I can't wait to marry you."

"Liam, how did I ever get so lucky?"

"Ericka, I'm truly the lucky one. Tomorrow, we are going to find the perfect wedding venue."

After finishing the bottle of champagne, the evening was getting late.

"Maybe we should go in. We still haven't unpacked," Liam suggested.

"Babe, can it possibly wait until tomorrow? I feel exhausted. I think I've had too much to drink." Standing up, I swayed, feeling faint.

Scooping me into his arms, Liam carried me inside. Gently slipping me under the warm covers, he kissed me goodnight, returning to the kitchen for clean up. My first day in Hawaii had come to an end. It was perfect.

The following morning, I woke to the aroma of freshly brewed coffee. Grabbing my bathrobe, I strolled into the kitchen. Liam was once again making breakfast.

"Geez, Mr. Lachowski, you're spoiling me."

"Good morning, sweetheart," Liam smiled with a wink handing me a cup of the hot brew. "Kona Coffee, made in Hawaii."

Enjoying a huge savory sip, I smiled. "It's delicious. Thank you."

"After breakfast, we're going to check out wedding venues. I've rented a car and made arrangements to show you several locations. They're all beautiful."

"I can't wait."

Taking my coffee, I sat down at the kitchen island. Liam set a plate filled with bacon, eggs, and hashbrowns in front of me. "Delicious," I complimented, tasting the scrambled eggs.

"Aren't you eating?"

"Of course," Liam laughed, rummaging through the fridge. "Hot sauce."

After breakfast, we showered and changed, ready for the day.

A white Porsche convertible waited for us as we walked outside.

"Wow, this is an impressive way to see the island."

"I had a friend of mine drop the car off earlier this morning. Glad you approve. I've made several appointments today at various venues. I'm hoping you'll fall in love with at least one or more. I much prefer the beaches on the North Shore. They're less crowded and more private than the beaches near Honolulu, especially Waikiki."

"If you decided on these venues, I'm sure that I'll love them. However," I paused. "I see nothing wrong with being married on the beach at your house. It offers privacy, and it's definitely romantic."

"Well, we can keep that on our shortlist. But, first, let me show you what's available, and then you can decide."

"Sounds good."

Sitting in the luxury of the Porsche, the warmth of the sun and the refreshing breeze felt relaxing. Quickly putting on sunglasses and a baseball cap, I couldn't imagine a better way to see the North Shore. Starting at Kahalu'u, we drove north along Highway 83, the Kamehameha Highway. It was breathtaking, with magnificent mountain views to the left and gorgeous views of the Pacific Ocean on the right.

Arriving at our first option Kualoa Ranch, it offered the best choices, a lush tropical garden, an ancient Hawaiian fishpond, or white sandy beaches, which I preferred. Used in numerous Hollywood film settings, Kualoa Ranch was spectacular. Their venue choices included Paliku Gardens located at the base of the sacred 1,000 ft. Kanehoalani mountain peak. It had beautiful views of Kaneohe Bay, lush green gardens, rolling pastures, and the iconic Mokoli'i Island, also known as the "Chinaman's Hat." Another option was Moli'i Gardens, a stunning two-tiered garden setting that bordered an 800-year-old fishpond. Jumanji and Low Camp both offered remote valley locations, which were phenomenal. However, my preferred option would have been Secret Island. A beach location that was only accessible by a catamaran.

I was impressed, and it made reaching a decision difficult. I couldn't imagine a better choice, and this was only the first venue. However, my heart was still leaning towards Liam's gorgeous Polynesian home and access to the beach.

Continuing north on the scenic highway, our next stop was Loulu Palm, which provided a magical setting for a fantasy wedding. It began as a seed, a twinkling idea in the heart of its creators, and had blossomed into a fantastic place to hold special gatherings. The beachfront location was surrounded by beautiful sprawling greenery, and the photo opportunities were endless. After touring the luxurious grounds, it definitely topped our list.

"Wow. Liam, you should have been a tourist guide, specifically a destination wedding specialist. These venues are exquisite," I smiled, walking towards the car.

"Sweetheart, after everything you've been through, you deserve the best," he winked, opening my car door.

Our last appointment for the day was Owen's Retreat, located on the beautiful coastline of Mokuleia Beach on the North Shore. It offered a fairytale-like setting with an ocean backdrop and unbelievable sunsets. It was pet-friendly and would allow Fritz to accompany me down the aisle. The scenic views were incredible, and the wildlife such as Laysan Albatross, Hawaiian monk seals, green sea turtles, and humpback whales added to the ambiance. The atmosphere of the waves gently washing ashore as the backdrop was perfect. Visiting Owen's Retreat, our last appointment for the day made my decision even more difficult. Like the two previous venues, it offered everything.

My heart was torn between choosing one of the gorgeous locations or the possibility of having our wedding at Liam's home and hiring staff to help. I was leaning towards the latter option, Liam's beautiful estate. However, I knew it meant finding local accommodations for family and friends, catering, and setting up on the beach.

Leaving our last venue, Liam made dinner reservations at an exquisite restaurant on Waikiki Beach in Honolulu. The sun was just beginning to set as we arrived. The evening sky was brilliantly bathed in pinks, violet, and orange hues. The Beachhouse at the Moana was impeccable. It offered an iconic setting amidst the Moana Surfrider and the tranquil cobalt waters of the Pacific.

"Good evening, sir," the maitre d' smiled, ushering us to our table near large windows overlooking the ocean.

"Liam, you never disappoint. What a perfect ending to a perfect day."

"Sweetheart, that perfect ending you mentioned, this isn't it," he winked mischievously.

"You're incredulous, but I love you."

Ordering a bottle of Moet & Chandon, Liam made a toast.

"Babe, here's to an unbelievable wedding at the desired venue of your choice."

"Here's to us and our perfect day. I love you."

Dinning on a feast of Alaskan King Crab along with asparagus and roasted garlic potatoes, it was delicious. Afterward, saving room for dessert, we enjoyed lemon cheesecake.

Later driving back to Liam's estate, the stars were once again out in abundance, and the luxury of the convertible offered a complete panorama of the night sky. Sitting next to Liam, I felt like the luckiest girl on earth. Suddenly a shooting star streaked across the vast darkness.

"A shooting star, I exclaimed excitedly. "Did you see it?"

"Yes. So, what was your wish?"

"You're not supposed to know. If I told you, it wouldn't come true."

"Did you make a wish?"

"No. She's sitting right next to me."

"I love you. Have I told you how perfect you are?" I blushed.

"Sweetheart, I'm far from perfect. I'm afraid you'll find out once we're married."

"Really? Well, I like a challenge, but on the off-chance, what does that imply?" I teased. "Not picking up your socks?" I laughed.

"Maybe?" Liam grinned.

"Whatever. I'll take my chances. I like to live dangerously," I giggled.

"Ericka, I love you. I hope you enjoyed your day. But, honestly, all I want is your happiness. Everything else is trivial.

"I love you too."

Laying my head against the seat, the exhaustion of visiting the wedding venues and the champagne was finally consuming me. Arriving at Liam's estate, he opened my door. Scooping me into his arms, he carried me inside.

"I can walk," I insisted.

"You look exhausted."

"I am," I smiled sleepily.

Carrying me into the bedroom, Liam removed my shoes and clothing and tucked me under the warm duvet. Suddenly, hearing his phone, he walked over to a chaise lounge. Unable to overhear the conversation, I was curious. After the call ended, he came over to kiss me goodnight.

"That was Harry."

"And?" I asked.

"They'll be here tomorrow evening. They are stopping in Honolulu."

"Oh my gosh, I'll get to see Amanda." Sitting up in bed, I was too excited to sleep.

"Well, that bit of news certainly revitalized you. Want to join me in a nightcap?"

"Certainly. How was their honeymoon?"

"Ericka, sweetheart, that's not a topic of my concern. However, I'm sure Amanda will be quite happy to answer all your questions," Liam laughed.

"I can't wait to hear all about it," I smiled, grabbing a robe as I followed him into the living room.

Pouring himself a scotch, Liam reached for a bottle of chardonnay. Filling a glass, he brought it over to where I sat on the couch.

"I know that I promised not to take care of any business dealings while we were in the islands, but Harry said there's a problem with the hotel in Singapore. It's going to necessitate a few phone calls tomorrow. I'm sorry. Perhaps having Amanda here will compensate for the few hours this will take. Afterward, I promise to make it worth your while."

"Liam, I love you. I know that your business is still a huge part of your life. It's okay. I think I'll survive."

"Wow. I know I'm marrying the right girl," Liam winked.

"Let's go to bed, the day isn't over, and I promised you a happy ending," Liam grinned, quickly downing his scotch.

Once more, he scooped me into his arms, carrying me into the bedroom. Slipping me back under the covers, he turned out the light. He was right. This was the perfect ending.

Waking the following day to the brightness of the morning sun as it peeped in through the curtains, I was excited. In just a few hours, Amanda and Harry would arrive. I had missed her and was anxious to know the details of their time in Tahiti.

"Good morning, sweetheart. What a night?" Liam smiled wickedly, giving me a quick kiss.

"Liam, I've never been happier. You've made my world complete, and I've finally decided on a wedding venue," I announced, sitting up in bed.

"Great. Is it Kualoa Ranch, Loulu Palm, or Owen's Retreat?"

"None of the above," I smiled.

"Really?" he teased, knowing my answer.

"Here. I want to get married here on the beach. Is that alright?"

"Babe, it's more than alright. I was hoping you might come to that decision, but I wanted to give you options. I wanted you to be sure. After all, it is your dream wedding."

"Liam, I'm sure. Thank you," I smiled, leaning over to kiss the love of my life.

Pulling me down to him, our kiss quickly became passionate. It was easy loving Liam, too easy, and I knew that we'd never make it out of bed if we continued. Amanda was arriving in a few hours, and I wanted to plan dinner.

"Liam," I whispered. "I have things to do. Amanda and Harry will be arriving shortly."

"Seriously, did you just bring Harry and Amanda into our bedroom? Isn't that a little crowded," he teased, kissing my neck.

"Liam, you know what I meant. I need to go grocery shopping."

"Sweetheart, I have staff that can prepare anything you would like. You don't have to shop or cook," he smiled, sitting up in bed. "It's not a problem. What do you have in mind for dinner?"

"Thanks for the offer, but I'd like to cook. I love Italian food, so I thought I would make a lasagna."

"Sounds perfect. If you make it, I've no doubts it will be amazing. Give me your list of needed ingredients, and I can place an order with the local grocery store."

"Alright. I'll concede to let you order the groceries. However, I'm taking over your kitchen this afternoon."

"The kitchen is yours. No worries," Liam grinned, pulling me out of bed. "But first, I need coffee, lots of coffee, and breakfast. After that, the kitchen is entirely yours."

Grabbing our robes, we hurried to the kitchen, where Liam made coffee. Then, deciding on Belgian waffles and bacon, I smiled, watching my handsome guy pour the batter into a waffle iron. He was sexy, brilliant, managed a billion-dollar empire, domesticated, and most importantly, mine.

After we finished breakfast and cleaned up the kitchen, I decided to take a shower and dress for the day. I couldn't wait to see Amanda. Finally, I was ready for the day, styling my hair and putting on jeans with a tunic top.

Walking into the living room, I discovered Liam dressed in shorts and a polo shirt. He was lounging on a wicker chaise in the Lanai and appeared deeply entrenched in a conversation on his phone. I wondered again if it was possibly Harry. Motioning me over, Liam smiled, pulling me down to his lap.

"Sorry. It's Singapore," he whispered, muting his phone.

As the call ended, I noticed he appeared perplexed.

"Is everything alright?" I questioned.

"Yes, and no," he answered. "We've got a minor problem with the progress of the hotel. It should be an easy, inexpensive install. The worst part is that it requires me to be there. Sorry. Unfortunately, I have to fly to Singapore this next week. So I'll fly home with you to San Francisco and get you resettled in Marin before I leave. Hopefully, I'll only be gone a few days."

"You don't have anyone that could oversee the problem for you?"

"I do, but my reputation is on the line with this job. It's a huge undertaking, and I simply need to be there in person. I promise to be back as soon as possible."

"Okay, I understand," I replied with a silly frown.

"Do you have a list for the grocery store?"

"Yes. I have listed the ingredients for the lasagna, along with the ingredients for a strawberry vinaigrette salad. Plus, we will need garlic bread, and I thought I would bake Amanda's favorite chocolate cake for dessert. So, I've listed those ingredients as well."

"Great. Give me just a moment while I have those delivered for you."

With a quick call, Liam placed the order. The items were set to be delivered within the hour.

"Also, I forgot to mention. I've arranged for Amanda and Harry to stay in one of the guest rooms. There's no need for them to find other accommodations. The house is huge."

"Aww, thanks. You've thought of everything. I love you, Mr. Lachowski," I smiled, giving him another quick smooch.

"We have a few hours before they arrive. Why don't we take a walk on the beach? It's a beautiful day."

"Sounds nice," I replied, quickly removing my shoes. Pulling me up from his lap and the wicker chaise, he reached for my hand. Closing the double doors to the Lanai, we strolled down to the water's edge. It was warm and inviting.

"Do you swim?" I inquired.

"Yes. Quite often, in fact. It was one of the reasons I built on the beach. I've always loved the water."

"I suppose the fact you live in Marin means you also have a love for being near the bay or ocean as well."

"I do. But I don't swim. I have a heated pool. That's my idea of enjoying the water. Our climate is rather cool, and the water in the bay, well, I'm sure it's safe to swim, but I'd rather err on the side of safety and cleanliness," I laughed. "Plus, we have some powerful currents in the bay."

Watching in the distance, as a young family with children chased after their puppy, which was running loose down the beach, Liam appeared deep in thought.

"Ericka, I would love to meet your sons and their families. You know that I've never had children of my own. I can only imagine the joy of having children and grandchildren. Please don't misunderstand. I would never try to replace their father. It's not my intention. They have an amazing mother," Liam smiled, stopping to give me a quick kiss. "I know they are brilliant young men."

"Of course. Liam, I would love for you to meet my family. When you get back from Singapore, I'll arrange it."

"Thanks. That would be wonderful."

Strolling farther down the beach, Liam put his arm around me, pulling me close as we walked. But, it was apparent, he had more to say.

"Sweetheart, I'm thrilled that you decided to get married here on the beach. As I said, when I built the house, I had no idea that I would ever find anyone to share it with. I feel fortunate and blessed to have found you, and now the possibility of having your sons and their family here is a bonus. I can only imagine the joy of having children here during the Holidays and especially Christmas."

"Well, let's hope they don't discover how wealthy you are. I'm afraid their Christmas list might explode," I laughed.

"I would take that as an honor. I would love to fulfill their wish lists. Especially ensuring they get into the best colleges. Ericka, you're not only making my dreams come true by becoming my wife, but you're giving me the chance to have a family. Perhaps, I was born to play the role of grandpa," Liam laughed.

"Liam, the kids would be lucky indeed to call you grandpa or whatever name you would choose," I smiled as tears moistened my eyes. I knew the importance of family and to be able to once again share that experience with someone was huge.

Suddenly, Liam's phone buzzed.

"No problem, buddy. You know the house. See you soon."

"Well, Harry and Amanda just landed. A bit early, I might add. Suppose we better turn back."

"Oh my gosh, I've not started the lasagna or even the cake," I froze.

"Sweetheart, don't panic. I'm sure they won't mind. They weren't expecting you to cook. No worries. I'll make dinner reservations. I don't see this as a problem," Liam laughed.

"Oh, you wouldn't, but I wanted to prepare a homemade meal for everyone."

"Babe, you're cute. I didn't marry you with the expectations of you suddenly becoming Susie Homemaker.

"Oh, Mr. Lachowski, trust me, you're going to regret that. I have skills."

"Oh my, I do love your tenacity," he laughed.

"You better hope everything has arrived. I'm cooking."

"Please, be my guest. As I said, the kitchen is yours. Oh, there's a fire extinguisher under the sink," Liam roared with laughter.

"You're digging yourself a hole, Lachowski. I suggest you stop with the snide remarks while you are ahead. After all, you will be eating and," I stopped short, putting him on notice.

"Did I just hear the slight hint of a threat?" he grinned.

Quickly pulling me into his arms, he held me through my emotional outburst.

"Oh Ericka, loving you is going to be an adventure. I love you."

Reaching the house, my anger had vanished. It was simply impossible to be mad at Liam. I loved this man more than life itself. However, finding all the ingredients waiting for me helped.

Once inside the kitchen, I began the process of making the lasagna.

"Can I help?" Liam asked.

"There's not much to do, but I could use a glass of wine."

"At your service," Liam teased, popping the cork from a bottle of white zinfandel.

"Thank God you have double ovens," I smiled, taking a sip of wine.

Placing the noodles on the stove to boil, I grabbed the ricotta cheese from the fridge and prepared the sauce. Once I had all the layers together in a large pan, I put the lasagna in the oven and began the process of making Amanda's favorite chocolate cake. It was a simple recipe and didn't require a lot of effort to make. Finally, everything was in the oven, including the cake.

Suddenly hearing Amanda's voice, excitedly I ran to the living room.

"Wow. Something smells delicious. Are you cooking?" Amanda laughed.

"Of course. How was the honeymoon?" I inquired, giving my best friend a huge hug.

"Best time of my life," Harry interjected.

"Wonderful," Amanda answered.

"Geez, I'd swear you've got a glow about you," I smiled.

"It's probably from the sun. I would highly recommend Tahiti," Amanda blushed.

"The sun?" Liam questioned with a laugh. "Right. I think you could use a beer, buddy."

Grabbing two beers from the fridge, and after pouring a glass of wine for Amanda and refilling my drink, the guys took their beer and walked out to the Lanai. Finally, leaving Amanda and me alone.

"Are you baking a chocolate cake?" Amanda asked with a huge smile.

"Yes, but not just any chocolate cake. It's your favorite recipe."

"Wow. I'm impressed. You're certainly becoming domesticated."

"Well, you haven't tried it yet. But, fingers crossed, it's as good as the ones you bake."

"Geez, Ericka, this house is gorgeous. You seem happy. I never expected to see you in Hawaii."

"I know. I felt a little down after you left. So Liam suggested we fly to Hawaii and check out wedding venues. Who wouldn't be happy in this house, in Hawaii with a man like Liam?" I smiled.

"Ericka, I'm happy for you. I'm excited about your wedding. Have you set a date?"

"No. Not yet. I still have to check with the boys and see what dates work best for them. Liam and I are flexible. But, of course, he does have to be in Singapore next week."

Hearing the loud beeps of the timer, the lasagna was done. Amanda followed behind me as we ran to the kitchen. Removing the pan from the oven, it looked delicious. One dish down and only the cake remaining. Mission almost accomplished. I smiled.

"I'm putting my house in Marin on the market," Amanda blurted without thought of the impact it would have.

"You're what?" I gasped. "Did you just say that you are selling your house?"

"Yes."

"Amanda, you can't move," I insisted.

"Ericka, we have a lot to talk about. I'm moving to Vancouver. As you know, Harry has a home there, and he's still working with Liam. It just makes sense. Plus, I need a change."

"Wow. I'm speechless. I don't know what to say."

"Just be happy for me. Who's to say that you might not do the same after you're married. Our kids are all grown, and those homes hold many memories. Although good memories, our lives have changed.

Not to say that we didn't love our husbands, but sometimes change is good. We'll talk later."

Hearing the deafening beeps of the second timer, it was just the distraction I needed. The cake was baked. Thoughts of Amanda moving and leaving Marin were overwhelming. Taking the cake out of the oven, it looked perfect and smelled heavenly.

"Would you mind making the salad while I whip up the frosting?"

"Sure."

"The ingredients are in the fridge. Strawberries, lettuce, and the vinaigrette are already made as well."

Warming the garlic bread, I had accomplished the goal of cooking my first dinner for Liam and our friends. Mission accomplished.

Hurriedly lighting candles while setting the table with silverware and china, it looked elegant.

"Amanda, why don't you inform the guys that dinner is ready. I'll bring out the bread, salad, and lasagna.

As everyone was seated at the table, Liam gave me an approving glance as he opened another bottle of wine, filling each glass.

"Sweetheart, it looks delicious. Well done," he grinned.

"Thank you," I smiled. "Enjoy."

After dinner, I served the cake to everyone's delight. It was delectable.

"Geez, the cake is simply amazing. Thank you," Amanda remarked.

"No problem. I know how much you love it. It's so good to have you both with us."

"Here's to good friends and good times," Liam toasted.

After dinner, we took our drinks out to the Lanai. Enjoying hours of light conversation, Amanda and I were quickly falling asleep.

"I think we should get these young ladies to bed," Liam mentioned glancing at Harry. "I think you'll find everything you need in the guest room. If not, please let me know."

"Thanks, buddy," Harry smiled, reaching for Amanda's hand.

"It's nice having you here," Liam remarked. "Goodnight."

"Goodnight," Harry replied with a smile.

"Babe, let's go to bed. You look tired," Liam grinned.

The following day, Liam surprised us all with a helicopter flight.

Seeing the island from the air was spectacular, especially observing whales as they swam and frolicked in the dark cobalt waters of the Pacific. Amanda and Harry stayed with us for three days. We played the role of tourists and enjoyed bonfires on the beach late at night. At the end of the week, we all boarded the jet for the flight back home to San Fransico. Finally, taking a limo to Marin.

Chapter Fourteen

The following morning after we returned to Marin, I walked over to Amanda's house for coffee. Harry had returned to Vancouver on business, and Liam had left for Singapore. So we were alone and overdue for a long conversation.

"Come in. I'm in the kitchen," Amanda yelled. "Sorry about the boxes. Just walk around them. Coffee is ready."

"Wow, Amanda, you're really selling," I asked, still in denial as she poured us a cup of the hot brew.

"Yes. I'm really selling. Ericka, sit down. We need to talk," Amanda answered. "Why do you seem to be having such a hard time with it?"

"Honestly, I don't know, and I know it's none of my business, but I just need to understand how you could possibly sell this house. It holds the memories of your marriage to Bob. You raised your family in this house. And more importantly, why on earth are you moving to Vancouver? I'm sorry. I just don't get it. I know you're married, and Harry is a great guy, but why doesn't he move to Marin?" I questioned, taking a sip of coffee.

"Ericka, you're right. You don't get it. I love Harry." Amanda replied, taking a huge sip of coffee. "Ericka, we can't live in the past, no matter how much we loved our former husbands. Do you think me selling the house and moving to Vancouver is like discarding Bob and the life we had? How is that even possible? You know that we carry their memories everywhere we go twenty-four hours a day, three hundred sixty-five days a year. The years that I had with Bob, both the good and the bad, never left us. Maybe life would be better if their memories faded with their passing, but we know first-hand life doesn't work like that. Becoming a widow is hard. Regardless of how it happens, be it after numerous years of caregiving as happened in our situation or suddenly due to an accident or other unexpected misfortune. Becoming a widow is hard. I love you like a sister, and I need you to understand," Amanda stood refilling her coffee.

"Ericka, my life has changed. I've met and married a man whom I love. He's asked me to move to Vancouver, and I'm sorry if you don't get it, but somehow I believe you will someday. We don't always plan the direction of our lives, sometimes it's thrust on us, either good or bad, and we're just left to deal with it. I'm dealing with it the best I can, with my heart. Maybe you're right, maybe I'm being foolish, but in my heart, I know it's the right decision. I love Harry. Honestly, I would follow him anywhere. Ericka, it's not houses or material things that matter in life. It's the people we're connected to. As I said, I love you like a sister, but I'm remarried now, and Harry is the love of my life. His job is in Vancouver. Knowing that Liam works and lives in Vancouver, are you telling me that if he asked you to move, you would give up your relationship with him to remain in Marin? Ericka, I know you. You would sell or move in a nanosecond, just like me. I see what you've found in Liam. Do you even know how lucky you are, me included, to find love for the second time? Seriously, we've been blessed. We can never bring our husbands back. But sacrificing ourselves by being unhappy for the rest of our lives serves no purpose, especially now that God has brought these two wonderful men into our lives. Ericka, think about it. Liam loves you, and he would spend his last penny to make you happy, and trust me, he has a lot of pennies," Amanda smiled. "I love you."

"Amanda, I love you too. You're right," I cried, becoming emotional. "Everything you've said makes sense. I get it. Just to prove my point,

I'll even help you pack or possibly find you a buyer with what few connections I have left in the world of real estate. I'm sorry. Can you ever forgive me?"

"Ericka, I love you. No worries. There's nothing to forgive. Just be happy and if Liam asks you to move, decide with your heart, and you'll make the right decision. Now, get out of here and take Fritz for a walk. I'm sure he missed you. I've got work to do, and Hazel is demanding attention as well."

"Let me take Hazel. I'll take them both for a long walk."

"Thanks. Her leash is hanging on a hook by the front door."

Grabbing Hazel and her leash, I left to get Fritz. The fresh air would be refreshing for me as well as the dogs.

After a long walk, I returned home somewhat rejuvenated, less emotional, and most of all, no longer worried about Amanda selling and moving to Vancouver. Hearing the buzz of my cell phone, I smiled. It was Liam.

"How's my girl?"

"I'm fine. Where are you? You can't possibly be in Singapore."

"No. I have a short layover in Hawaii of all places. So I decided to fly first class and make the jet available for Harry. We have a hotel opening in Madrid next week, and I might need him in Spain at a moment's notice. I miss you. Are you staying busy?"

"Yes. I just walked the dogs, and earlier I had coffee with Amanda. She's selling and moving to Vancouver, but I'm sure you already knew that."

"Yes. Sorry, I have to go. We'll talk about that later. I love you. See you soon."

"I love you too. Take care."

Taking Hazel back to Amanda, I was curious about their honeymoon.

"Knock, knock," I teased loudly, opening her front door. "I've brought Hazel."

"I'm in the bedroom closet," Amanda yelled. "Come on back. I'm sorting through clothes to give to Goodwill. I will never wear a lot of them, and they should go to someone who would put them to good use."

"Great. Do you need help?"

"You can grab some boxes and fold the clothes to fit inside."

Following Amanda's instructions, I began picking up clothes from the floor pile intended for Goodwill.

"Amanda, I never asked. How was your honeymoon? Did you like Tahiti?"

"It was wonderful. Harry took such good care of me. We had a cabana that sat high above the water. You know, like the ones you've seen in all the brochures and on television. We even had a ladder to descend into the water, which was crystal clear. Tahiti would be a great location for your honeymoon."

"Did you enjoy having the use of the private jet?"

"Are you kidding? It's sheer luxury."

"So," I laughed. "Are you an official member of the mile high club?"

"Geez, Ericka, we were on our honeymoon, and you know it has a stateroom, right? So what do you think?"

"Well, I'll take that for a 'yes,'" I laughed.

"You're silly, but I still love you," Amanda blushed.

"Liam and I have decided on Phuket, Thailand, as our honeymoon destination. He suggested it. It looks amazing and the resorts, even though they are five-star and world-renowned, still offer exclusivity. We were looking for a private setting on a beach, and Phuket covered all the things we wanted in a resort."

"It sounds phenomenal. I'm sure you've made the right choice. Harry and I will have to check it out. Ericka, you know that Liam and Harry are still working. Harry hasn't mentioned considering retirement. Do you think Liam is close to retiring? I was just curious," Amanda questioned, heaping more clothes onto the Goodwill pile.

"Liam said once we were married that he'll probably step away from most of his corporate responsibilities. But, Amanda, you know the control these guys like to have regarding their business dealings. It makes you wonder if they would ever walk away. Liam is in Singapore, and it sounds like Harry might soon be sent to Madrid. I'm sure running billion-dollar corporations entails a lot of work. But, unfortunately, a lot of it requires their personal attention. So I guess it's simply a tradeoff. We might have to learn to live with it for the present time."

"Yes. It certainly sounds like it. Harry mentioned he might be going to Madrid. Maybe if we were able to tag along, it might not be so bad. Just remember, it's their hard work and tenacity which got them where they are today, and we're certainly benefiting from all their efforts. For heaven's sake, just look at the size of my diamond. I'm still awestruck every time I glance at it," Amanda laughed.

"You're right. They are generous," I giggled, trying to keep up with the clothes as Amanda tossed them in my direction. "What are your plans for this evening?"

"None to speak of. I just want to get the house packed up as quickly as possible. That way, I can move out and just leave it in the hands of a competent realtor. Too bad you quit the real estate business. I could simply turn it over to you," Amanda laughed.

"Well, that isn't going to happen. Good luck finding a listing agent."

Helping Amanda go through her closets and deciding what to keep and discard or give to Goodwill took hours. Finally, after several hours, we had managed to go through most of her closets. I was exhausted.

"I think this is where I say goodnight," I laughed. "We can finish tomorrow. I'm going home to crash on the couch, enjoy a glass of wine, and maybe if I can manage to stay awake, write. Don't work too hard. You're not in a hurry to move out. Besides, I'm going to miss you," I frowned.

"You're right, I'm not on a time limit, but the sooner I can pack all of my belongings, the sooner I can move in with Harry. Have you seen his house in Vancouver? It's gorgeous and spacious. I might need a maid," Amanda laughed.

"No. However, I have seen Liam's penthouse. It's your typical bachelor pad. Even at his age, it's sterile and uninviting. It needs a complete renovation. At first, I thought it might be a fun project, but after thinking about it, it would be easier to sell and start over."

"Well, maybe you'll get the chance to help him either renovate or move."

"Perhaps. See you tomorrow."

"Goodnight."

Walking back to my house, the thoughts of it being empty without

Liam were disheartening. We had spent enough time together that missing him had become a huge problem. Greeted by Fritz, my four-legged fur baby, I lovingly scooped him into my arms. They say animals are sensitive to your needs. It certainly seemed to be the case with Fritz. He always knew when I needed comfort and support.

Reaching for my laptop, I lounged back on the sofa. I was only a few short chapters away from the end of my current manuscript. I had been working on it since I left Marin. Perhaps, it would offer the distraction I needed. But, instead, I felt lost without Liam.

Startled by the unexpected buzz of my cell phone, I jumped. It was Liam.

"Hey, gorgeous, I had a few minutes and wanted to call. What did you do this afternoon?"

"Oh, I helped Amanda clean out her closets. I packed up things she no longer wanted. She's going to take them to the Goodwill Store."

"Great idea."

"Liam, I miss you, and to be honest, I feel lost without you. I need you. Can't you just come back?" I cried, trying hard not to become emotional.

"Sweetheart, I love you. But, unfortunately, it's not how life works. Remember you said you would try and arrange for me to meet your family, why don't you visit them. It would be a great time to discuss the wedding. I'm sure they would love to see you."

"You're right. I haven't seen the boys in a while, and the school pictures of the grandkids prove they are growing up too fast. Okay. I'm going to give them a call. I love you. Keep safe."

"I love you too, sweetheart. See you soon."

Reclining back on the sofa, thoughts of seeing the boys, my lovely daughters-in-law, and especially my grandkids lifted my spirits. Getting the family together was way overdue. Just the mere thoughts of seeing them gave me goosebumps. Then, reaching for my cell phone, I placed a call to Keith. Fortunately, he answered.

"Hey, mom, what's up?"

"I just wanted to check in and see how my handsome pilot and his family were doing?"

"We're all fine. How are you doing?"

"Good. I called because I was thinking of coming for a short visit. I miss you, Briella, and the boys. Also, I was hoping to see Greg, Samantha, and the twins. What are the chances of us all getting together this week? Do you think you could arrange it? I want to see everyone. The grandkids are growing up so fast."

"Mom, I have an idea. I'll call Greg, and if it's alright with you, I'll fly everyone up to San Francisco this weekend. I'll rent a van and drive us to Marin. How does that sound?'

"Oh my gosh, like music to my ears. That would be wonderful. Do you think you could get your brother to come on such short notice?"

"Mom, don't worry. He'll be there. I'll call him as soon as we hang up. Now, don't plan anything or cook a lot of food. You know Greg loves to show off his culinary skills. We'll take care of everything. See you Friday evening. I love you."

"I love you more."

Lounging back on the sofa, I could hardly contain my excitement. Once again, Liam was right. He knew how to fill the empty void of him not being here, and he was right that it had been too long since I saw my family. I was more than excited. I couldn't wait to share the news with him and let him know the kids would be here when he returned. Then, finally, I would have everyone together. After meeting Liam, we could discuss the date and make arrangements for the wedding.

Regardless of Keith's sweet advice not to go to any trouble for their visit, I needed to stock the fridge and pantry with things I knew the kids loved and clean the boys' old rooms. I had turned Keith's room into a sewing room, and Greg's room had unfortunately been used for storage. I needed to clean out his room and make space for the boys to sleep. I was going to be busily happy for the following two days. I had a lot to do before Friday arrived.

Slipping under the warm covers on my bed, I turned out the light. Even though I missed Liam terribly, I had exciting things to look forward to. My kids were coming home. Sleep became elusive as thoughts of things I needed to do raced through my mind.

The following morning, as the brilliance of the morning sun crept into my bedroom, I rubbed my eyes. There was no time to sleep in. I had to make a list of everything I needed to accomplish before Friday. I bolted up from the bed, racing for the shower. Suddenly the sound of an incoming call stopped me in my tracks. Reaching for my cell phone, it was Liam.

"Hey, sweetheart. How's my gorgeous girl?"

"Oh, Liam, I couldn't be better. How are you?"

"Wow. What happened to the Ericka I spoke with last night?" he laughed.

"Liam, the kids are coming home this weekend. Can you believe it? As usual, you were right. I can't begin to tell you how excited I am."

"Ericka, Babe, I can hear the excitement in your voice. I'm thrilled for everyone. Promise to take lots of family photos for me. What day will they arrive?"

"Keith is flying everyone into San Francisco on Friday evening. He's renting a van, and they're driving to Marin. I can't wait to see them."

"When are you coming home?"

"Sweetheart, that was the reason for the early call this morning. Unfortunately, I'm going to be delayed until next week. I'm so sorry. I'm truly disappointed that I will miss seeing everyone. Can you please give my apologies to your family?"

"Liam, of course. What happened? I thought you were only going to be away for a few days?"

"Well, as you know, that was the original plan. However, things changed. I've been waiting on a shipment of Daikin HVAC units to arrive. I was just informed they've been delayed at the port in Tokyo. I'm sorry. I have to be here at least until I know they've shipped. Then I can leave someone in charge of their installation. Sweetheart, I'm so sorry. I promise to make up for our lost time."

"Liam, I understand. I love you, and I know this is beyond your control. I'll just see you when you return. No worries. Remember your quote from the movie *Love Story*? It just came to mind, '*Love means never having to say you're sorry.*'

"Ericka, where did you come from? Honestly, Babe, I don't deserve you. I love you more than you could ever know. I can't wait to get you back in my arms. I love you. I'll call you tomorrow."

"I love you too. We'll talk tomorrow."

Sitting down on the bed, I felt like the breath had been knocked out of me. Unfortunately, Liam wouldn't be here to see the family this weekend. I was more than disappointed. I was devastated. However, I would try to make the best of it. There was nothing to do but carry on. The kids were coming, and I was excited to see them even if they wouldn't get to meet Liam on this trip.

After a quick shower, I dressed for the day. I made a mental note of things I needed to do that kept me from stressing over the fact that Liam was delayed in Singapore until next week. Suddenly, hearing my cell phone buzz, it seemed like Grand Central Station. It was Amanda.

"Hey, girl, do you have any plans today?"

"Oh, Amanda, I'm glad you called. Liam has been delayed in Singapore until next week. Can you believe it? I'm so disappointed. The kids are flying in this weekend, and I wanted to have everyone together. Now, he can't make it."

"Well, it sounds like you could use a little retail therapy. I need my shopping buddy. I'm going to take a day off from packing and drive into the city. Want to join me?"

"Amanda, I would love to go, but I have a list of things to get done before Friday evening. What takes you into San Francisco, and what are you shopping for?"

"I'm looking for some new designer dresses. You know, nothing off the rack, something I could wear out for the evening with Harry. He's flying in on Friday night. That is if Liam doesn't send him to Madrid."

"Sorry. It sounds like fun. You've always been my fashionista. My guru of high-end designer labels, but, honestly, I don't have the time, but give me a raincheck. You know I love to shop. However, if you see anything jaw-dropping in black in my size, put it on hold."

"Alright. I can't believe I'm shopping by myself."

"You're a big girl. I think you'll do just fine. Are you giving Harry's Black Amex Card a trial run?" I laughed.

"How did you know?"

"Seriously, Amanda, you are Mrs. Harry Morgan. It comes with perks," I laughed. "Enjoy the benefits. Call me when you get home. I'll run over and see what you bought."

"Okay. Talk to you soon."

Running out the door, I had several stops to make, the grocery store and a big box store for extra bed linens and towels. I knew the kids always enjoyed the heated pool, which meant having lots of extra towels available. Also, time permitting, I needed to get a manicure, pedicure and schedule a hair appointment for Friday morning.

Arriving back home, I was exhausted. Bringing in all the grocery bags and shopping bags, what little energy I had was gone. Opening a bottle of white zinfandel, I poured myself a glass and took it into the living room. Lounging back on the sofa, it felt good to accomplish so much in one day. I had twin air mattresses for the older grandkids, the fridge was now fully stocked, and I had enough bed linens and towels to survive the weekend. The house would again be filled with boisterous laughter and four rambunctious grandchildren. Laying my head back on the sofa, thoughts of Liam consumed me. He had lived his entire life without a family of his own. I couldn't wait to introduce him to mine. We would soon become the family he never had. Wiping tears from my eyes, I couldn't imagine not having the experience of raising children and later the joy of welcoming grandchildren. Feeling tired and emotional, I made my way into the bedroom. Grabbing Fritz, we climbed into bed for the night. As I was just about to drift off, my cell phone buzzed. I smiled. It was Liam.

"Hey, sweetheart, how was your day?"

"Busy."

"You have no idea how much I miss you."

"Oh, Liam, trust me, I do. Are you still stuck until next week?"

"Yes. I'm afraid so. If anything changes, you'll be the first to know. What kept you busy today?"

"Nothing exciting. I shopped for groceries, purchased twin air mattresses for the older grandkids, and bought an extra supply of bed linens and towels. Oh, I also decided at the last minute to bake chocolate cupcakes tomorrow for the grandkids."

"Darn, I'm missing your cupcakes. I know you're excited to see your family. Just enjoy the moments you have, and most of all, make memories. In the end, that's all we have. I love you. Get some rest."

"I love you too."

Laying my head against the pillow, Liam's voice was the last thing I remembered before falling asleep.

Chapter Fifteen

"Mom, we've just landed in San Francisco. We'll be home soon. Love you."

Those words were music to any mom's ears. Putting down my phone, I began to do the flight of the bumblebee, making a mad dash around the house. I ensured everything was spotless, in its place, and ready to comfortably accommodate a family of nine, including myself. I couldn't wait to see everyone. As Liam said, it had been too long. It was time to enjoy being with my family and making memories that would last a lifetime. After making the house inviting, I sat down to enjoy a cup of coffee before the happy chaos commenced.

"Mom, we're home," Keith announced, walking in with everyone in tow.

"Oh my gosh," I smiled, running to throw my arms around everyone. I felt my heart would burst as I began giving everyone enormous bear hugs. "Wow. It's so good to see everyone. It's been way too long. How was the flight?"

"Well, considering Keith was flying the plane, suppose it was alright," Greg laughed.

"Last time I fly you anywhere," Keith countered.

"Ya'll haven't changed," I laughed, putting my arms around Keith first, then Greg. "Your dad would be so proud of you," I added, not wanting to let go of my boys.

"Hey, mom," Briella smiled. "How are you?"

"Never better seeing all these smiling faces," I grinned. "You look beautiful as always. Oh my, this isn't possibly Jeffrey and Bobby. You've grown so much. Just look how big you are," I smiled, giving them each a huge hug.

"Mom, it's so nice to see you," Samantha smiled, stepping forward as she lovingly placed her hand over her belly, giving me a giant embrace.

"Samantha," I screamed with joy. "Are you expecting?"

"Yes, ma'am," she beamed.

"Oh my gosh," I cried as tears of joy escaped my eyes. I was thrilled beyond words.

"I'm just four months. The baby is due in June, and we just found out this week we're having a boy," Samantha smiled. "We were waiting to tell you this weekend."

"Samantha, I couldn't be happier for you and Greg. A little boy is perfect. Abby and Bella will be amazing big sisters. Where are the girls?"

"Oh, they're coming. They fell asleep on the ride in from the airport. Greg just went out to wake them and get them out of their car seats. Something smells wonderful. Did you bake cupcakes?"

"Of course. I know how much my grandkids love my chocolate cupcakes," I smiled with pride.

Stopping to enjoy the moment, I glanced around the living room, noting all the happy smiling faces. Suddenly, I was overwhelmed with thoughts of Bob. The last time the kids were all here was for his memorial service. Discreetly wiping tears from my eyes, this was a joyous occasion, and I didn't dare let my family see me cry. I would cry later when they had to leave.

"Nana," Abby giggled, running towards me.

"Oh, wow, just look at you," I laughed, scooping her into my arms. "You're getting so big. You're almost grown," I teased.

"No. I'm a princess. Daddy says I'm his princess."

"Yes. A beautiful princess," I smiled, kissing her sweet angelic cheeks. "Where's your sister, Bella.

"Daddy's got her."

Looking up, Greg walked in with Bella, who was still sleeping in his arms.

"Greg, the girls are adorable," I smiled, giving them both a quick kiss. "Your bedroom is ready. Why don't you take her upstairs to bed? She looks worn out."

"Thanks, mom. I'll be right back."

Herding everyone into the family room, I knew it was getting late, and the kids should probably be in bed. However, I wanted just a few moments to take in the feel of having my family at home.

"Can I get anyone something to drink or perhaps something to eat?" I asked.

"Mom, sit down and visit with the kids. They've missed you, and we're only here for the weekend. Greg and I can wait on the kids," Keith smiled, giving me a quick kiss.

"Speak for yourself," Greg laughed, walking into the family room.

"Samantha, if you're tired and need to lie down, I have the beds ready in Greg's room," I inquired, taking a seat next to the boys.

"I'm fine. Thanks, mom."

"Are you both still playing Little League Baseball?" I asked.

"Yes, but Jeffrey wants to play soccer next year. But, Nana, he's got a girlfriend," Bobby playfully interjected with a laugh.

"I do not," Jeffrey yelled in defiance.

"Boys, no yelling. Remember, we discussed using our inside voices," Briella stated, giving Jeffrey a stern glance.

"Nana, daddy's going to take us fishing. Grandpa took us fishing," Bobby explained in childlike fascination with a toothless grin.

"I remember. That sounds like fun," I laughed as memories flooded my mind.

"Do you want to go fishing?"

"I'm not exactly fond of fishing, but I would go with you."

"Hey, daddy, Nana said she would go fishing with me."

"I heard," Keith laughed.

"Bobby, Jeffrey, it's bedtime. Say goodnight to Nana and go brush your teeth," Briella smiled.

"Goodnight, Nana. Can we go swimming tomorrow?" Jeffrey asked sweetly.

"Of course, if it's alright with mom and dad."

Giving the boys a quick hug and kiss, Briella took them upstairs. I smiled, noticing that Bella had fallen asleep in Greg's arms. Walking over, I gently kissed her forehead.

"Guess it's time to take my little princess upstairs to bed," Greg smiled. "I'll be right back."

"Mom, Greg, and I want to talk with you. Come sit next to me."

"Is something wrong?" I asked curiously, taking a seat beside Keith.

"No. Not really. Let's wait for Greg."

"Alright." I suspected it concerned Liam and our upcoming wedding.

"Mom, it's so good to be home. I've missed you," Greg smiled, walking into the family room. He took a seat next to me on the sofa and reached for my hand.

Having my sons seated next to me was wonderful. However, I knew something was heavily weighing on their minds. Glancing at Samantha, and Briella who had just returned after putting the boys to bed, they both smiled.

" Mom, you know how much we all love you, and you know that we only want your happiness, right?" Keith began.

"Of course."

"Isn't the fact that you're engaged happening rather soon after losing dad?"

I knew this would be the topic of their discussion, and I knew they had never met Liam. Unfortunately, the worst part was that he wasn't here to answer any questions they would have regarding him. Most importantly, without him here, the boys wouldn't be able to see for themselves how much Liam and I loved each other. They wouldn't get to see what a kind, gentle, caring spirit he had not only for me but for them and our entire family. I had to convince them that what Liam and I had found in each other was nothing short of a miracle. Finding love for the second time in life didn't happen for everyone, especially someone my age. I loved their father with every ounce of my being, but he was taken from us after an extended illness. I knew that Bob would want my happiness, and just like the incident with the bottle of Aramis, I knew without a doubt that I had his blessings. Now, I just needed theirs. I just had to convince them that what Liam and I shared was real. Holding my breath, I began.

"Keith, Greg," I smiled, reaching for both their hands. "First, I don't have to remind you how much I loved your father. He was the love of my life, and I took care of him for many years. To be honest, those years were not easy. It was hard on him and me. I knew your dad never wanted to go to a skilled nursing home. He required a one-on-one attendant, and very few provide that level of care. There were days when I didn't know how I would make it to the next. The degree of care he needed was almost inconceivable. It was overwhelming. I knew there was no way for either of you to give up your careers and relocate to Marin. It would have been a huge burden on you and your families, and neither your father nor I wanted that. So, I did the best that I could for him, and in the end, hospice stepped in to help. Now, let's talk about Liam," I smiled as tears gently filled my eyes.

"Mom, wait. Greg, get the Jameson. You do have a bottle, right?"

"Yes," I smiled, wiping tears from my eyes. "It's in the liquor cabinet."

"Bro, bring some glasses."

"Really, Keith?" Briella asked. "You're getting Irish Whiskey for your mom."

"Of course," Keith grinned. "Why not? The kids are all in bed."

Walking in with three Glencairn glasses filled with Jamesons, Greg laughed. "Wow, mom's a connoisseur. Look at the glasses I found."

"Those were your dad's," I pointed out.

"Sorry, girls, would you both like an orange juice or milk?" Greg teased.

"We're fine," Briella smiled. "However, I'll get us a glass of ice water."

"Mom, take a sip and continue," Keith encouraged.

"Yes. We don't have all night. Some of us would like to go to bed," Greg interjected, taking a huge gulp.

"Greg, really, this is important," Keith chided. "Okay, mom, tell us about Liam. We want to know everything."

"Seriously, bro, you've already looked him up online and his corporation. So you already know everything there is to know about him," Greg laughed.

"Greg, we need to hear mom's version. Not the internet."

"Boys, it's getting late, and I'm sure the girls are tired, so I'll keep it short. What do you want to know?"

"Do you love him?" Keith asked. "I suppose that's the most important question?"

"Yes," I smiled once again, wiping my eyes.

Noticing my emotions, Samantha handed me a tissue.

"Mom, please don't let the boys upset you," she smiled.

"Yes. Mom, they mean well, but truly it's none of their business. Samantha and I told them not to interrogate you, but I suppose they're a little overprotective," Briella added.

"It's alright. I understand. I know they miss their father, and what might seem like a short time to them since he passed has felt like an eternity to me. But, truly, no one could ever know the degree of loss, loneliness, and sadness that I've experienced. Only someone who has lost either a spouse or a loved one," I replied.

"Keith, Greg, I do love Liam with every ounce of my being, but there's so much more. It's like someone up above brought him into my life. The evening in Crescent City when I met Liam at the Fishermen's Restaurant was Déjà vu. I can't even explain it. There was an instant connection. Like we were fated to meet. It was so easy falling in love with him. It happened so naturally. To be honest, I couldn't imagine living a day without him. Liam knows me better than I know myself. To say that he takes care of me and loves me would be an understatement. He read my books and flew me to Paris overnight on his private jet and proposed at the top of the Eiffel Tower," I paused with a smile. "I fell in love with him before I even knew he was wealthy. Money to him isn't an extravagance. He worked hard to make his start-up company the conglomerate it is today. Yes, he's worth billions. However, his financial status doesn't consume him. He makes breakfast for me each morning.

He knows I have a waffle addiction. He loves Fritz and has a labrador named Ebony. He loves children, even though he's never had any of his own, and most of all, he can't wait to meet each of you. Trust me. He's not trying to replace your father. He's simply the best man I know. I love him beyond words," I cried. "We've found our wedding venue. We're getting married on the beach at his estate in Hawaii. I only have two questions for you. First, I truly hope you'll give us your blessings. Second, I would be honored to have you both walk me down the aisle," I smiled, wiping away tears from my eyes.

"Oh, mom, you have our blessings. We would love to take that walk with you," Keith answered, wrapping his arms around me.

"Yes, mom, we love you. We only want your happiness. You certainly have our blessings, and we would be honored to accompany you down the aisle," Greg cried softly, embracing me in his arms.

"Mom, we can't wait to meet Liam," Samantha cried. "You'll have the cutest little princesses to be your flower girls," she added, wiping her eyes.

"Mom, Liam has to be special. He fell in love with you. We love you so much. You deserve the very best," Briella cried. "And if you need ring bearers, we've got you covered."

"Looks like we're having a wedding, in Hawaii, on the beach," Keith announced.

"Why don't we all turn in for the evening. It's late, and it's been emotional. I'm so happy you're all here. I love each of you. I'll see you in the morning. Get some rest," I smiled, giving them each a hug.

Walking upstairs to my room, my heart was overflowing with love for my family. My kids were home. However, I held back tears, knowing the one person on earth whom I wanted to be here wasn't. I missed him more than he could possibly know. Picking up Fritz, I slipped into bed under the warmth and comfort of my duvet. Feeling the effects of Jameson's, I felt relaxed. Hearing the buzz of my cell phone, I prayed it was Liam. After talking with the kids, I simply needed to hear his voice.

"Hey, sweetheart, did the kids arrive?"

"Yes," I cried quietly, trying to gain control of my emotions.

"Babe, is something wrong? You're crying."

"Oh, Liam, the boys gave us their blessings tonight. I had a long talk with them, and they can't wait to meet you. They've even agreed to walk me down the aisle."

"Thank God," Liam answered. "Babe, why all the tears?"

"I'm missing you like crazy. I've never missed anyone as much as I miss you."

"Well, I've got some good news. The parts shipped today, and I'm flying home on Monday. After that, I'll get a flight into San Francisco. I'm going to reserve a suite at the Fairmont. Do you want to pick me up at the airport?"

"Oh, Liam, is that even a question. Of course, just send me your arrival information."

"Will the kids still be with you? I'm looking forward to meeting them."

"No. I'm sorry. They have work on Monday."

"Babe, please stop with the waterworks, alright? No more tears. I love you."

"I love you too. I'll try, but no promises.

"Get some sleep. I didn't mean to call so late. I just wanted to hear your voice."

"Liam, you've made me the happiest woman in the world. I can't wait to marry you. I love you.

"Ditto, Babe. Goodnight."

Laying my head on the pillow, as always, Liam's voice was the last thing I heard before drifting off.

Waking up the next morning to the aroma of freshly brewed coffee, I grabbed my robe and rushed downstairs to the kitchen. Greg was making pancakes.

"Good morning mom, I've taken over your kitchen. I hope you don't mind."

"Greg, you're a world-class chef, opening your own restaurant. I'm honored," I smiled, giving him a quick kiss.

"Nana, Uncle Greg is putting chocolate chips in the pancakes," Bobby grinned. "Do you like chocolate chips?"

"I love chocolate chips. They're my favorite!"

"Good morning, mom," Keith smiled, giving me a quick kiss. "I hope you slept well. We want to apologize for last night. We're sorry if we made you feel like you were being interrogated. Honestly, that wasn't our intent."

"No apologies needed. I wouldn't have expected less of you. I know you all just want my happiness. Now, no more talk about weddings. I need coffee," I laughed, pouring myself a cup.

"Nana, thanks for the air mattresses. We liked them," Jeffrey commented.

"I'm sorry, boys. There are only so many places for beds in this house. I hope you and Bobby didn't mind."

"Nana, it was like Boy Scouts. We love camping," Bobby giggled.

"Good morning, mom. The girls are so excited to be with you," Samantha smiled, reaching into the fridge for milk.

"Hey, mom, how did you sleep? I hope the boys didn't get you up too early. It's hard to keep them in bed on a Saturday morning," Briella smiled, hugging me.

"I slept well. How could I not? My kids are home," I grinned.

"Nana, daddy's making pancakes. They've got chocolate chips," Bella laughed playfully.

"We love chocolate chips," Abby chimed in.

"I know. Daddy's a great cook."

Quickly getting plates and silverware, I knew the kids were hungry.

"Mom, let me help with that," Briella smiled, taking the silverware to the table.

Once the table was set and Greg had finished making pancakes, eggs, and bacon, I reached into the fridge for milk and orange juice.

"Food's ready. Time to eat," Greg announced, refilling everyone's coffee.

Keith went outside and herded all the kids back inside to the dining room table. As everyone took their seats and the kids settled into their chairs. Keith offered to say a short prayer before we ate.

"God, we thank you for this special time with our family. Bless our food and each one here. Thank you for this day and for bringing Liam into mom's life and ours. Amen."

As everyone began cutting into their pancakes and passing around the maple syrup, I heard the front door open.

"Oh my gosh, you've started without me," Amanda laughed. "Wow, it's so good to see everyone. Those can't be the same kids I saw last Christmas. You've gotten so big," she teased.

"Hey, Amanda, it's so good to see you," Keith stood, giving her a huge hug. "I hear congratulations are in order. Harry's a lucky man. Is he here?"

"No. I'm afraid he's in Vancouver."

"Vegas and Elvis, right?" Greg laughed. "Join us for breakfast. There's plenty."

Sliding out a chair for Amanda, our table was complete, minus one handsome guy in Singapore and one in Vancouver. Looking around the table, I missed Bob. However, I felt his presence. I knew he was here.

"Okay, we have to hear all about your crazy wedding," Greg insisted. "It sounds hilarious."

"Greg, why don't we wait until after breakfast. Then, we can have coffee by the pool."

"Yes. Your mom's right. There's a lot to tell, and those pancakes look delicious."

"Please, help yourself. I'll get you a cup of coffee. Sugar or cream," Greg asked, getting up from the table.

"Just cream. Thanks."

"My pancakes have chocolate chips," Abby giggled, stuffing her mouth with pancakes.

"Abby, we don't talk with food in our mouth," Samantha whispered. "Sorry."

"The twins are adorable, and Jeffrey and Bobby have grown into young men already. Wow, you're so handsome. Just like your dad," Amanda remarked.

"Thank you," Briella smiled.

Greg returned with the coffee and brought out another platter of pancakes and bacon.

After everyone had enjoyed breakfast, we walked outside to the patio with our coffee. The boys chose to play video games in the family room while the girls watched *Frozen* on their Ipads. Although it appeared technology was huge with my grandkids, I smiled, knowing my generation found bicycles to be their main source of fun and entertainment.

"Okay, tell us all about your Vegas wedding," Greg asked.

"First, I want to know about your ring. It's absolutely stunning," Briella questioned, reaching for Amanda's hand for a closer inspection.

"There's not much to tell. Harry surprised me with it at the Grand Canyon when he proposed. It's five carats. I believe he got it at Cartier in Vancouver."

"Well, I must say, you made out like a bandit," Briella added. "It's gorgeous."

"Mom, your ring is stunning as well," Samantha interjected.

"Thanks, sweetheart."

"Mommy, mommy," Abby screamed from the kitchen. "Bella opened the refrigerator."

"I'm coming," Samantha stood. "Abby, tell her to close the door."

"Oh my gosh, I just noticed," Amanda gasped. "Are you pregnant?"

"Yes. Our baby is due in June. We just found out it's a little boy."

"Congratulations."

"Thank you."

"Ericka, you never told me."

"I only found out last night. I must say that I'm thrilled. The girls needed a little brother."

"Daddy, come inside. We want you to play Mario Kart," Bobby yelled.

"Excuse me. It seems I'm wanted in the family room."

"Okay, can we get back to the wedding in Vegas and Elvis?" Greg laughed.

"Well, there's not much to tell. It was Harry's idea. At first, I wasn't sure, but Harry had this wild idea, and the more I thought about it, I decided, why not. As you know, we got married at the Chapel of the Bells by an Elvis impersonator. I'll have to admit it was fun and unforgettable. The wedding photos made the best Vegas souvenirs," Amanda laughed. "Your mom was my maid of honor, and of course,

Liam was the best man. I'm not sure what your mom has told you about Harry, but he's best friends with Liam. They've known each other since college, Harvard. He's one of Liam's business partners, and Liam introduced us. The best thing about Harry, besides the fact, I'm madly in love with him, is that he was born and raised in New Orleans. We have so much in common."

"Wow, that's quite a story. I'm sure it was fun and, as you said, unforgettable."

"Yes. I walked down the aisle to Elvis singing, *Can't Help Falling In Love.* Liam surprised us after we took our vows. He arranged our honeymoon in Tahiti and let us use his private jet. It's all happened so fast. Seriously, it seems like a dream. Did Ericka tell you that I'm selling my house and moving to Vancouver?"

"No way? You're moving? You've lived in that house forever."

"I know. Harry is still working. He hasn't retired yet, and business keeps him in Vancouver. So, I feel my place was with him. You'll have to bring the family and come up for a visit after we get settled."

"I would love to, but as you know, I've just opened a restaurant. So it's keeping me extremely busy these days, and of course, we have a baby coming in June."

"Well, our door is always open."

"Hey, Uncle Greg, would you like to come inside and play video games with us? We just beat daddy in Mario Kart," Jeffrey asked. "Sure, that's an old game, and your dad lost. I'm not surprised," Greg laughed. "Well, I'm the cooler brother. You've just met your match."

"Ericka, have you heard from Liam? When is he getting back from Singapore?"

"He called last night. He wasn't supposed to get back until the end of next week. I believe they had a shipment of heating and cooling systems for the hotel that got held up in Tokyo. However, they've left the port, and he's flying in on Monday. I've missed him so much. You have no idea. Amanda, I'm crazy in love with him."

"I know," Amanda smiled. "Trust me. I know," she reiterated. "I can't wait for the wedding. Did you get a chance to discuss it with the boys?"

"Yes. Last night."

"How did that go?"

"Well, better than I expected. Unfortunately, they've never met Liam, so it's hard for them to form opinions of someone they don't know. But it went well. They've given us their blessings and agreed to walk me down the aisle."

"That's wonderful. I'm so happy for you."

"Thanks. We just need to set a date. I'm thinking July or August. The baby is due in June."

"So, how did your little shopping expedition turn out. Did you find any bargains?"

"Are you kidding? Honey, where I shop, they don't know the word 'sales.' However, I found a cute little dress for you and a few things for myself. I have your dress. After the kids leave, come over and try it on. I think you'll like it and you might want to wear it when Liam arrives. It's that sexy little black dress that every woman needs in her closet."

"Thanks, Amanda. You're the best. I'm going to be so lost when you move."

"Ericka, we're still going to be best friends. I'm only moving to Vancouver, and believe it or not, I have a strong feeling you'll be relocating to Canada very soon. After all, you've got to do something with Liam's penthouse. I'm sorry, but it sounds deplorable," Amanda giggled.

"I think we should go inside and see what the kids are doing," Keith mentioned as Briella followed him inside.

"Actually, I've got to be going. I've got tons of boxes scattered all over the house. I've got to get busy. It's not going to pack itself."

"Good luck. It does look like a daunting task."

"Let me say goodbye to the kids. It was so nice seeing everyone, and thanks for breakfast."

"Amanda, you're family. I love you. Now, go home and pack," I smiled. "Geez. Did I just tell you to go home and pack? I'm losing it. I don't want you to leave," I frowned.

"Ericka, it's okay. Enjoy your kids. They don't come home very often, and those grandkids of yours are growing up way too fast."

Walking through the house, Amanda said her goodbyes to everyone.

"Keith, did you or Greg want to do anything while you were home? Like go into the city or take the kids to the zoo," I asked, walking into the family room.

"No. Not really. We just came up to spend time with you. Greg and I are so busy with work that it's great just to relax. However, we want to go out to the cemetery and put some flowers on dad's grave before leaving. Would you like to come with us?"

"Of course, honey, why would you think I wouldn't come?"

"Oh, I don't know. Perhaps, it's the thought of making you sad or emotional. But, mom, I miss him so much. I think of him every day. You have no idea," Keith answered, wiping tears from his eyes.

"Sweetheart, I know. It's okay," I smiled, pulling my handsome son into my arms. "Sometimes I forget that you and Greg are still dealing with dad's passing too. I'm sorry. I love you, and if you ever need to talk, please promise you'll call me. Dad was so proud of you and Greg. You followed in his footsteps, becoming a pilot, and Greg has taken the initiative to open a restaurant. I'm so proud of my boys. Let's ask the kids if they would like to go swimming."

"I love you, mom."

"Oh, honey, I love you more. Now, let's find the kids' swimsuits."

"Who wants to go swimming?" I asked.

"I do," Bobby screamed.

"Bobby, no yelling," Jeffrey scolded. "Let's get our swim trunks."

Watching as the boys raced up the stairs, I walked into the living room. Briella was knitting a gorgeous baby blanket.

"Briella, the boys are going swimming. Do you know if Samantha wants to let the girls swim?"

"I don't know. I think she went upstairs to take a short nap. Greg was playing video games earlier in the family room with the boys, but I think he took Fritz and the girls to the park. I suppose we'll have to wait until they get back."

"Oh, okay. I didn't know Greg left with the girls."

"Yes. I'm sure they'll be back soon."

"The blanket is beautiful."

"Thanks, mom. I love to knit, and when Samantha said they were having a little boy, I remembered I still had tons of blue yarn."

"Well, it's lovely, and I'm sure Samantha will love it."

"Is there anything I can do? Do you need help with lunch?"

"Thanks, but I'm going to ask Keith if he would like to grill some hamburgers and hot dogs for everyone. Also, I made a huge potato salad yesterday, and I bought tons of chips and snacks for the kids."

"That sounds delicious. If you need any help, let me know."

"Thanks. I will. Wow, you're back," I smiled as the girls came in with Greg.

"Nana, Nana, we took Fritz to the park," Bella giggled excitedly, walking in with Fritz, still on his leash.

"Bella let Fritz go down the slide," Abby laughed.

"Girls, Jeffrey and Bobby are going swimming. Would you like to join them?"

"Yes. Daddy, can we go swimming? Please?" they both screamed.

"Okay, but be quiet. Mommy is taking a nap. I'll go up and get your swimsuits. Stay here with Nana. I'll be right back."

"Mom, do you still have their water wings from last summer or the kids' life vests?"

"Yes. No worries. They're in the garage."

"Great. I'll be right back with their swimsuits."

Quickly changing the girls into their suits and ensuring they had on safety devices, Greg and I took them outside to the patio and pool. The boys were loud and chaotic as they splashed water everywhere, jumping into the pool.

"Boys, Abby and Bella want to get into the pool. Be careful, and don't splash water in their faces," Keith warned.

"Keith, would either you or Greg like to grill some hamburgers and hot dogs for lunch."

"Mom, I'm the cook. Can you watch the kids until Samantha wakes up from her nap?" Greg asked.

"Of course. Let me run inside and put on my swimsuit. I might as well get in the pool with the girls. I'll be right back."

"Thanks, mom."

Getting in the pool with the twins was so much fun. Bob's decision several years ago to have the heated pool put in for the grandkids turned out to be a great investment. Watching as the kids swam and played, as usual, my eyes moistened. I knew Bob was here. I smiled, sensing his presence.

For the remainder of the day, the kids enjoyed the pool, and Greg, as expected, was a grill master. Everyone loved his burgers and hot dogs, and my potato salad was a big hit with the family. Finally, my chocolate cupcakes made another appearance to the delight of the kids and a few adults as well. Sitting by the pool watching the grandkids enjoying themselves, life was good even though I missed Liam. Almost as if he sensed my need for him, my cell phone buzzed. I smiled, seeing his name scroll across the screen.

"Hey, sweetheart, just calling to say I love you and miss you."

"Oh, Liam, I love and miss you too."

"How's the family?"

"Wonderful. The grandkids are enjoying the pool, and Greg just grilled hamburgers and hot dogs. I wished you were here."

"Babe, you have no idea how much I wanted to be there. I'm also calling to let you know that I'm catching a ride with one of the guys headed back to Vancouver. He has a private jet, and it's less complicated and stressful than flying commercial. I'll get home sooner, probably late Sunday night or at the latest early Monday. Once I arrive in Vancouver, I'll take the plane down to San Francisco. Please give everyone my sincere regrets for not having been there today. I love you. See you soon.

I love you too. See you Monday."

Reclining in the wicker chaise lounge, I took in all the happy smiling faces of my children and grandchildren. I smiled. I knew that marrying Liam would complete my family in a way that we hadn't experienced since losing Bob.

Later that evening, Greg revealed his true genius as a chef. He grilled steaks to absolute perfection, asparagus, corn on the cob, and made cheesy mashed potatoes, along with a delicious rendition of mac and cheese for the kids. Having a chef in the family certainly had its advantages.

The following day after another hearty breakfast, Keith drove us out to the cemetery. Stopping to purchase flowers, the visit was a somber occasion. Overhearing Samantha trying to explain where grandpa was to the twins brought tears to my eyes. Even though it had been two years since Bob passed, it still felt like the cut from an open wound. Some things in life were painful. I had learned that you never got over a loss. You simply found ways to manage your grief.

Driving through the massive wrought-iron gates of Woodlawn Memorial Cemetery, the grounds were immaculate. Bob and I decided before his passing he would be laid to rest amid the serenity of the rolling hills. Parking the van at the bottom of a lush grass-covered slope, Greg helped Samantha out of the car along with the twins. I stepped out after the boys and Brielle.

"Mom, are you alright?" Keith asked, walking over to where I stood. Lovingly he embraced me in his arms.

"Yes. I'm fine." Discreetly wiping my eyes, I fought back the tears.

Together as a family, we slowly made our way up the hill to Bob's grave. The boys placed the beautiful bouquet against Bob's headstone. After Keith and Greg had their moment with their dad, the kids became rambunctious.

"Mom, we're going to take the kids back to the car. Stay as long as you need," Keith smiled, giving me a quick kiss.

I took a seat on the concrete bench I had requested to be put near Bob's grave. The sun suddenly broke free above the billowy white clouds. It felt warm and inviting. Deciding to walk over to Bob's grave, I knelt. Taking one of the red roses from the arrangement, I gently laid it on his grave with a kiss. I knew the family was waiting, but there were things I needed to say.

"Sweetheart, I love you. I'll always love you. We're all fine, but somehow I sense you already know. Everyone misses you, but no one more than me. I've met someone, as you know. I felt your presence in the house on the beach. Babe, the bottle of Aramis, how was that even possible? Keith, Greg, and the family have given me their blessings, and I know without a doubt you were there to give me yours. I love you. Rest in peace," I cried, wiping a myriad of tears from my face.

The moments spent at the gravesite were cathartic. Finally, walking away, I had closure. Slowly making my way back down to the car, I was ready to embrace a new life with Liam.

Arriving back at the house, Greg opened a bottle of champagne. We had a wedding to plan and dates to discuss. The kids' visit had been perfect, just what I needed as Liam had known.

Saying goodbye to the kids and grandkids later that evening was difficult. However, the coming months held the promise of a new life with Liam and the exciting addition of a new family member. Racing over to Amanda's, Liam was finally on his way home, and I had a new dress to try on. However, unbeknown to me, life was about to throw me a curveball.

Chapter Sixteen

Waking up the next morning, sleep had been elusive. The excitement of Liam's arrival was overwhelming. The kid's visit had offered a happy reprieve, but I couldn't wait to see him, feel his warm embrace, and let him know how much I missed him.

As the warm water from the shower cascaded over me, it felt invigorating. Hurriedly getting dressed, I ran downstairs to make coffee. I needed coffee lots of coffee. Surprisingly, one cupcake had managed to escape the grasp of the grandkids. Peeling back the wrapper, I poured myself a cup of the hot brew and took the cupcake into the family room.

Noticing video games stacked neatly next to the television, Liam was right. Memories remained long after the days' end. Then, suddenly, I found a small pink sock stuck between the sofa's cushions. I smiled. It was the perfect memento of the kid's visit.

"Hey, anybody home?" Amanda called, bounding through the front door. "Coffee, I need coffee. Are there any of those chocolate cupcakes?"

"Sorry, I just ate the last one."

"That figures. They were delicious."

"I just made a pot of coffee. Help yourself."

"Thanks."

Reaching into the cabinet for a cup, Amanda poured the steaming beverage into a mug and sat down on the sofa.

"I bet you miss those cute grandkids?"

"Of course," I answered, taking a sip of coffee. "They're growing like weeds."

"You don't have to tell me. I couldn't believe how tall Jeffrey was, and Bobby looks more like his grandpa every time I see him. The girls were adorable. I know they're looking forward to having a little brother."

"Yes. No doubt about that. I thought Harry was flying down this weekend," I asked, changing the subject. "What happened?"

"Liam sent him to Madrid. I was afraid that was going to happen. So now, he's stuck in Spain for the remainder of the week."

"I know you're excited to see Liam. I thought he was supposed to be here by now."

"Oh, excited doesn't even begin to cover it, but I haven't heard from him. He took an earlier flight. One of the guys who works in the Vancouver office offered him a ride on his private jet. He promised to call once he arrived, but so far, I haven't heard a word."

"I'm sure he'll call soon. Don't worry."

"I've got to run. I just wanted to come over and check on you. See how you have been since the kids left. Thanks for the coffee."

"You're welcome. Don't worry about me, I'm fine. The weekend was fun but hectic, and I'm just going to relax."

"Well, if you feel like packing a few boxes, come over. I need all the help I can get."

"Sorry. Don't count on it today. The last thing I want is to be covered in sweat and worn out from packing boxes when Liam arrives, but have fun."

"Enjoy tonight. Where are you staying in San Francisco?"

"The Fairmont."

"Wear your new dress. It looked stunning on you."

"Definitely. I have the perfect accessories and heels."

"Great. Talk to ya later."

Checking the time, it was early 9:00 a.m. I was consumed with nervous energy waiting for Liam to call. Grabbing Fritz, his leash, and my cell phone, I decided to take him for a morning walk. Nothing like a brisk walk and fresh air to calm my nerves. Checking my cell for incoming calls, there were no missed calls.

Returning from my walk with Fritz, I picked up my laptop. The house was quiet, and writing seemed the perfect distraction. Turning on soft music, I focused on finishing my book. Excitedly hearing the buzz of my cell phone, I grabbed it from the coffee table, expecting to see Liam's name scrolling across the screen. It was Keith.

"Hey, mom, I was just calling to say how much we enjoyed being with you this weekend. Thank you for everything. Thanks for putting up with four rambunctious grandkids. They had so much fun."

"Sweetheart, you never have to thank me. I loved every moment. How was your flight home?"

"Great. The weather was good, and you know I enjoy flying. The kids slept. This will be short. I just wanted to call and say I love you. Please give Liam our warm regards. We look forward to meeting him soon. I love you."

"I love you more. Take care of those precious grandsons and Briella."

"I will. Love you."

Checking the time, it was 11:00 a.m. Walking into the kitchen, I made a turkey sandwich and poured a glass of iced tea. Bringing the food into the family room, I curled up on the sofa once again. After finishing the sandwich, I returned to writing. I was in the zone, simply taking dictation as the characters ran amuck on my pages. Finally, after writing for over two hours, I checked my phone for missed calls. There were none. A sense of worry began to consume me. Liam had promised to call once he arrived in Vancouver. It wasn't like him not to call. I just needed the assurance of hearing his voice to know that he was safe.

As the afternoon slowly passed, I wandered aimlessly through the house, desperately waiting to hear from Liam. Busily, I washed clothes, dried them, folded towels and bed linens, vacuumed the carpets, and finally went outside to start the pool sweep. Walking into the house, I was surprised to see Amanda.

"What are you doing here? Sorry. I'm not helping you pack today."

"Ericka, Harry just called," Amanda paused. Her expression was cause for alarm. She looked whiter than a ghost, and she was visibly shaking. "We need to talk. Let's sit on the sofa."

"What's wrong. For heaven's sake, you're shaking. You look like you've seen a ghost. You're scaring me," I asked nervously.

"Oh, Ericka, I don't even know how to say this. Unfortunately, Liam's plane never reached Vancouver."

"What do you mean, it never reached Vancouver? Did they stop somewhere?"

"Ericka, the plane went down somewhere between the southern coast of China and the Philippines. I'm so sorry."

"No. Why are you telling me this? It isn't true. I know it's not true," I panicked in unbelief. "Harry is mistaken. I'm sure Liam will be calling any minute."

"Ericka, look at me, he's not going to be calling, and I would never lie to you. Honey, I'm so sorry. Harry is leaving Madrid in an hour. He's flying back to Vancouver. He's utterly devastated."

"Amanda," I cried bitterly, allowing the details to sink in slowly. "I can't lose Liam. I can't do this twice in a lifetime. I lost Bob. I can't lose Liam," I sobbed hysterically. "He's the sun, moon, and stars in my world. I don't exist without him."

"Ericka, honey, I know how hard this is for you. But, trust me, I understand. I love you."

"No. You don't. We are engaged. We are getting married. Amanda, I can't do this. I can't do this a second time. Do you hear me?" I cried in complete despair. "I love Liam. You have no idea."

"You're wrong. I do know. I know how much you love him, and I know for a fact he loved you more than anything in the world."

"What am I going to do? Amanda, I don't want to be here anymore. Life is too hard," I sobbed. "I can't do this."

"Ericka, that's nonsense. You're stronger than you know," Amanda wept, holding me in her arms. "We'll get through this. I promise. Just like we did when our husbands passed."

Walking over to the liquor cabinet, Amanda found the bottle of Jameson's and poured us each a drink.

"Here, toss this back. It might help."

Jumping nervously at the buzz of my cell phone, I looked down at the screen, praying to see Liam's name appear. It was Harry. What did he want at a time like this?"

"Ericka, I'm so sorry. It's truly unbelievable. Is Amanda there with you?"

"Yes."

"Oh, thank God. If you feel you need a sedative, Amanda can drive you to the nearest hospital."

"Harry, I don't need a sedative. I just need Liam."

"Ericka, I understand. Unfortunately, I just lost my best friend. I'm completely devastated."

"Nobody could ever understand how I feel right now. Nobody," I cried.

"I just heard from the guys in Vancouver. There was a Filipino fishing trawler in the area. They witnessed the jet going down. Ericka, there were only six people aboard the plane, counting the pilot, co-pilot, and cabin attendant. Four bodies have been accounted for, and there were two surviving passengers. They've been taken to a hospital in Manila. We don't know the condition of the two survivors, and it would take a miracle for them to make it, much less one of them to have been Liam. It's a real long shot, so please don't get your hopes up. The witnesses on the trawler said it would have taken a miracle for anyone to have survived the crash. Unfortunately, we have no way to know the identity of the survivors taken to Manila. I'm so sorry."

"Harry, get me on a flight to Manila. I want to leave as soon as possible."

"Ericka, can you just wait for me to fly into San Franciso. I'll go with you."

"No. I'm not waiting. Do you understand? I'm leaving tonight."

"Ericka, there's no rush. First, we don't know who was taken to the hospital or even which hospital. Second, we don't know their condition. I'm trying to get there as fast as possible, considering I'm in Spain. I'm leaving Madrid within the hour. Just take a deep breath and stay calm.

Amanda will stay with you, and I'll be there as soon as I can. You're strong. We all love you. Hang in there. See you soon."

"Amanda, I've got to pack. I'm going to the Philippines."

"Ericka, that's crazy. You're going to stay here and wait for Harry. We'll go to Manila once Harry arrives.."

"No. I'm calling Keith and see if he can get me a flight."

Reaching for my cell phone, my entire world was spinning out of control. I felt as if I was losing my grasp on reality. But, thank God, he answered on the first ring.

"Keith, I need your help. I have to get a flight to the Philippines as soon as possible. I need to leave now," I cried.

"Mom, calm down. What's going on, and why do you need to get to the Philippines of all places? You're acting irrationally."

"Liam's plane went down. There were two survivors. He might be in Manila. But, baby, please help me. Please," I sobbed.

"Are you sure? Who told you?" Keith asked, assured that I had finally lost my mind.

"Amanda."

"Mom, I want to talk to Amanda. Can you please put her on the phone?"

"Yes, but we're wasting time. I have to get to the airport. Can you fly me to Manila?"

"Mom, that's absurd. I can't fly you to the Philippines. I mean, technically, I could. I do fly internationally, but I don't personally own a Lear jet or a long-haul aircraft. So I borrowed my friend's aircraft this past weekend. Let me talk to Amanda."

Handing my cell phone to Amanda, I overheard their entire conversation on speaker.

"Hey, Keith," Amanda cried.

"Amanda, for God's sake, what's going on? Mom's demanding a flight to Manila. She said Liam's plane went down."

"Yes. Harry just called, and I came over immediately to let her know. Keith, they've retrieved four bodies and possibly two survivors. But, no one knows their condition or even who they are. We don't even know the name of the hospital where they might have been taken. Only the fact it was in Manila. There's a good possibility they may no longer be alive. I'm so sorry. Men onboard a Filipino fishing trawler watched the plane go down in the ocean. They said it would take a miracle to survive that crash," Amanda anxiously explained. "Harry is flying in. He told your mom to wait for him. He's in Madrid, but he's leaving within the next hour. Keith, your mom, insists she's not waiting."

"Amanda, I'm coming. I'm leaving San Diego as soon as possible. I'll get a hop, and I should be there within the next hour and a half. Don't let mom leave, go to the airport, or do anything stupid. She's not thinking rationally. We'll figure it out once I arrive. Do you know where she keeps the Jameson's? Pour her a drink. I'm leaving for the airport."

"Thanks, Keith. Do you need me to pick you up in San Francisco?"

"No. I'll get an uber, taxi, whatever. Don't leave mom alone. Just try to keep her calm and let her know that I'm on my way. Find the Jameson's."

"I'm already one step ahead of you. I've poured her a drink. We'll see you when you get here."

"Okay. Thanks, Amanda. See you soon."

"Ericka, Keith's coming. He's on his way. Why don't you lie down? It's getting late. You've been through a lot of emotional drama. You need to rest."

"Amanda, don't you dare treat me like an imbecile. I heard the entire conversation. Don't you dare tell me to sleep, rest? You have no idea what I'm going through," I snapped. "I'm going upstairs to pack. Go home. Wait for Harry. I don't give a damn. Leave me alone," I screamed.

"Well, if you're so hell-bent on going to the Philippines, I'm going too."

"Amanda, Keith is coming. We don't need you. Stay here."

"Ericka, I know Keith is coming. For heaven's sake, I just spoke with him. But, if you're determined to go, I'm going with you."

"Suit yourself. But you're acting crazy."

"Honestly, Ericka, you infuriate me. But I get it. I know you're freaking out. Go pack. I'm pouring myself another shot of Jameson's."

I was falling apart at the seams, and Amanda was along for the ride. We were both losing it. I worried Keith would think we were both becoming irrational. I needed to focus all my energy on getting to Manila. Racing upstairs, I threw my suitcase on the bed, opened my closet, and began dumping clothes inside. At this point, I was starting to feel light-headed, and I had no idea what I had even thrown inside. Forcing it to shut, I pulled it downstairs, sitting it next to the front door.

"Okay. I'm ready to leave as soon as Keith gets here. Aren't you going home to pack? You said you were going?"

"I'm not leaving you. I'll wear some of your things. I know you. You've probably put everything in your suitcase, including the kitchen sink."

"Amanda, you're acting completely nuts?"

"Seriously, Ericka, I'm truly sorry about Liam, but you're losing your freaking mind. I can't wait for Keith to get here. I can't do a damn thing with you. Sit down. I'm making you some coffee."

"I don't need coffee," I ranted, pacing the floor.

Finally, after what seemed like an eternity, Keith came running in.

"Oh, mom, I'm so sorry," he said, pulling me into the safety of his warm embrace.

Nestled inside my handsome son's strong arms, I cried rivers of tears.

"I have an idea," Amanda quipped. "I have Harry's Black Amex Card. I'm going to charter a jet. It's going to take Harry too long to get here, and I know time is of the essence."

"Amanda, do you think that's a wise decision. You do know that's going to cost a small fortune.," Keith gasped.

"It's only money. I've got this. What are best friends for? We need to get Ericka to Manila, just in case there's even a remote chance Liam survived."

"Oh my gosh, Amanda. I take back every mean thing I've ever said to you," I sobbed.

"Well, that might take a while," Amanda teased, picking up her cell phone.

"It's arranged. We can leave as soon as we can get to the airport. I need to leave a message for Harry and let him know we've already left. I'll ask Mrs. Whitman to watch Hazel and Fritz. Afterward, I'll get my car and meet you both out front. Ericka, don't forget your passport. Keith, did you bring yours?"

"Seriously. Amanda, I'm a pilot. I fly internationally."

Within minutes, we were on our way into San Francisco and the airport. Then, boarding the Bombardier Global, we were on our way to the Philippines.

"Wow, put this on my Christmas list," Keith smiled, taking in every aspect of the luxurious aircraft.

"Well, you never know. Stranger things have happened. Liam's a wealthy man and very generous."

"Oh, Amanda, you're talking as if he's still alive," I cried. "Do you think there's hope?"

"Mom, there's always hope. I love you. Why don't you rest? It's going to be a long flight?"

Laying my head against the seat, thoughts of Liam consumed me. Every moment we had ever shared scrolled through my mind like a movie reel. He had to be alive. He just had to be. I knew that I wouldn't come back from this if he wasn't one of the survivors. Losing Bob was unbelievably hard, and I didn't have the strength to do it again. Tears softly ran down my cheeks. I remembered every kiss, every night we had spent together, the mornings he made pancakes for me, the flight to Paris, his proposal at the top of the Eiffel Tower, and our moments on the beach in Hawaii. He was my world, my entire reason for being. I was lucky enough to find love for the second time, and I prayed that he would be alive waiting for me. I wouldn't accept another reality.

Sleeping through most of the flight, I simply got up for short intervals finding Keith sitting beside me. He had lovingly covered me with a blanket. Keith was my rock. I knew Greg would have stepped up if it were possible, but the restaurant and Samantha being pregnant demanded he remain at home. I had the best sons on earth, and I willed Liam to survive to meet them. His survival was paramount. I couldn't imagine life without him. He was my reason for being, breathing, existing. There would be no life for me without him. I wept.

Arriving in Manila, the long flight had been grueling. Even though I had slept, it was at best restless. I was tired both emotionally and physically. Keith had made a list of possible hospitals where the survivors might have been taken. It would be an exhausting process of elimination.

Stepping inside a taxi service provided by the charter company, we were on our way to the first hospital. Driving through the streets of Manila, I hardly noticed the vast differences between our countries and their economies. I only had one thing on my mind. That was finding Liam and, most importantly, finding him alive.

Parking at the front entrance of the first hospital, I held my breath. Taking Keith's hand, we ran inside, with Amanda following close behind. Walking up to the hospital receptionist, Keith inquired if their staff had admitted anyone with the name Liam Lachowski or any recent survivors of a plane crash. After checking their records, they assured us he was not a patient, nor had he ever been brought to the hospital. Keith showed a recent photo of Liam with his cell number written on the back. He pleaded again with the hospital worker to ensure he wasn't a patient. Reluctantly they kept the photo. Unfortunately, they gave us the assurance he had never been admitted. However, before leaving, they recommended checking another hospital.

We ran back to the car and followed their directions to the next medical facility. Once again, we bolted inside and over to the reception desk. Similarly, the scenario played out much the same as the first hospital. According to hospital staff, Liam wasn't there, and he had never been admitted. Letting my emotions consume me, I fell into Keith's arms.

"Keith, I don't know how much more disappointment I can take. I'm so scared we won't be able to find him. He has to be in one of these hospitals. He just has to be," I cried, feeling completely overwhelmed.

"Mom, if he survived, we'll try to find him," Keith paused. "But mom, I need you to know, there's no guarantee. We still haven't learned the identity of the bodies they retrieved. I love you more than life itself, and it kills me to tell you, but our efforts could be futile. Also, there are almost one hundred level-3 hospitals. Unfortunately, I don't have half of them on my list. Do you have any idea what a huge undertaking this will be or the time it could take? Mom, I'm so sorry. This could take days."

"Sweetheart, I know, but I feel he survived. I can't explain it. I'll not stop looking until we've thoroughly exhausted every effort to find him."

"Keith, it's strange, but I think your mom might be right. If anyone could have survived that crash, Liam had a good chance. Maybe better than anyone else on board. He's in great shape for his age. Let's keep going. Where's the next hospital?" Amanda asked.

"It's in the next district."

"Okay. Let's go," Amanda insisted, hurriedly stepping inside the car.

For hours we drove through the downtown streets of Manila, checking out various hospitals to no avail and marking each one off our list. It was more than discouraging, to say the least. Finally, we were directed to a small Catholic Hospital, Saint Francis, near the outermost part of the city near the coast. It was a long shot at best.

Walking inside, we were praying to find Liam. Approaching the desk, we inquired about incoming patients who might have survived a plane crash. To our astonishment, we were informed they indeed had received one of the two survivors. However, at the moment, he remained unidentified and in a comma. Turning to face Keith, my knees buckled from beneath me. Catching me in his arms, Keith held me as we followed behind one of the nuns. She escorted us down a narrow hallway. Reaching the end of the hall, we held our breath as she slowly pulled back the curtain dividing the beds. I gasped. It wasn't Liam. However, the man was covered in gauze and unconscious. His condition was horrifying, and there was no way he could answer any questions we might have or in any way help us find Liam.

"Oh my Lord," I froze, utterly shocked. "That poor man."

"Thank you," Keith stated. "I'm sorry to say he isn't the person we're looking for. Is he expected to make it?"

"It's hard to say. He's burned over fifty percent of his body and has internal injuries. His recovery doesn't look good, but he's in God's hands," the young Sister replied.

I shuddered at hearing his prognosis. It was looking less likely that Liam might have survived. But, if he did, I now had the worries of his injuries."

"There's a hospital a few miles from here. I suggest you go there," she smiled.

Once again, getting back inside the car, I now feared finding Liam. If that man's injuries were any indication, for the first time, I allowed myself to think death might be kinder. Wiping tears from my eyes, I was almost to the point of giving up. However, I would never allow Keith or Amanda to sense my concern. They had given me the support and means to do the impossible, to leave Marin without waiting for Harry. I owed them more than I could ever repay.

Arriving at the next hospital, I willed my body to move, to get out of the car. For the first time since leaving Marin, I was losing hope. I felt the possibility of failure. Keith held me as we walked inside and to the reception desk.

"We're trying to find a man who might have been brought in as a result of a plane crash. We were told there were two survivors, and we've recently located one of them at Saint Francis. Did you receive any patients recently under those circumstances?" Keith inquired.

Waiting for a moment, the lady responded with a smile. "*Yes.*"

"Oh, Ericka," Amanda cried. "What if it is Liam?" she smiled, wrapping me in her arms.

Immediately, I asked to be taken to his room, without any further questions, even regarding the person's injuries.

"Mom, please don't get your hopes up, remember the odds aren't good. Please tell me you understand?" Keith asked with a worried stance.

"I understand."

Following behind the nurse, she led us down a long hallway. Reaching midway, I froze dead in my tracks. I heard a voice, a very recognizable voice. Sprinting down the hallway, like a deranged woman, I frantically began pulling back each curtain that separated the hospital beds. Holding my breath, my hands shook as I held onto the last curtain. Slowly, I pulled back the white drape, afraid to open my eyes.

"Sweetheart, what took you so long?" Liam smiled, sitting up in bed.

"Oh my God, you survived," I smiled as my legs buckled. Keith caught me in his arms.

"You must be Keith. Would you mind helping your mom onto the bed next to me? I worry she might faint."

"Liam, are you alright?" I cried, reaching over to gently rub his face.

"Except for a few broken bones, I'm fine."

"How did you find me?"

"Does it really matter? I'm here," I sobbed uncontrollably.

Amanda's phone began blowing up.

"I think you better answer that. It might be Harry," Liam smiled.

"Amanda, Liam made it," Harry excitedly yelled loud enough to be heard by everyone in the room. "We've located him in a hospital in Manila. We've found both men, and we're getting them back to the states as soon as possible."

"I know. We're here."

"What?" Harry asked in a state of total confusion.

"We're here with Liam. I'll call you soon with all the details. I love you," Amanda replied.

"Now, get me out of here," Liam winked with a grin.

"Liam, don't you think you should stay, at least for a while."

Buzzing for the nurse, Liam was determined to leave the hospital.

"Please bring me a set of crutches. My ride is here," Liam grinned.

"Sir, you've got a broken leg and several broken ribs."

"Thanks for the reminder, but I've got a flight to catch.'

Walking out of the hospital, Keith helped Liam inside the car.

"Please tell me you brought the jet. I don't relish the thoughts of flying commercial under these circumstances."

"Well, we flew over in a jet, but it's not exactly yours or one of the companies," Amanda laughed. "I chartered a jet out of San Francisco."

"Good girl."

"Someone I know was losing it and refused to wait for Harry."

"Thank God. We have a wedding to plan," Liam smiled.

Chapter Seventeen

Reaching the states, Liam agreed to let me nurse him back to health. I suggested we should stay at my home, but he insisted the Fairmont Hotel would be the better option, at least for the first week. We both agreed room service sounded nice, and not having stairs to contend with would be less stressful.

Liam covered the cost of the charter before Amanda left the airport. She was anxious to get home, wait for Harry's arrival, and finish packing. Keith left immediately upon our arrival in San Francisco. He had numerous domestic flights on his schedule. Now, we were alone, just the two of us.

Arriving at the hotel, I held onto Liam as we checked in and entered the elevator. Unlocking the door to our suite, we both took a deep breath, relieved the long ordeal was finally over.

"Now, where were we before life kicked us in the gut," Liam smiled. "Oh, I remember," he winked with a wicked grin.

Pulling me down to the bed, Liam turned out the lights.

"Hey, I want to know more about the crash and how you miraculously survived."

"Tomorrow," he whispered, kissing me on the nape of my neck.

"Mr. Lachowski, if you ever scare me like that again, I'll personally kill you myself," I smiled, returning his kisses with a vengeance."

"Maybe not," he laughed. "Let me give you some reasons to keep me," he smiled with a mischievous wink, pulling me gently into the warmth of his embrace.

Despite his injuries, our night was spent in each other's arms. Little did he know, he was the center of my universe. He hung the moon and the stars in my world.

Waking the following morning, we were reluctant to get out of bed. It felt like a warm cocoon sheltering us from the world. Then, however, Liam's phone began blowing up with messages from Harry.

"We should meet Harry and Amanda for breakfast. He's dying to know what happened," Liam smiled, sitting up in bed.

"Of course. I could never repay Amanda for her kindness. She came through for us."

"Yes. Don't forget your brilliant son, Keith. He's earned my respect—what a great guy. I can't wait to meet the rest of your family. Ericka, I want you to know what you're bringing to our marriage money can't buy. I love you, and I can't wait to make you mine."

"Liam, I'm already yours," I smiled as my eyes moistened.

"We should get dressed. If I stay in bed with you, I promise breakfast isn't happening."

Reaching for Liam's crutches, I helped him dress. Afterward, ripping through the contents of my suitcase, I pulled out a pair of dress pants and a sweater. Then, quickly styling my hair, we were finally ready to meet Amanda and Harry downstairs for breakfast.

Entering the restaurant, Harry got up from his seat.

"Oh, my God, buddy, I thought I had lost you," he smiled, giving Liam a huge hug.

"Not a chance."

"From what I heard, it's a miracle you survived. I want to hear all the details."

"First, I need coffee, lots of coffee."

"Sure."

"I received a call from the office on my return flight. They gave me up-to-date details. Let's eat. Then I'll fill you in."

Glancing at Amanda, she looked happy. I knew she was thrilled to have Harry at home for a few days. Hopefully, with his help, packing would be a breeze. I smiled. Our lives had changed dramatically since these two remarkable men appeared in our lives, and I wouldn't change a thing.

"Do they know what caused the crash?" Harry questioned, finishing the last morsel of his blueberry pancakes.

"No. I suppose it will take the FAA a while to determine what happened. Ed offered me a ride back to Vancouver. You know how I hate flying commercials, and I was anxious to get back. Unfortunately, it seems somebody was missing me," Liam winked with a smile giving me a quick kiss. "I'll always live with the fact he didn't make it. I was told the crew didn't survive. We lost four people, and as you know, Larry is still in the hospital. His prognosis is good, but he's facing a long recovery from the extensive burns."

"I'm sorry to hear Ed didn't make it. I've flown with him numerous times. He's meticulous with the maintenance of his jet. I feel for Linda and the kids," Harry sympathized, taking a slow sip of coffee.

"Well, we're going to make sure they have everything they need. I know it won't bring Ed back, but we'll do what we can."

Hearing the news that another woman had become a *widow,* I cringed. Life was hard and didn't come with guarantees. But, staring at Amanda and seeing the happiness she had found with Harry, I knew starting over was possible. We were living proof.

"Do you guys have any plans for today?" I asked.

"Oh, you mean other than packing?" Amanda laughed. "I'm afraid not. Now that I've got this strong guy here, I'm going to take advantage of every second."

"Geez, Amanda, that could easily be taken out of context," Liam laughed.

"Well, now that you've mentioned it, maybe a few boxes could wait," Amanda giggled.

"Babe, let's get out of here. I like the way you think," Harry grinned.

Leaving the restaurant, Amanda and Harry were on their way back to Marin. Reaching for my hand, Liam winked.

"I think we have unfinished business upstairs," he smiled.

"Oh, Mr. Lachowski, I like the way you think," I reiterated with a laugh.

Unlocking the door to our suite, the world effortlessly fell away. I knew that life came with an expiration date. However, since I had almost lost Liam, I was determined not to waste a moment. Even if it meant we could only hold each other due to his injuries.

Watching movies, curling up in bed together, and room service became our routine over the next two weeks. Finally, Liam regained his energy and felt well enough to return to normal activities.

"Why don't you come with me to Vancouver? The kids aren't with you, and I need to check in with the office. I'm sure Amanda will be up in a few days with Harry."

"That sounds wonderful. I'm not letting you out of my sight. Amanda and I could shop for my wedding gown. But, first, I have to pick up Fritz."

"Not a problem. Let's go," Liam grinned, calling for a car.

Arriving at the house, it felt odd to have Liam in tow. Unlocking the front door, Fritz met us with an abundance of kisses. However, the horrific memories of Amanda giving me the news of Liam's possible demise still lingered. It cast a shadow over the previous joys which had recently filled every corner. My home was simply a repository of memories. Both good and bad memories which had been stored in it over the years by family and friends

Taking Liam's hand, I pulled him into the family room. Reaching for a bottle of chardonnay and glasses, Liam uncorked the bottle filling our glasses.

"Here's to us," Liam toasted.

"Us," I smiled.

"Liam, I want to get married. I don't want to wait."

"Is there a reason?"

"Us. I almost lost you," I cried. "I want to get married as soon as we can make all the arrangements. What do you think?"

"Sweetheart, I would marry you this instant if it could be arranged. I would have married you in Vegas."

"Liam, I want to get married next weekend."

"Wow, sweetheart, that's soon."

"I know. It probably sounds crazy, but I want this more than anything I've ever wanted."

"If it means that much to you, I'll make it happen. However, you haven't considered your family, their schedule, Amanda and Harry, or my bum leg.

"I know, and I'm sorry. But, Liam, don't you see, it doesn't require them, only *us*," I smiled, wiping tears from my eyes.

"Alright, let's fly to Vancouver, you can shop, and I'll make all the arrangements."

"Hey, anybody home?" Amanda asked loudly, making her usual entrance. Except for this time, Harry was with her. "Is everyone decent, everyone dressed," she laughed.

"We're in the family room," I answered.

"I saw ya'll get out of the car. Tired of luxury?" Amanda giggled, walking in with her arms around Harry.

"No. We just stopped by to get Fritz. We're flying to Vancouver."

"Oh my gosh, we just finished packing, and we were thinking of leaving tonight."

"The jets at the airport. You can fly up with us," Liam grinned.

"Sounds like a party," Harry laughed.

"We're getting married," I smiled.

"Of course you are," Amanda acknowledged.

"No. We're getting married next weekend."

"What?"

"We're not waiting. I almost lost Liam, and as he's always said, 'we're in the last inning of our lives.' So I'm not wasting a single moment," I replied as my eyes welled with tears. Kissing away my tears, Liam pulled me into his arms.

"What about the kids? I thought you were waiting till July or August after the baby was born?"

"I was. All that changed when I found Liam in Manila. Amanda,

I so regretted not getting married in Vegas. Harry was right. When you know something is right, you don't wait. Sometimes life doesn't afford us another opportunity. I pray the kids can make it. I really do. I wanted the boys to walk me down the aisle, but if for some reason they can't, I can live with that. What I can't live with is waiting any longer to marry this handsome man. We've been given a second chance, and just like Harry, it's happening. Minus Elvis," I laughed.

"Well, I hope Vancouver has bridal boutiques. We've got some shopping to do," Amanda cried, giving me a huge hug.

"Geez, let's get these girls and the dogs to the airport," Harry laughed. "I need a drink."

Later that evening, as the jet lifted skyward into the darkness of the evening, the bright lights of the Bay Area came into view. I knew, just like Amanda, that I was going to leave Marin. There was only one place that I wanted to be, and that was with the man who owned my heart.

"Sir, can I get anything for you, Harry, or the young ladies," Stacy inquired.

"Yes, two mimosa's for the young ladies, and we'll have a double shot of Michter's Bourbon," Liam smiled.

The flight into Vancouver was short but eventful as Amanda and I scrolled through page after page of bridal gowns. There wasn't enough time to place a special order, but I wanted to get an idea of the latest trends.

Arriving in Vancouver, a limo waited for our arrival. Dropping Harry and Amanda, along with Hazel, at his residence, we continued to Liam's penthouse. As the limo approached Liam's building, its modern design seamlessly blended in with the surrounding towers. However, quickly remembering the interior of the penthouse, I smiled.

Unlocking the door, Ebony anxiously greeted Fritz and us.

"Hey, girl, I've missed you," Liam bent slightly as he lovingly rubbed Ebony behind her ears, "Daddy's home."

"Oh my gosh, you redecorated," I gasped, noticing all the new décor. "It's gorgeous."

"Sterile or impeccable?" Liam laughed.

"Impeccable."

The white leather furniture had been replaced with a dark brown chenille symmetrical sofa accented with colorful floral throw pillows and centered with a colorful Persian Serapi hand-knotted wool rug. A large intricately carved mahogany coffee table added elegance to the room while matching brocade curtains elegantly draped the wall of windows. It was no longer sterile but cozy, warm, and inviting.

"Unbelievable," I smiled, thoroughly scrutinizing each piece. "When did you decide to change your décor?"

"The very night you referred to it as sterile and uninviting. I called my interior designer, and she came in the next day. You were right. The space was dated and definitely needed a touch of elegance. I'm glad you approve."

"So, Mr. Lachowski, you did this for me? We weren't even engaged. You took a big risk."

"Oh, sweetheart, trust me, it wasn't a risk at all. I would never have let you get away that easy," he laughed, picking up my left hand. "I believe you accepted my proposal."

"Yes. We have a wedding to plan, and we don't have a lot of time."

"Tomorrow," Liam winked seductively, tossing his crutches on the sofa. Then, reaching for my hand, he playfully pulled me down the hall towards the bedroom.

"Liam," I laughed. "You should be resting. You're still healing."

"Let me be the judge of that," he grinned.

For the remainder of the night, passion consumed us. Lying in Liam's arms, the floor-to-ceiling windows brilliantly reflected the vastness of the city skyline. Watching as the lights slowly faded with the arrival of the morning sun, we hadn't slept at all. My first night in Vancouver had been perfect.

Later that afternoon, Liam insisted that I take his Black Amex Card and shop for the wedding dress of my dreams. Unfamiliar with the stores and currency in Vancouver, I reluctantly agreed. His words to me were quite simple.

"Shop till you drop."

Chapter Eighteen

Our first stop was meeting Amanda at Masson's Bridal Boutique in downtown Vancouver. I was anxious to find my perfect wedding dress. I envisioned a simplistic design, a cream, silk, sweetheart bodice with an A-line silhouette, and for Amanda, after much thought, I decided on a light coral tea-length gown. A beach wedding set against the backdrop of the cobalt blue waters of the Pacific Ocean would enhance the color of her dress. The additional accent of turquoise jewelry would result in exquisite wedding photos.

"Welcome to Massons's Bridal Boutique. I'm Marie Masson, the general manager," an older distinguished woman smiled. "Follow me to the back, and I'll have Jeanette pull some designs for you. Is there any particular designer, color, or type of fabric you're interested in?"

"So, you must be the bride to be," she inquired, glancing at me as she unlocked the dressing room door.

"Yes. Ericka Reed, soon to be Ericka Lachowski. How did you know I was possibly the bride?"

"Your smile. My brides always exude a unique charm or essence. Je ne sais quoi, for lack of a better term," she smiled. "It simply means an indescribable, elusive characteristic."

"About your questions, I'm looking for a cream, silk, sweetheart bodice with an A-line silhouette."

"I love a bride that knows what she wants. It makes my job a lot easier," a young woman smiled, overhearing my response. "I'm Jeanette. I'll be pulling dresses for you today."

"Thanks, Jeanette. We're also shopping for my maid of honor, Amanda."

"Do you have something in mind for her as well?"

"Yes. We're specifically looking for a coral tea-length gown."

"May I inquire how soon the wedding will take place?"

"Yes. Next weekend."

"Wow. Okay," Jeanette paused. "Such short notice. A special order wouldn't be available. So, that means off the rack and in stock."

"Would you care for champagne?"

"Yes. Thank you"

"Jon will serve you while I search our available stock. It shouldn't take long. You've been very specific with the details. I'll be right back. Enjoy the champagne."

"Thanks."

"Geez, Ericka, this place looks rather expensive and hoity-toity," Amanda giggled. "I hope Liam's paying.

"Yes. His exact words were, shop till you drop."

"Okay. That's all I needed to hear," Amanda giggled.

Enjoying our champagne, I prayed Jeanette would find exactly what I was looking for. But, unfortunately, I wasn't a shopper like Amanda."

Quickly returning, Jeanette brought out a rack of available wedding dresses and numerous tea-length coral gowns. At first glance, it looked promising. Holding my breath, I walked over for a closer inspection. My heart sank as I pulled the first gown and then the second. Disappointment washed over me as I dismissed the third and fourth gown. Then, as I reluctantly searched farther toward the end of the rack, I saw it. Tingles of excitement invaded me as I took it from the rack.

"Oh my gosh, this is the one," I beamed, holding it up for Amanda's approval.

"It's gorgeous. Try it on," Amanda remarked excitedly.

I prayed it would fit as I walked into the dressing room.

Stepping into the exquisite silk gown, Amanda painstakingly buttoned the numerous tiny silk buttons lining the back. Afraid to look, I shut my eyes and held my breath. Then, slowly, turning to face the mirror, I opened my eyes. Staring in unbelief, I smiled. It fit perfectly. No alterations would be necessary.

"Oh my, Amanda, I absolutely love it," I cried as mascara ran down my cheeks.

Quickly grabbing tissues, Amanda began wiping the mascara from my face and handing me more tissues. Ericka, don't let the mascara touch this dress. Be careful.

"What's wrong?"

"Geez, did you see the tag on this gown? It's Dolce & Gabbana, and it's seventeen thousand dollars," Amanda exclaimed.

"Well, your wedding dress wasn't exactly cheap."

"You're right. It wasn't," Amanda laughed. "Ericka, it's stunning. How does it make you feel?"

"Regal. Like royalty."

"Liam will die when he sees you in this dress," Amanda smiled.

"For heaven's sake, watch your words. Don't use words like that."

"Oops, sorry. You know what I meant."

"Now, did you see anything you liked?" I asked, hoping it would only be a quick process of elimination.

"Yes. As a matter of fact, I did," Amanda smiled.

Pulling a tea-length, off-the-shoulder, coral Mikado gown from the rack, it looked perfect.

"Try it on," I insisted.

Taking the garment into the dressing room, I watched Amanda put on the gorgeous gown. Staring in the mirror, she looked stunning. It fit her body like a glove.

"I think we have another winner," I smiled.

"Oh, yes," Amanda beamed.

At last, we had our wedding attire.

Deciding not to purchase a veil, I wanted to wear a Haku Lei, a Hawaiian crown of flowers woven with pink rosebuds and baby's breath.

Purchasing jewelry along with shoes to match our gowns, we were set. Now, only the men required formal attire.

Walking out to the limo with our cherished purchases, the chauffeur had waited patiently. Deciding to eat lunch before we returned, we chose a nearby Italian restaurant, Luigi's. It was quaint and set off from the main street. Walking in, it reflected an old-world charm. The air was infused with the aroma of sausage, tomatoes, garlic, spices, and warm bread. Ordering my standard fare, tasty lasagna, with a limoncello, we stuffed ourselves with salad, and warm bread, saving room for tiramisu.

Afterward, the chauffeur took us to the penthouse. I was anxious to show off Liam's new décor. Taking our purchases, we entered the elevator for the short ride to the top floor. Walking in, the guys were sitting outside on the patio enjoying drinks.

"Hey, sweetheart, am I still a billionaire?" Liam laughed

"Liam, that's not funny. Even though I did spend more than I expected," I smiled.

"I think the more appropriate question is, 'Did you find the dress of your dreams?'"

"Yes."

"That's all I wanted to hear. Do I get a sneak peek?"

"Mr. Lachowski, that's a hard 'no.'"

"I found my gown," Amanda announced excitedly, walking over to sit on Harry's lap.

"Great. I can't wait to see it. Please tell me Lachowski paid for it?" Harry laughed.

"Umm, of course," Amanda smiled, glancing at Liam.

"Thanks."

"As long as you girls are happy, we're happy," Liam winked, pulling me over for a quick kiss.

"Now, we have to set up catering, flowers, and reserve hotel suites for the family. Oh, and find an officiate. Definitely, not Elvis," I laughed. "Sorry, Harry."

Liam laughed. "That's the easy part. It just takes money."

"Any honeymoon destinations?" Harry inquired. "Amanda and I loved Tahiti."

"Yes. Phuket," Liam announced.

"Wow. Impressive," Harry grinned. "The Phi Phi Islands are beautiful. White sandy beaches, turquoise waters, and fascinating rock formations. Don't forget Tapu, James Bond Island. It's famous for the movie *The Man with the Golden Gun*.

"Geez, Harry, you sound like a tour guide," Amanda laughed.

"Well, I've been there several times. Phuket is world-renowned, and yet it still offers exclusivity. I'll take you."

"Yes. Let's go this summer."

"Alright, Mrs. Morgan, Phuket it is."

"We should be going. I need to run some numbers on the project in Madrid."

"What's the short-term projection on that one? Is it still coming in ahead of schedule?"

"July. But, we should put some extra personnel on that one. It would be a smart decision considering we're already accruing so many cost overruns."

"Well, go home, run the numbers, and let me know. Then, I'll call the office and see who's available to send to Madrid."

"Okay, doll, we should be going. Daddy's got work to do," Harry laughed.

"Amanda, don't forget we're going shopping tomorrow. I'll pick you up around 1:00 p.m."

"More shopping?" Liam grinned. "I think you girls are becoming shopalcoholics."

"Tomorrow we're shopping for my wedding trousseau."

"Oh. She means girlie things, lingerie?" Amanda laughed.

"Well, sweetheart," Liam winked wickedly with a smile. "Please, shop till you drop.

Saying our goodbyes to Amanda and Harry, the evening was getting late.

After Liam enjoyed his usual nightcap of bourbon and I finished a glass of white zinfandel, he reached for my hand, pulling me towards the bedroom. Slipping into bed, the city skyline lights bathed the bedroom in a soft romantic ambiance. Snuggling inside the warmth and safety of Liam's arms, the scent of his cologne, patchouli, and sandalwood, combined with the taste of bourbon on his lips, was hypnotic. Liam was my weakness, my aphrodisiac, and the night belonged to us. Once again, we simply shut out the world.

Waking up the following day, the energizing aroma of coffee drew me to the kitchen. Grabbing my robe, Liam was cooking breakfast.

"Good morning, sunshine," Liam smiled. "I'm making your favorite waffles. "Have a seat. I'll pour you some coffee."

"What did I ever do to deserve you?" I laughed, unable to take my eyes off him. He was Adonis personified in the flesh, wearing only his pajama pants, exposing his buffed physique.

"So, shopping today?" he grinned, giving me a quick kiss as he handed me the hot beverage.

"Of course. Weddings require a lot of shopping," I smiled, enjoying a sip of coffee.

"Babe, you do know, clothes are optional on our honeymoon?" he laughed.

I giggled. "Geez, Mr. Lachowski, you make me blush."

"Here. Eat. You're going to need your strength to keep up with Amanda today. I hear she has a 'black belt' in the shopping arena."

Placing a large stack of waffles covered with warm maple syrup and bacon on the kitchen island in front of me, he returned to the stove to make his plate and sat next to me.

"Amazing," I smiled, tasting the delectable fare.

"I aim to please," Liam winked.

"What's going to keep you busy today?"

"Oh, you mean besides making all the wedding arrangements," he smiled. "Working on the Madrid project. I've got to bring it in before the completion deadline, and it's looming overhead, like a dead albatross around my neck."

"Well, you can always go shopping with Amanda and me?"

"Sweetheart, that's cute, but I hate shopping. I'll manage."

After breakfast, I jumped in the shower, dressed, and got ready for another shopping marathon with Amanda.

"I've arranged a limo service for you today. Enjoy yourselves. I'll see you when you get back. Oh, I love black," Liam smiled wickedly, giving me a quick kiss.

Arriving at our first shop, Elegant Secrets, we browsed through their lingerie collection. However, after spending over an hour in the shop, it didn't appear to offer the color, styles, and material I had in mind. Quickly, we moved on to the next shop

Arriving at Victoria's Lingerie, it appeared to be precisely what I was looking for in honeymoon apparel, romantic, chic, and sexy.

"Welcome to Victoria's. I'm Brittany. Please feel free to look around. Let me know if you need assistance or have questions. We're having a sale on last year's fashions."

"Thank you," I smiled.

"Did you catch that?" Amanda questioned. "They're having a sale. Maybe I should stock up."

"Seriously, Amanda, what would you do with a stockpile of lingerie?"

"Ericka, I am a newlywed, or have you forgotten? I'd model for Harry."

"Oh, geez, did you have to go there?" I laughed.

I browsed through the lingerie and purchased a sheer black lacy gown with a matching robe and elegant undergarments. It would be perfect and age-appropriate. Amanda left the store with a shopping bag filled with lingerie and undergarments.

"I'm starved. Where should we go for lunch?" I asked.

"I know the perfect place. There's a little bistro down on the waterfront. Harry and I love eating there. We often stop in for lunch after we've taken a long stroll along the harbor with Hazel."

"Sounds great."

Entering the limo with our purchases, we were on our way to lunch.

As the limo made its way along the waterfront, the scenery was breathtaking. The still blue waters of the bay reflected the numerous boats safely anchored in the harbor. The community was bustling with tourists and locals who filled the countless shops, while others chose to stroll or jog along the seawall.

Bayside Bistro was charming. The cool breeze wafting in from the bay was refreshing as we ate outside under the brightly colored awning.

"What looks appetizing to you?" Amanda questioned.

"Clam Chowder," I replied after carefully reviewing the menu. "Let's add a bottle of white zin. I think it'll nicely complement our meal. "What are you ordering?"

"The turkey club sandwich with cranberries and a side salad."

"That sounds delicious."

Sitting outside with a glass of wine, enjoying the natural beauty of the harbor, my cell phone buzzed, interrupting my zen moment. It was Keith.

"Hey, mom, I got your voice message. I can't believe you're getting married next weekend. Isn't that a bit soon? I thought we had agreed to wait until after Samantha had the baby."

"Oh, sweetheart, we did, and I can't explain it, I really can't, but I don't want to wait until July or August. I'm sorry. I know it's sudden, and I understand if you, Greg, and the family can't make it. Honestly, I do. I did have my heart set on you both walking me down the aisle. It'll probably be one of my biggest regrets."

"Mom, I'm sorry. It breaks my heart, but there's no way either Greg or myself can be there on such short notice. Are you sure you won't reconsider changing the date?"

"Honey, I love you and Greg more than life itself, but after I almost lost Liam, it changed my perspective on so many things. Time for sure. We're given so little of it. You were with me in the Philippines. You know the trauma I went through just trying to find out if he was possibly one of the survivors. If he was alive or dead," I explained.

"Keith, please let Greg, Briella, Samantha, and all the kids know that I feel truly awful. Oh, so that you know, I'm in Vancouver. I flew up with Liam, and Amanda is here. I love you. You'll be missed more than you could know."

"Okay, mom, I've got to run. We love you too. Take lots of photos."

"I love you more."

Sitting back in my chair, I covered my face as I cried.

"What was that about?"

"The boys. They're not going to make it to the wedding. They won't be walking me down the aisle. I'm devastated."

"Ericka, you had to have known when you rescheduled the date this soon that there was a real possibility they wouldn't be able to make it on such short notice. I'm truly sorry."

"I know. I tried to sound convincing to Keith and make it appear that it wasn't a big deal and that I was sorry and understood why they couldn't come. But, Amanda, I lied. It is a big deal. No one will ever know how important it was for me to have them by my side on my wedding day and walk me down the aisle. Am I a horrible mom for not waiting?"

"Ericka, no, not for a single moment, and I'm sure they understand. You were traumatized by the crash and almost losing Liam. Heck, we were all traumatized. You flipped out. I thought I was going to have to admit you to the nearest hospital for the insane," Amanda laughed.

"I wasn't that bad."

"Oh, yeah, what reality were you living in? Don't get me wrong. I knew you were going to take the news hard. Who wouldn't? I get it. We've both been through the devastation and loss of our husbands. If you want to marry Liam this afternoon, tonight, whenever I want you to know as my best friend, I'm going to be right next to you. I love you. Now, finish your wine and no more tears. Girl, we've both been through so much in our lives. Who attends, the date, the time, or the location is inconsequential."

Later that evening returning to the penthouse, I needed another shoulder to cry on.

"Sweetheart, how was your day?" Liam inquired as I walked in.

"Oh, Liam, the boys aren't coming. Keith called. I'm devastated," I cried, tossing my shopping bag on the coffee table.

"Come over here," he patted the couch, pulling me into the comfort of his arms.

"Babe, if you want to reschedule the date again, it's okay."

"That's just it. I don't want to reschedule the wedding. I only wished it could have worked out differently so my boys could have walked me down the aisle," I sobbed.

"Well, I do have some good news for you. All the arrangements have been made. We have an officiate, catering, flowers, and décor.

I was only waiting for you to decide on the cake. I promised to call back with your choice of flavor after you've checked out their online cakes, the design, and the number of layers. So why don't we turn in for the night? I think you're exhausted. You've been shopping nonstop for two days."

Grasping my hand, he pulled me towards the bedroom.

"You're right. I do feel exhausted."

"Why don't you take a warm bath? Then, I'll get you a glass of wine."

Afterward, slipping under the cozy covers, I fell asleep as soon as I rested my head on the pillow.

Waking as the morning sun washed over the room with a soft glow, I felt rested. Sitting up in bed, Liam walked in with a tray containing hot coffee and filled with scrambled eggs, sausage, toast, and assorted fruit.

"I think someone could use a little pampering this morning. How are you feeling?"

"Better. Thank you. It looks delicious. Have you eaten?"

"Yes. I went for a short run along the seawall at the harbor. When I returned, you were still sleeping, so I decided to let you sleep in and cook breakfast."

"You're spoiling me," I smiled.

"Ericka, you've been through a lot this past week. A lot of emotional trauma, and I feel I was to blame. I'm truly sorry you had to go through the ordeal of flying to the Philippines and the worry of not knowing if I had survived. But, sweetheart, as long as I live, I'll never forget seeing your beautiful face when you walked into my room."

"Oh, Liam, how could you possibly blame yourself for what happened. I thank God you survived. It was a miracle. Seriously, if I had lost you, I'm not sure I could have gone on without you."

"Babe, I've made arrangements for us to fly to Hawaii this afternoon. I talked with Harry this morning; they are going with us. Are you okay with leaving Vancouver a little earlier than expected? Did you have any last-minute shopping you wanted to do before we left?"

"Liam, I'm so ready."

"Great. I've got the crew on standby for a 4:00 p.m. departure.

Later that afternoon, as the limo parked next to the jet, Amanda and I picked up Fritz and Hazel and carried them on board. They were now a common fixture on most flights. Finally, we were on our way to the islands. In a few short days, I would gain another title, Mrs. Liam Lachowski. I couldn't wait.

"Good evening, sir, welcome aboard," Stacy smiled. "Can I bring you anything before departure?"

"Yes. We'd love champagne," Liam smiled. "Thanks."

Returning with four fluted glasses of the sparkling beverage, the party had started.

"Here's to Liam and Amanda," Harry toasted. "Amanda and I wish you both a lifetime of happiness," he grinned.

"Yes. All the happiness in the world," Amanda smiled as her eyes welled with tears.

"Thanks," I smiled.

As the jet lifted skyward, the lights of Vancouver appeared like a vast sea of brilliant diamonds. I knew when I returned that I would never leave. Vancouver would be home. Laying my head against Liam's shoulder, the love I felt for him was like nothing I had ever experienced. I had loved Bob with my entire being, but this was different. I could only reason it was that I came so close to losing him. Giving Liam a quick kiss, I smiled. "I love you."

"Ditto," he winked with a smile.

Arriving at Liam's estate, the days went by in a blur. Amanda and I shopped for last-minute items and made hair and nail appointments. At night, we sat on the beach under the brilliance of a star-filled sky and reminisced over the past year while enjoying several glasses of wine. Then, finally, our day arrived.

"Good morning, sunshine. Are you ready to take that walk and meet me on the beach this evening?" Liam whispered, kissing me awake.

"Oh, Mr. Lachowski, you have no idea."

Later, the house was a flurry of activity as catering arrived, florists, the photographer, and the crew returned to finish the small thatched-roof gazebo, palapa, which Liam requested. Finally, the bakery arrived to set up our beautiful two-tiered wedding cake. Walking through the house, my eyes moistened. It would soon be filled with new memories.

These memories would remain here forever, transforming the beautiful house into a home.

"It's time," Amanda smiled. "We should get dressed."

Walking into the master suite, we opened the glass doors. The cool ocean breeze gently wafting in through the delicate curtains gave the room an ethereal ambiance.

"Ericka, please be careful with the mascara. I know it's supposed to be waterproof, but there's no guarantee," Amanda smiled as we applied our makeup. I chose to style my short hair in curls simply adorned with the Haku lei.

"Amanda, are you sure you've got this? I mean styling my hair," I questioned, heating the curling iron as I sat down in front of the mirror.

"Yes. Don't be silly."

Finally, done with hair and makeup, it was time to get dressed. Slipping on a blue garter for something blue, I gently took my dress from its hanger. Then, carefully stepping inside the stunning silk sweetheart bodice dress, Amanda began the tedious task of buttoning each tiny silk button that lined the back. Suddenly, hearing a light knock, Amanda walked over to the door.

"For the bride," the young man said, handing her a beautifully wrapped box with a card.

"Something for you. Any guesses as to who sent this?" Amanda teased.

"Maybe," I laughed.

Anxiously removing the ribbon and wrapping paper, it revealed a blue velvet box. Opening it, I gasped. It contained a diamond eternity necklace with matching earrings.

"Oh my gosh, this cost a fortune."

With trembling hands, I opened the card.

> *"Ericka, from the moment I met you, everything led to today. I'm waiting on the beach."*
>
> *Love, Liam*

"Oh, Amanda," I cried. "I love that man."

"I know."

Amanda finished the arduous task of buttoning the back of my dress. Taking a glance in the mirror, I smiled. It was exquisite. The luxurious appearance of the silk elegantly draped the length of my body.

"Wow. You look stunning," Amanda cried.

"Amanda, no tears," I smiled.

With shaking hands, I positioned the diamond necklace around my neck, closing the clasp, and then I added the exquisite earrings.

Finally, adjusting the colorful Haku lei wrapped in pink rosebuds over my hair and stepping into my Louboutin heels, I was ready. Hurriedly, I helped Amanda with her dress. She looked stunning in her coral gown and turquoise jewelry. Once again, hearing a knock at the door, Amanda walked over.

"For the bride and bridesmaid," the young girl smiled, handing Amanda a large box.

Quickly opening the box and removing the tissue paper revealed a beautiful bridal bouquet of pink roses and baby's breath. Also included was the bridesmaid bouquet, a smaller bouquet of white roses and carnations.

Taking one last look in the mirror, we were ready. Walking into the living room, it was inundated with glowing candles and flowers. The aroma of the fresh flowers was hypnotic

"Hey, mom, we heard you might need someone to walk you down the aisle," Keith smiled, walking into the room with Greg.

"Mom, do you need two little flower girls?" Samantha questioned with a smile.

"Hey, mom," Briella smiled. "I brought you two handsome ring bearers."

My knees buckled just as Keith caught me in his arms.

"Oh, mom, we love you. There was no way we were going to miss your wedding," Greg smiled. "Liam sent the jet for us."

I was breathless as my handsome sons, dressed in tuxedos, stood ready to escort me down the aisle. First, two adorable little princesses dressed to perfection, each wearing a Haku lei of pink rosebuds, walked down a satin runner to the beach, scattering rose petals. Next, two handsome young men carrying our wedding rings walked towards the beach. Finally, Amanda slowly walked down the satin runner.

"Mom, are you ready?" Keith asked.

"Yes. I have never been more ready in my entire life," I smiled.

"Let's take that walk. Shall we?" Keith and Greg smiled, each looping their arms through mine.

Walking between my handsome sons, they escorted me towards the palapa. The sound of waves gently washing ashore was the only music needed. An unbelievable sunset bathed the sky in brilliant hues of pinks, purples, and orange.

Looking up, our eyes met, and my heart stopped. Dressed in an Armani tuxedo and looking like the day I first saw him, the love of my life was waiting. Slowly approaching the palapa and Liam, I was breathless. Walking down to meet me, Liam took my hand. "You look amazing," he whispered.

"It is an honor to stand before you this evening and officiate the marriage of Ericka Reed and Liam Lachowski. Who gives this woman in marriage?"

"We do," Keith and Greg smiled.

"The bride and groom have chosen to write their vows. Liam, please take Ericka's hand," the officiate said.

"Ericka," Liam paused, staring into the depths of my eyes. "I've loved you since the day we first met in Crescent City. I knew from that moment that we would be standing here today. I promise to love you, to be your best friend, to care for you in sickness and in health, to cherish you, to protect you, and walk by your side until I take my last breath. I give you my entire being. But, most importantly, I give you my heart. I love you," Liam winked with a smile.

"Liam," I paused as he gently wiped away my tears. "You came into my life at its lowest point. Your love has brought me here today. It's given me a new beginning. I've loved you from the day we first met. I give you my heart, my entire being. I promise to love you, to cherish you, to care for you in sickness and in health, to walk by your side until I take my last breath. I love you," I smiled.

"Liam, please place the ring on Ericka's left hand and repeat after me."

"Ericka, I give you this ring as a sign of my love and commitment until death parts us," Liam smiled, placing the ring on my finger.

"Ericka, please place the ring on Liam's left hand and repeat after me."

"Liam, I give you this ring as a sign of my love and commitment until death parts us," I smiled, placing the ring on Liam's finger.

"I now pronounce you husband and wife. Liam, you may kiss your bride."

Turning to face my family, I saw him fleetingly out of the corner of my eye. An ethereal image of Bob appeared for a brief instant with a smile I would recognize anywhere. I knew he came to give me his blessings. Just like the bottle of Aramis, it didn't matter if anyone ever believed the coincidence at the beach house. I knew that love was strong enough to transcend the veil of heaven and earth. "I love you," I whispered.

The journey, which I began in sadness, turned out to have a happy ending. I found love for the second time. Miracles happen. I was living proof.

Two years later

I finally finished my manuscript, *A Widow's Journey.* It skyrocketed to number one overnight and remained on the New York's Best Seller's List for two years. I was invited to address numerous organizations and women's groups across the country.

We welcomed our new grandson, Michael Erick Reed, only four short months after we married, and Liam has a new title, grandpa, which he loves. So, as expected, the grandkid's Christmas lists continue to expand expeditiously. Yet, Liam continues to tell me that I gave him the most important thing in life. Something which money can't buy, *family.*

Greg's restaurant was a huge success, and he's now in the process of opening a second location. Keith gave up flying commercially and now flies private jets for Liam's Corporation.

Liam and Harry finally retired to the golf course. At least it keeps them close to home.

Amanda and I continue to be best friends, and we love living in Vancouver. We spend holidays together and celebrate birthdays and anniversaries together.

I learned that becoming a widow is hard. There are no handbooks. However, I believe when you're faced with life-changing moments in your life, you only have two choices. One is to let it consume you, and the other choice is to allow it to mold you into something new. I chose the latter.